Dirk van den Boom

Arrival

DIRK VAN DEN BOOM

THE EMPEROR'S MEN

ARRIVAL

Editor: Rob Bignell

www.atlantis-verlag.de

1

"Nice to see you go."

The words couldn't be misunderstood. The coldness in Karl's voice emphasized their meaning. Rheinberg decided not to return this kind of farewell. When he left the house and walked to the sidewalk, he felt their eyes burning on his back.

The eyes of Helga, his sister, with the mixture of sadness and defiance that had already accompanied him all day since yesterday. The eyes of her husband Karl, clearly filled with hatred and contempt.

That had been apparent yesterday as well, in spite of the thin shell of courtesy covering their interaction. Karl received his brother-in-law in his small brick house in Yard Street. The shell had cracked quickly, the cracks had widened, and in the afternoon after a lunch of bland and overcooked potatoes and fish, it had finally broken. Karl had resumed his monologues and, as always, warmed quickly to the topic.

The system of exploitation, he repeated again and again, and capitalism. Feudalism of the mind and the corruption of monarchy. Freedom for those and retaliation for this, and then of course his greatest enemy: the favorites of the Emperor, the naval officers. Karl knew what he was talking about, or at least he pretended so. For six years he worked as a shipyard worker in Wilhelmshaven, and in this city there were only yards building for the imperial fleet. Since the Second Navy Law has been in force, they created constantly in day and night shifts the weapon that His Almighty Majesty ordered to be built. Karl earned every penny of his life with work as part of the system of exploitation, for which he seemed to feel only hate. When he brought out his pamphlets, publications of the social democratic presses, with waving flags and pictures of their leaders and heroes, especially Marx and Engels and Lassalle and whoever else, Lieutenant Commander Jan Rheinberg had enough.

Helga had noticed it right away. She was his sister, and at the same time the black sheep of the family, had ran away from home when barely 18 and then married a revolutionary, a simple worker, unworthy in every respect. Her father had never contacted her again, which was not surprising for the old, inflexible, rigid school principal and retired cavalry officer. Only mother sent her letters every now and then, often with money, because she lacked it all the time. Even during the first eight years of Jan's career, when his parents had to subsidize his upkeep and put thousands into his training, before he was finally promoted to First Lieutenant and by that had achieved some financial independence, the letters came – just as had those pleas of his mother that he should visit Helga.

So he visited her at least once a year, and since his transfer to Wilhelmshaven six months ago, about once a month, to the highest displeasure of her husband. Jan himself felt no joy during these visits, but he did his duty – just as he had always done, even when his father had declared to him that he would give his only son to the naval academy, as people like him were sought after in the ever-expanding corps of officers. The "Seeoffizierskorps," His Most High Majesty's most precious favorites, and thus a safe career for a hard-working young man who had just passed a high school exam with highest honors and actually preferred ...

But it only mattered what his father wanted.

Jan had done his duty. And as left the house of his revolutionary in-law on that chilly October Sunday morning, he remembered the bitter cold in his voice as he had answered Karl during the previous evening. His words had been honor and commitment, patriotism and loyalty, and the meaning of the Most High authority without which a political system would break down into exactly the anarchy and arbitrariness that Karl and his followers surely strived for. He had lost control, was actually not such a fanatical supporter of the monarchy – or, to be more precise, of the current monarch. Nevertheless, Lieutenant Commander Rheinberg had a good, strong voice, which had come to maturity in Muerwik, as an instructor, a post he had held up until six months ago. A hated and beloved work, hated because of its monotony and poorer pay; loved because he taught, and education was important to him.

Every night he read texts in Latin: Cicero, Sallust, Ambrosius. Latin he had actually preferred to ...

What mattered now lay before him. In four hours, he had to report to the light cruiser *Saarbrücken*, one of the oldest ships of the Imperial Fleet, but only after visiting the White Castle and picking up his commander's written instructions. The trip would go to the West Africa station, and the anticipation in Rheinberg outweighed the frustration that had accumulated during the last day and the silent, bitter morning in the house of his sister.

He shouldn't have been so loud. Karl normally distributed his cheap, damaging propaganda only in the pub and his home, but very wisely not at the shipyard, and its content was supposed to roll off him like spray water on his rain jacket. But the cold anger that always rose suddenly in him when he came upon stupidity was difficult to manage. He and Karl didn't understand each other; their worlds were totally different, only held together by the bridge of his sister.

They had both been adamant, stubborn and ungracious. It had to end in dispute. It always did.

The weather was wet. Jan pulled up the collar of his uniform jacket. The very existence of this uniform in his house was an insult to him, Karl had emphasized that morning. Then Rheinberg had decided not to wait until noon and left right away. The officers' mess was undoubtedly a friendlier place, and apart from that there was more than enough to do to bring the *Saarbrücken* back into service before it embarked on its great journey.

This simple thought noticeably improved Jan's mood. He even dispensed with the tram and went the distance on foot. He had to clear his head, and nothing worked better than a Sunday's walk. He touched the crackling paper in his uniform pocket with his right hand, the letter from his father, sent three days before his death, in which he told his son formally and without flourish that he had heard the news of his promotion and appointment as second-in-command with pride and appreciation. Then he said he hoped that Jan would continue to serve the Emperor faithfully, thereby continuing the honorable tradition of his ancestors.

Jan's response didn't reach him in time.

He shooed the brooding thoughts away. He could neither make the unexpected death of his father undone, yet the existence of annoying Karl Jansen, and he went to visit him only for his mother's and finally the sake of his sister, who apparently loved this man. Commander Rheinberg's sacrifices were considerable, because his superiors had reported the improper connection of his sister to the highest levels, and twice he had been forced to wait for a promotion longer than others. Ultimately, however, his zeal and his unwavering devotion to duty paid off, and he was finally promoted to a leading position on one of the fleet's largest ships.

As Jan thought about it, he found himself humming happily. When he reached Adalbert Square, with its exact rows of trees and the shimmering construction of the naval station at its end, which was commonly called just the "White Castle," he almost regained something like a good mood. He considered the fit of his uniform before passing the guards and was placed into a waiting room after a short presentation and explanation of his visit's purpose. He had to wait a long time yet wasn't bothered. The room was plain, but the chair comfortable and a boy brought him coffee and pastries after his behest. Usually collecting orders wasn't always handled so formal, but this was the last great journey of the *Saarbrücken*, and after their return she would seal her fate as an accommodation ship. Marine officers and engineers of other units strangely had always just some important task in port to do, long enough to take a last look at the sleek, powerful ship that seemed to come from another time. The old warhorse BREMEN-class ship had been the pinnacle of German engineering when it was built in 1902, and although 12 years later her sister shipshad been more or less all replaced by modern turbine cruisers, Rheinberg still was proud of the old lady.

Captain von Krautz was still in the hospital with the flu. Station Chief Admiral von Herringen himself would pass the necessary orders to Rheinberg in his capacity as Executive Officer, and this was an honor for the sick commander, who had been in charge of the ship for the last seven years.

Rheinberg felt no excitement and no fear. He saw himself where he belonged, and he would prove himself. This course would lead him to his own command of a cruiser in due time. And his chance to prove himself was imminent, there was no doubt. The war, for which the Emperor in his wisdom had prepared his fleet so carefully, would soon arrive, as everyone who possessed sufficient intelligence knew. Rheinberg had no shortage of intelligence, and he expected the future with anticipation. War meant battle, and victory above all. That there would be victory was certain.

"Commander!"

The voice of the adjutant interrupted his thoughts. A few moments later, Rheinberg found himself in the presence of an old admiral. Von Herringen was a tall figure with powerful, white whiskers. He had taken office just about a year before, and Rheinberg had the feeling that he would not hold it for long. The man was close to retirement age, and if there would actually be a war, then it took an officer who was as adept in civil affairs as in military matters. No one had any illusions about what war would mean for the city and region of Wilhelmshaven. The city most certainly would be declared a fortress, and that automatically would make the admiral also a civilian governor.

"Sit down, Commander!"

Rheinberg accepted the invitation. Von Herringen settled behind his wide desk and nodded at a sheaf of papers, which lay on the front edge of the tabletop.

"Take this, it's the marching orders. They are sealed so that only Captain von Krautz can open them, as soon as he is discharged from the hospital. How is he doing?"

"Admiral, the captain is already quite lively. He has weathered the influenza very well and will take up his duties by tomorrow."

"That's good, that's good. You will find your ship to be pretty tight on the way."

"Admiral?"

Von Herringen pointed again to the paper bundle. "There have been some additions in the last minute. You know that international tensions are rising. Should it come to war, it will affect our colonies as well as the fatherland. The governor of Cameroon has requested additional troops. He will not get what he would have liked, but he will have at least one full army company. You will have to put them on the *Saarbrücken*."

"That will be very tight indeed, Admiral!" Rheinberg said. A full company, or about four platoons of 40 men each, with all the equipment ... an organizational nightmare.

"I know. There are also ammunition, additional guns, and 25,000 Goldmark to deliver to the governor. You will need to lash a large stash of cargo on deck so that there will be room for the soldiers below deck. Many of them will not feel too well, especially when it gets rough. The company commander, a Captain ... Becker ... seems to have been at sea quite a few times and might comfort our passengers. He will report with his men Monday afternoon, so you should be ready to receive them."

"Yes, Admiral. We'll figure this out."

That was easier said than done. But it was hardly for Rheinberg to discuss these details with von Herringen. Why they didn't send a steamer together with the *Saarbrücken*, he could not explain. 25,000 Goldmark. He had to be extra cautious.

"I'm sure you will," said the stationmaster. "You will take coal in Portugal; the authorities there will be informed of your itinerary. If war breaks out, you will not stop in Morocco, as all the coasts up until Togoland will be hostile. So don't dare full cruising speed and save coal. If you arrive a day later, that's not so bad. I don't want the *Saarbrücken* to fall into enemy's hands on her last big journey."

Now Rheinberg couldn't control himself. Von Herringen had sounded so determined and sure. "Admiral, can we really expect a declaration of war soon?"

Von Herringen allowed himself a thin smile. "Who am I to foresee the highest counsel from Berlin? But what I hear is encouraging. I'm sure that soon some questions will be clarified inquite unambiguous ways. You need to prepare yourself. It's all in the instructions."

"Yes, Admiral."

"One more thing. No, two things. For one, you get a new chief engineer, Marine Chief Engineer Dahms, a short-term replacement. He will report tomorrow."

"Yes, Admiral. And the second?"

Von Herringen sighed. He looked out of the window for a moment, lost in thought. The drizzle had been replaced by a chill. The fall began to show its unpleasant side. There would be heavy sea. Rheinberg deplored the infantry already.

"The reports of social democratic agitation in the file and the ranks of the non-commissioned officers are piling up. I don't know how many stokers and mates have connections among the socialists; they often don't profess openly. We are still united by the bond of love for the emperor, especially here in the fleet. But I just need to ask you especially to keep your eyes open."

This "you especially" Rheinberg could understand in two different ways – as an appeal to his genuine responsibility as an executive officer directly in charge of the discipline in his crew, or as an indication toward his in-law, about whose existence von Herringen knew with absolute certainty. Rheinberg decided not to discuss it. In any case, he had gotten the message.

Luckily he could confine himself to a simple "Yes, Admiral!" an appropriate response in any situation.

For a few minutes the conversation turned to chit-chat, then Rheinberg was allowed to leave. When the young officer left the White Castle, the rain had eased. The cold air that blew from the Jade Bay smelled like a storm. Nothing that couldn't be tackled by a good light cruiser but nothing any experienced sailor longed for. An overloaded vessel, as the *Saarbrücken* would become, could use calmer waters.

Rheinberg glanced at the clock. Three hours still remained until he had to return to the ship, but on the other hand there was obviously more to do than expected. His boy had put his luggage on board a long time ago. Rheinberg started thinking about a rotating schedule for his and other's cabins in order to optimally use the capacity of the *Saarbrücken.* During the walk to the fitting port, he quickly came to the conclusion that he himself would share his humble cabin with the captain of the embarked infantry, and that meant that he had to be put up for vigils as the infantryman should enjoy his sleep in the night. It was an act of politeness – Rheinberg was sure that Becker would have accepted any other arrangement without complaint – but it was helpful that Rheinberg loved vigils, because during that time the ship was really his.

When he reached the *Saarbrücken*, she was under steam. That meant all cargo had been loaded and that the engineer tested the engine, as well as checked the electric circuits. Rheinberg knew that the deputy chief in the engine room, Engineer Dortheim, has returned to his duty some days ago. He decided to take him aside and ask him about his new boss, who would arrive tomorrow. Officers like himself, the Marine Engineers knew each other well, although of lower prestige and status. For a long time, this was a cause of friction, and some of Rheinberg's comrades were not too reluctant to emphasize the difference through all sorts of snide remarks. Rheinberg had never held this belief and was always looking for a good relationship, even though he would stand as a simple lieutenant above even a veteran engineer in the ship's hierarchy. The biggest distinction of rank became clear in the permission to marry: While naval officers received their permission to enter into a marriage directly by His Majesty, the dispensation for Marine Engineers was issued by command posts. There was no clearer sign of the social separation between the two groups, and the engineers had long urged that for them an imperial dispensation should be required as well. As it had been rumored, the Emperor was inclined to grant this, but the Admiralty, led by Fleet Admiral Tirpitz, still strongly opposed it.

Rheinberg didn't concern himself with such matters. He served as first officer, being responsible for the functioning of the crew, and there was nothing more important for a technically complex entity like a light cruiser as a good team in the engine room, especially well-trained officers who had to be sure that the ship's command treated them decently. And that exactly was Rheinberg's intention.

His opinion might have been shaped by the fact that he himself had been frequently a victim of teasing and derogatory remarks. He was a commoner, and although no officer corps was as bourgeois as that of the Navy, the fifth consisting of noble sons still enjoyed special consideration. He had not had it as bad as those comrades who had not even had an old cavalry officer as a father. His roommate, Valentin, with whom he had served as a midshipman, had been a merchant's son. No one was punished with more contempt than a *Koofmich.* Valentin had left the Navy one year after his promotion to lieutenant.

Rheinberg couldn't blame him.

The guard protecting the gate to the deck of the *Saarbrücken* came to attention when he recognized Rheinberg. The first officer had already been a first lieutenant aboard the cruiser and had, as executive officer, commanded some squadron exercises in the North Sea. Nevertheless, the ship spent most of its time in the harbor, and Rheinberg had been busy with courses or dealing with administrative matters. It was a positive sign that the guard only allowed access to the ship after checking the ID of the approaching officer. Rheinberg nodded approvingly then stood on the wet steel deck and closed his eyes for a moment. All the anger, all the musings, fell away from him. He forgot about Karl and his sister and the fact that he had received this rank and position two years later than other comrades of his year. It was here where he was now, and he was where he belonged.

"Commander?"

Rheinberg opened his eyes and looked into the round face of Navy Medical Dr. Hans Neumann, the ship's chief physician. Neumann was the opposite to Rheinberg in every respect. Where Rheinberg was tall and wiry, he tended toward chubbiness. Where Rheinberg had a narrow face and a sharp, thin nose, radiating an aura of austerity – sometimes even without intending to – Neumann exuded comfort and joviality. And where Rheinberg fit into his uniform as if it were perfectly tailored, Neumann's was always either too big or too small.

Rheinberg owed this man a lot. He wasn't only a good doctor but had become a friend during the last six months. He had helped Rheinberg learn when rigidity came to an end and where a kind word in dealing with the crew, helped much more – something they didn't teach in naval school. Most didn't even learn it as young officers. Some covered their insecurities by being the martinet. When Lieutenant Rheinberg was on the wrong track, Dr. Neumann had saved him just in time, and Jan was eternally grateful to him for this assistance.

"Hans," replied Rheinberg. "You've been on board a long time?"

"For three days now. I've heard that we take a bunch of mud-eaters to Cameroon."

"News spreads quickly."

Dr. Neumann grinned and tugged at his not too well fitting uniform jacket.

"The big vomit will not be long in coming," he croaked. "This is a great ride."

"You'll handle that. Who else has been reporting in already?"

"Klasewitz is on the bridge."

Johann Freiherr von Klasewitz, a commander like Rheinberg, albeit with fewer years of service, and second officer, was exactly the sort of person with whom Rheinberg had always had trouble because of his middle-class background. Twice they've clashed seriously, and it had taken some time before the nobleman had recognized Rheinberg's authority, although with recognizable reluctance.

"Then I'd better let him be alone," Rheinberg said with a faint smile. "Are the new crewmembers on board?"

"So far as I've noticed, yes. I've examined already half of them."

"Did they get all of their assignments?"

"Right after embarkation. The crew must first get used to the ship. This time we have around 20 percent new staff. I suggest that we begin soon with the skirmish drill."

Rheinberg looked at his clock. "I want lunch according to the normal routine. After lunch, leisure is limited to one o'clock. Instead of a small service, I want to damage control drills per division, up until dinner. After dinner, I want to talk all the division heads in the mess."

"Not all heads probably are available," Neumann said. "We still wait for some deck officers and NCOs. All in all, we've assembled quite a new crew. I understand that some men will arrive, together with the captain, day after tomorrow."

"The drills are taking place anyway. Where no division heads are present, take the alternate or we let experienced NCOs lead. When Captain von Krautz comes on board, I don't want to have to answer for a potentially poorly experienced crew without at least having tried to do something about it."

"Talk to Klasewitz about it. He will be pleased."

Rheinberg sighed. The second officer had never met someone like Dr. Neumann in his early career. The baron was like a martinet and would use each drill for merciless punishment, if he was not kept under control. Rheinberg wanted to postpone the conversation with the man as long as possible.

"We load coal on Thursday and on Sunday we have orders to sail. Not much time left. Housing the infantry is my biggest problem. We need to create additional space for hammocks. It will be even tighter than we already had it. We also need to ensure that peace prevails among the men."

"We will manage, if we make good progress. But the autumn storms are expected. It would have been better if we would have sailed two months ago."

Rheinberg shrugged and tapped the bundle with the orders in his breast pocket. "It's the way it is."

Neumann nodded. He cast a searching look at the sky. The clouds began to tear in some places. Hesitant sunlight danced across the brackish water of the harbor.

"I'd fancy a beautiful and sunny fall," muttered the doctor.

"Me too. We'll see. Seen my boy somewhere?"

"He is waiting for you but now ..."

Neumann turned. "Chief Petty Officer!"

The massive, ponderous form thatslid down the ladder was well known to Rheinberg. Chief Petty Officer Harald Köhler was the senior NCO on board the *Saarbrücken*, just 50 years old. His beard was trimmed as impressively as the rest of his massive frame, and no one would've guessed his age. Köhler bristled not only from power, but as an elder of the NCOs, he was also the official spokesman for all NCOs and men. All complaints, all the problems, came to him first. The fact that everyone actually spoke frankly to him said much about the respect he commanded as well as his popularity. Rheinberg had learned to rely blindly on the older man during the last few weeks. If he remembered correctly, it was Neumann who had pointed him toward the importance of veteran NCOs.

Köhler saluted smartly.

Rheinberg looked around and grinned. "See von Klasewitz somewhere, Köhler?"

"No, sir, Lieutenant Commander."

"Then stop the motions. Tell my boy that I'm on board and he should lay out a fresh uniform for me. I want to conduct a survey by noon, and I don't want to fail myself."

Köhler returned the grin. "I'll gather him personally. Surely playing cards somewhere ..."

"Fine. Any news?"

The question sounded casual, but was not meant that way. Köhler's judgment had weight for Rheinberg. "Everything in order so far. A fine ship, but you knew that. The crew is still a little bit confused and must grow to know each other; we have plenty of newcomers. They abuse us a bit as a training ship, I guess. We'll make it, though. I would suggest that we start with battle drills, at the latest, after the coal."

"Better even before, but that won't work. We have to deal with our guests from the infantry first."

Köhler grimaced. "Would be easier if they would've sent our comrades."

Rheinberg knew that the NCO was referring to the Marines. He shrugged. "No, it will be the infantry. Treat them well. It would be a good idea if you could become friends with one of their senior sergeants, drink a few beers with him, and gather ideas in regard to the needs of his men. I can't use surprises on an already overcrowded ship."

"Yes, sir."

Rheinberg dismissed him. Köhler tapped his index finger against his forehead and turned away.

Rheinberg sighed and glanced at the bridge.

Neumann patted him reassuringly on the shoulder.

"Now you should go."

"Yes, now I'll have to. See you later." Neumann nodded and disappeared.

Rheinberg proceeded without further hesitation to the bridge. It was not too far. When he entered the spacious command center with the all dominating wheel, he found only two men present. Quartermaster Börnsen stood behind the steering gear like the *Saarbrücken* was already on a grand voyage against the English. He fixed the slightly agitated water of the port with an intensity as if at any time the appearance of a torpedo was to be expected. Rheinberg rolled his eyes. The second officer was the other person on the bridge, a symbol of the perfect imperial officer, tall and muscular and with his angular face sporting a magnificent beard trim comparable to that of the Highest

Majesty. This was not unusual among the officer corps, and the mere fact that Rheinberg preferred his face clean-shaven had been already enough to encourage von Klasewitz's contempt toward him. The second officer, who also held the position of the artillery officer, smiled maliciously. Although he ranked lower than Rheinberg, his promotions had not been postponed, and his noble rank made him a better person anyway. Rheinberg's father had taught him unconditional respect for the nobility from the cradle, but the young man hadn't lost his mind before entering the military academy. Von Klasewitz was a pompous puppet, trying to compensate for his inability with unnecessary rigor and disciplinary arbitrariness. In fact, the only thing he was really familiar with was his artillery; with everything else, especially with people, he was not familiar at all.

He had come so far only because his father had found a sympathetic ear at the court and because the Admiralty rather preferred nobility in senior positions. In contrast, Rheinberg had to work laboriously for what fate had given von Klasewitz.

"Commander!" The baron did not even move to attempt a half-hearted salute.

Rheinberg pointed a finger on Börnsen. "Did we receive new instructions, Mr. von Klasewitz?"

Incomprehension loomed on the picturesque face of the baron. "Why do you ask?"

"Do we have to sail now?"

"No, no ... we don't, don't we?"

Rheinberg suppressed a sigh. "What is the quartermaster doing here? The *Saarbrücken* will be moved early on Thursday, when we get to the take coal. Now the ship is moored, and we haven't everyone on board, including the captain."

Von Klasewitz pressed his lips together. "I believe that we must be ready at all times. The enemy –"

"Will most probably not attack today," Rheinberg completed the sentence. "The only mate that we could use on the bridge would probably be for signals. I don't see one. I only see Börnsen clutching the helm, as if it would fall off if he lets go."

Börnsen gave a nearly inaudible groan. Rheinberg admired him for his self-control. The mate was a good man; it was a shame that he was forced to this farce by his second officer.

"Börnsen, you can go," Rheinberg finally said.

He didn't wait for confirmation of the command but left the bridge together with the mate, leaving von Klasewitz alone.

The baron stared after him. His hands were clenched into fists until the knuckles went white out.

He said nothing.

* * *

Rheinberg had hoped to take infantry and coal on board separately. As always, it worked exactly not the way it was planned. Three things happened simultaneously: After the *Saarbrücken* had been transferred to the coal port and the filling up started, the signals mate on duty excitedly asked for him. The first officer was rushed to the bridge, in the suspicious expectation that something went wrong with the coal, causing an accident or a malfunction, which unfortunately occurred from time to time and sometimes could seriously injure someone. Fortunately, his assumption was not confirmed. The alternative wasn't much more pleasant.

"The infantry," repeated the mate, pointing to the bank.

Indeed. A day earlier than announced the army came marching and in full gear. Fortunately, they didn't just storm aboard. As a short, stocky man broke from the pack and purposefully headed for the gangway, Rheinberg knew that this could only be Captain Becker. In his mind, he already saw how the coal dust-covered crew would guide the immaculate marching infantry with a big smile through the coal dust-covered ship, so that at the end they would look like they had done duty at the boilers.

"Where is the duty officer?"

"Lieutenant Joergensen is below, monitoring the storage of the coal together with the deputy engineer."

Rheinberg sighed. Who had not yet appeared, was the new engineer, Marine Chief Engineer Dahms, whose job this was supposed to be. He was about to leave the bridge to meet Becker, when he saw a car pull up. Rheinberg focused his eyes and immediately another deep sigh burst out. Climbing out of the car, a little shaky, came Captain Harald von Krautz, the commanding officer of the *Saarbrücken*, whose return had actually been announced for later in the evening. But he had probably not been able to put up with the care of the nurses anymore, and Rheinberg could not resent him for that. But his return was inopportune, actually quite so. In the corner of his eye he saw the grins of the bridge crew in anticipation that the simultaneous arrival of the three officers could develop into something amusing. Rheinberg held back any rebuke. *Schadenfreude* was still the sincerest pleasure of them all, even if he was the object of it.

Rheinberg ran toward the men. Becker and Krautz had simultaneously reached the guard at the gangway, as he also jumped ashore. For a moment, the soldier on duty looked speechless at the three men. Becker opened his mouth, but von Krautz spoke first.

"Gentlemen, it seems to me that we have a small party here."

"Captain," replied Rheinberg. "It's all a bit awkward ..."

Von Krautz smiled. "I hope you're not talking about me?"

Rheinberg's face turned a little bit red. "Of course not, I –"

"He refers to me," interjected the infantryman with his deep voice. "And he's right, we didn't arrive at the planned time."

Now Rheinberg was a little bit embarrassed, because he had firmly resolved to provide their guests with a thoroughly warm welcome.

"Captain, I've certainly not meant it that way," he answered lamely, and looked at the broad grin on the faces of both men and capitulated. "Gentlemen, welcome aboard the *Saarbrücken*. Captain, I –"

Von Krautz raised his hands. "Nothing, Rheinberg! If you expect me to formally assume command, then you are in error. You have your fun with the comrades of the army, and I will disappear in my cabin until dinner." He bowed to Becker. "Captain, I put the fate of your men in the capable hands of my Executive Officer, Lieutenant Commander Rheinberg. I would be pleased to welcome you this evening as my guest in the mess. The food at the Imperial Navy is much better than in the army, I can tell you."

Becker returned the gesture. "Captain, I thank you. We'll see you tonight!"

Without further ado, von Krautz waved off his servant. The boy had carried the luggage out of the car and tried to lift the first suitcase on board. Then von Krautz turned and nodded to Rheinberg with about the same grin that had been seen on the bridge, and squeezed past him to the guard holding out his badge. Shortly thereafter, he disappeared aboard the light cruiser.

Rheinberg eyed Becker. The infantryman was a good four inches shorter than him but looked very strong. He had a healthy, ruddy complexion, and his wide, soft-looking face was covered with freckles. Rheinberg guessed him to be in his late 20s. His deep, dark voice did not fit the boyish appearance. When he took Rheinberg's proffered right, he pressed it firmly, which hinted at the strength in his arms.

"Commander, I really have to apologize for this mess. I myself had the intention to announce our arrival in time. It's all gone upside down. I've got a new deputy, and then lacked half the men, because the train from Oldenburg had an engine-failure. My troop is brand new; I know no more than a third of them. I'm just so tired."

Becker's smile was open and disarming. Rheinberg's bad mood melted away. He immediately took to the captain and only shook his head. "We take it as it is," he said. "I must ask you and your men to wait for another two hours before boarding. I want to finish with the coal before. It doesn't look like rain, so let the men sit and smoke a pipe. We can also bring out coffee. But please let us do one thing after the other."

Becker didn't even discuss it. He called a young man with the rank of lieutenant and introduced him as his deputy. Lieutenant Klaus von Geeren listened attentively to the explanations of his superior, then he turned and barked some commands. A short time later, the soldiers were sitting on their backpacks, and tobacco made the rounds.

Rheinberg threw a hard look at the cruiser. As expected, he saw Chief Petty Officer Köhler standing at the railing, like if he had just been waiting for the searching eye of the officer, and he gestured that they needed one-and-a-half hours. Rheinberg had calculated correctly. He raised his thumb and turned back to Becker.

"You, sir, I can already bring on board. There is a lot going on, but I will take the opportunity to give you a little tour of the ship."

Becker nodded. "I've looked forward to this for a long time. You've got a beautiful old pot."

"You ever had the pleasure sailing with the fleet?" Rheinberg knew that he had, but he wanted to give the captain an opportunity to brag about his experiences a bit.

"I already have had a stint in German South-West. I had been a substitute for a sick comrade and traveled with the cruiser on station, like now. It's been a while; I was a fresh lieutenant and the ship was an old aviso."

"Long time," confirmed Rheinberg. Those boats had been an ultimately very unreliable class of ships whose tasks were now taken over by the light cruisers. "Well, once again, welcome aboard!"

And with that he led Becker up the gangway to the deck.

"The *Saarbrücken* is one of the oldest ships in the fleet," he began at once with his introduction and proceeded before Becker. "It was completed in 1902 as the second ship of the BREMEN-class, the first having ten 10.5-cm quick-loading cannons." Rheinberg pointed toward the turret and passed on. "We have six of them now, and a 15-cm gun both in the bow and the stern. We needed the bigger punch."

"I suspect the conversion has affected the ship," said Becker and knocked on the gun barrel covered with a tarp.

"Some, yes. The foremast was put into the bridge due to safety considerations. The electrical system has been brought up to date. What we didn't get were turbines. The *Lübeck* has them, but we still breathe in the traditional way."

"Three-cylinder triple expansion engines, ten marine water-tube boilers with natural circulation," pontificated Becker.

Rheinberg raised his eyebrows and nodded. "You you're your stuff, Captain."

"I should have become a naval officer. No, it is one of my principles to pursue the most optimal preparation, no matter what the mission is. Many of my comrades allow themselves to be too surprised by the things they should have expected. My good lieutenant didn't even deemed it necessary to know where Cameroon actually is. He said he'll see once we arrive at the port of Douala."

Rheinberg grinned. “No real port. There is a beautiful harbor, but with a long pier because it is too shallow for us to get close.”

Becker nodded. “I have also told him. Then I sent him in seclusion for some hours, together with an atlas and a geography book about our colonies. I’ve made myself familiar with the cruiser even earlier. It’s just a magnificent piece of engineering. While what they are building today doesn’t have the curved bow or the decorations anymore – this still had a certain style and grace.”

Rheinberg could not help but agree with the infantryman. The new vessels were significantly more functional than the old *Saarbrücken.* He was ready to confess that this increased functionality had its merits. During the last 11 years, the technical development had not stopped. The installation of Parsons turbines in the sister ship *Lübeck* two years after the *Saarbrücken* had been built, becoming the first ship in the fleet with the new technology, was a good example.

Becker interrupted his thoughts. “How big is the crew?” They had reached the bow and stood directly above the rich ornaments.

“287 NCOs and enlisted men, 18 officers,” Rheinberg replied promptly. “And recently, yet another 160 infantrymen.”

Becker grinned. “We will make ourselves as small as possible, I promise.”

Rheinberg made a generous gesture. “We will manage somehow. However, the ship is pretty overloaded, and therefore we’ll load less coal than usual. Our speed will be a leisurely pace, because our Lady could swallow over 10 tons of coal per hour in full speed. We will remain at half speed, which extends our trip but preserves our coal reserves. In Portugal, we will fill up, and then sail slowly to Cameroon. Expect some weeks of travel, as the journey will take time.”

Becker sighed. “I suspect you will sweeten our time with some nice drills.”

“Exactly. Every one of your men gets an assignment. You all need to know where you have to be in the event of something unexpected. And we will practice until they know it in their sleep.”

“Great prospects.” Becker knocked on the rail. “But I am very confident that the old lady will deliver us to our goal.”

“So am I,” Rheinberg said. He turned and enjoyed the view of the bridge where a pale von Klasewitz stood and stared at the two men. "That's the second officer," said Rheinberg, when he realized that Becker had noticed the stare. "Keep dear to the captain or me, or even better, if there is anything to ask for, talk to Chief Petty Officer Köhler. He has been on board for ten years and knows corners of whose existence I'm not aware. If something doesn't work out, especially in regard to the relationship between your men and my crew, he is the contact person."

Becker nodded thoughtfully. "I have a sergeant, who should make friends with him ..."

Rheinberg was pleased that he was apparently going along very well with the captain. Again his eyes fell on the stiff figure of von Klasewitz who scrutinized them as if they were discussing the formation of a workers "and soldiers" council on the *Saarbrücken.* Rheinberg felt that Becker would "appreciate" this man just like him. This had perhaps something to do with the fact that the infantryman seemed to be a commoner like Rheinberg. That was a little bit rarer in the army than in the fleet. Becker, therefore, certainly did not always felt easy in the vicinity of highly respectable noble superiors like von Klasewitz.

Rheinberg continued his tour of the ship. Becker proved to be an extremely attentive companion, as he soaked up every piece of information despite occasional jokes and lighthearted swipes at the fleet. At the end of their round they arrived at Rheinberg's modest cabin. The commander made a sweeping motion.

"Be my guest, sir. I will endeavor to do the night watch, so that you can sleep in peace. If needed, I will be sleeping in the bathtub. My boy provides fresh linens."

Becker nodded. His eyes fell on the only shelf in the room. It was so full of books that they probably wouldn't slip even in the heaviest seas. He ran a finger over one spine and read the title aloud. "Edward Gibbon, 'The Decline and Fall of the Roman Empire.' 'The Notitia Dignitatum' in a new translation. Vegetius. Ambrosius ... hm, you have a soft spot for Roman history, Lieutenant Commander."

Rheinberg smiled sheepishly. "Since my early youth. My dad has promoted this interest; he said I could learn a lot from it."

"Your father wanted you to be a professor of history?"

Rheinberg's smile carried a painful touch. "No, he was determined from the beginning that I would become a naval officer. But the history of the late Roman Empire is mostly military history. A fascinating topic, anyway. I have in my parents' house a whole wall full of books. Only the most important works I've taken; I read them time and again."

Becker pulled with a little effort a thin book from the shelf. "Latin grammar. I'll be damned, this is the grammar book from secondary school. It is certainly among the most hated books of my youth."

Rheinberg grinned almost boyishly. "Latin is my passion. I was top of the class until graduation. I take it that it wasn't your favorite subject?"

Becker frowned. "I was passable in Greek. Latin gave me a permanent headache. Who thinks up something like the ablative case?" He gently pushed the book back in its place. "I follow your passion for military history. We can learn much from the ancient generals."

Rheinberg nodded. "We can, but unfortunately we don't do it often. Captain, I have to devote myself to other obligations ..."

Becker looked guilty. "I have stayed too long. I'll return to my men, and we shall meet again, once I go on board with the troops. One thing, though: In one of my boxes are 25,000 Goldmark for the governor of Cameroon. We should stow that one away safely!"

Rheinberg had almost forgotten the money. He tried not to show his disappointment about himself and acted as if he had expected this. "Of course," he replied firmly. "The purser will take care of everything. The ship's safe should be too small, but the Office of the Paymaster is doubly secured, and we will store the chest there. It is a safe place, and our Lieutenant Thies has already overseen large sums."

"Then everything is settled. I find my way back to the deck on my own; I have to learn that as soon as possible anyway."

"If anything is amiss, please contact me directly or Chief Petty Officer Köhler. With him, you are always in good hands."

The farewell was quick and courteous. Rheinberg rushed upstairs to personally provide for the immediate shipment of the gold. He was grateful for the reminder, even if not saying so.

Rheinberg would definitely get along very well with the captain.

2

The *Saarbrücken* lurched.

Autumn had gathered his forces on the day before the solemn departure and swept through the jetties and piers of Wilhelmshaven, so that even a day later, the marching band finally decided to succumb to the weather and left. The assembled visitors who had the endurance to bid the cruiser farewell waved goodbye to the ship while being totally disheveled by wind and rain. Normally, the departure of a ship was the reason for the so-called whooling – the crying, happy, sad, quiet, loud and uncontrollable ritual – with which the relatives, friends and brides dismissed the sailors on long voyages. This time the weather didn't really mean well for all of them. As the boatswain whistles were sounded, the regret about the final farewell gave way quickly to the joyous expectation to return to a warm and dry place. Rheinberg could clearly see from the bridge that the first had already begun to take up the way back to shelters as the *Saarbrücken* was only 20 meters away from the wharf. He didn't blame anyone, not even the men of the infantry, who had preferred to stay in the cruiser's interior. Their relatives, who were as a rule found in the vicinity of their home barracks further inside the empire, had already bid them farewell during another occasion.

At the last possible moment, the infantrymen had taken delivery of a disassembled Benz 4-ton truck that had been hoisted aboard. Apparently the governor desperately needed a large vehicle in Cameroon and didn't want to wait for a freighter. Köhler had cursed like a fishwife for hours and Rheinberg had allowed him to, because in the end the car parts were securely stowed in the most unlikely places on and below deck. Captain Becker had since been very, very kind to the old sergeant, something Rheinberg had noted with great joy. It was nice to meet officers every now and then who saw the men of lower rank as human beings.

Wind speeds up to 8 knots and a rough sea was nothing that could embarrass the very stable and safely-built cruiser, but the ship was overweight and some of the men on board lacked any experience with the sea. Rheinberg harbored some concerns and asked perhaps more than necessary for the well-being of guests. As the *Saarbrücken* finally took a westerly course along the North Sea coast and fought bravely against the waves and the penetrating wind, Rheinberg, who was in command at that time, was really happy to see a healthy and quite agile Captain Becker entering the bridge. A signalman took off his heavy raincoat and put the wet scarf over the metal plate above the stove, which made the bridge a relatively pleasant place. The temperature outside wasn't freezing, but the biting wind and the incessant rain – sometimes as showers, sometimes as a wet foam – increased the chill.

"Volkert, give the captain a cup of coffee," was Rheinberg's first command. Midshipman Thomas Volkert was on his first long journey with this ship and had so far proven himself as quite capable. The young officer looked lanky, sometimes had too pale of a face and was still working hard to develop the necessary authority. Rheinberg had decided to place the man under his personal care, in order to avoid the danger of falling too much under von Klasewitz's bad influence. The young guy had it rough enough, since after a very long evening in the officers mess it slipped out of him that he still was a virgin, which had of course spread among the crew. Von Klasewitz especially found it very funny to rub the ensign's nose before the assembled troops. Volkert was more of a shy type, and he struggled to handle this properly. Rheinberg was not sure why someone like him had ever gone to the fleet, but the ensign showed some profound knowledge about the navigation techniques and a knack for the mechanics of the ship. All this had to be encouraged without the impression that he was under the special protection of the ship's officers, but that impression would surely not materialize, so long as von Klasewitz acted like he did.

Becker, clutching the steaming metal cup with both hands, placed himself next to Rheinberg, who himself stood next to the quartermaster behind the large windows of the bridge and looked at the gray-blue waves with a critical eye.

"Your men and yourself are doing well, Captain?"

Becker nodded and took a sip. “I’m fine. Just wish I could say that about all my men. Your ship’s doctor does his second round today, and the number of green faces has not diminished.”

“It takes time. And we have time. The wind is strong, although not as strong as in the beginning. Strength 6 this morning. But we have to fight against him and can’t achieve more than 10 knots without increased coal consumption.”

“We don’t want to go faster anyway in order to save coal,” said Becker.

Rheinberg nodded. “But in order to keep the speed, we need to force the machines, because we fight the wind. That costs us extra. Here, see for yourself ...”

Rheinberg led the infantryman to the card table. In addition to his current appointment as executive officer, he was the navigation officer of the cruiser, and no one knew the charts as well as himself and von Krautz. A chart was spread on the table, showing the whole western part of Europe. The fine lines of the planned course of the *Saarbrücken* registered clearly.

“We may keep close to the coast,” Rheinberg said, “but we won’t be able to get coal again soon. I mustn’t tell you how fragile the political situation has become. The station chief himself spoke of war on the horizon. I don’t want to be in a potentially hostile port when the lid flies off. So we avoid Belgium and France and make a stopover in Portugal. What we hear from there is also not really encouraging, but they will give us coal.”

“That’s far. How far exactly?”

“A little more than 2,400 NM,” explained Rheinberg and immediately saw the slight confusion in the eyes of the captain. He calculated in his head. “Around 4,500 kilometers.”

Becker smiled gratefully and bowed his head. “I’m still learning, Lieutenant Commander.”

Becker and Rheinberg spoke very friendly to each other and without any formalities, but here, in the presence of subordinates, such behavior was inappropriate. Nevertheless, both the mate as well as the signalman noticed the relaxed atmosphere among the two officers and grinned widely at their jokes without fear of reprimand.

"How long will it take us with ten knots average speed?" persisted Becker.

"We expect to make it in eleven days if nothing worse happens in regard with the weather. We will not stay in Portugal for long; we take coal and water, and off we go to Cameroon. The whole coastline of the West Africa station is British and French, except for Togoland. We should therefore strive to steam as directly as possible to Douala."

Becker nodded. "So there will enough time then for my men to gain sea legs."

Rheinberg looked down at the man. "You seem to have them already."

"One never forgets. But I'll keep to myself how I felt during my first long voyage."

"Oh, no, please share that with me!" Rheinberg said with a grin, then he turned back to look over the bow of the *Saarbrücken*, the spray splashing as they broke through a new, powerful wave. After a critical look at the gray overcast sky he shook his head. "This will be a long night," he muttered to himself.

"You'll have late watch?"

"Yes, so you can get some sleep. I'll have some rest in the afternoon – and otherwise the coffee will help."

Becker raised his now empty cup. "This one wakes the dead."

"Which is very helpful on a warship," smiled Rheinberg.

The captain set down the cup and took another look at the raging sea. He stood upright as a wave crashed on the bow which made the ship lurch mightily. The deafening sound of the steaming masses of water pressing on the little bridge made all conversation impossible for a moment. Then the cruiser had fought free. Rheinberg threw again a critical look toward the sky. A bright crack had formed in the dense, deep black clouds, and it seemed to expand.

"We're lucky," the first officer said loudly as he could make himself understandable to some extent. "The weather seems to have calmed a bit."

Another twenty minutes passed before the storm subsided and the wind decreased markedly. The first sailors showed themselves on deck, where the cargo covered with tarpaulins and lashed items were examined for completeness and integrity. The noise level fell significantly.

Rheinberg now seemed relaxed and threw the helmsman an approving glance.

"Decent work, Hansen!"

"Thank you, Commander!"

Becker tapped Rheinberg on the shoulder. "Thanks for the coffee. I'll go below deck and look after my men. They'll be glad as the rocking has subsided somewhat. Where are we now? The men will be asking."

"Longitude and latitude?"

"I'd like something a little bit more illustrative."

Rheinberg turned to the charts again, and after only a brief orientation he pointed with his index finger on one particular area. "North of Ameland, in Dutch waters. When we have a clearer view, one can see for himself. But if you're looking to port ..."

Becker followed the now outstretched arm of Rheinberg and squinted. In the still relatively high waves, he barely could make out a strip of land in the distance.

"Ameland?"

"Yes."

"That is enough for me, if someone asks. I'll leave now."

Rheinberg tapped with his right hand to his cap.

"You are always welcome back, sir."

* * *

Rheinberg could not help himself, but during the journey through the Channel and along the French coast, he never ceased to be restless. During his readiness watch and even outside the actual duty time, he caught himself unable to relax and had to roam restlessly across the deck. The crew quickly got used to it, and the division chiefs soon realized that it wasn't the intention of the first officer to conduct unannounced inspections. He was greeted, but Rheinberg's absent facial expression made it clear that he was not interested in listening to status reports. For several minutes, he stood at the rail, armed with binoculars, while the *Saarbrücken* struggled through the rough seas of the channel, and he watched carefully, as the coast of France appeared in the misty spray. His father had taught him two things from which he couldn't or wouldn't dissociate himself completely: the traditional enmity with France on the one hand and respect for the courage of French soldiers on the other. As a cavalry officer and a young man, the older Rheinberg had fought in the Franco-German war and shared in the euphoric victory over the old enemy, a victory that brought the Empire reputation, land and financial resources. France as an enemy has always been one of the fixed and inevitable pillars of self-esteem, and Rheinberg had to learn that in his training, too. Deep inside him, something struggled against this setting, a quiet, nagging doubt, an unspoken question, and he found himself in an amazing harmony with his unpopular brother-in-law, Karl, who spoke of the chance to overcome the hostility to France by the "unity of the working class." Although Jan didn't care for Karl's socialist rhetoric, the idea of reconciliation with France had a certain attractiveness. The descriptions of his father, who had always expressed respect for the fighting courage of his enemies, may have contributed to it. Why should men who fought with equal vigor and dedication for their respective homelands automatically be his enemies? They seemed to have more in common than they wanted to otherwise admit, and this made Rheinberg think.

He would never have dared to express it openly, not even to Karl. And he felt the impact of decades of indoctrination as he nervously watched the French coast in anxious expectation, not least bearing in mind the worsening political situation on the continent. War was in the air, and this war would drive Germany and France against each other again, of that there was no doubt. Rheinberg believed that the German Empire would again prevail in this struggle, which was as expected as the Amen in church.

He and his ship might become involved right from the start. Most of West Africa consisted of French possessions, interspersed with some British colonies. The German colonies were in a difficult strategic position. Togo as a small colony was a narrow strip of land sandwiched between the French and British territories, and Cameroon, although of greater length, was surrounded by potential enemies. The borders had been amicably agreed to in 1884 at the Berlin Conference, chaired by Chancellor Bismarck, yet it was clear that in case of war all this would be quickly called into question. Africa would be a theater of war, and the German troop presence was small, one of the reasons that the *Saarbrücken* carried a company of soldiers with her, despite the fact that an additional company would ultimately make no difference. The cruiser, however, could accomplish something as a raider to disturb supply lines, but here Rheinberg's realism won over his confidence: His ship was old and slow, and he knew about the new French and British cruisers. The Germany Navy had better and newer ships, which didn't help the good old *Saarbrücken*, and the conversion to the new guns made since was only a marginal difference. The light cruiser was armored relatively weak and ammunition was limited; it wasn't a ship of the line and had not been built for a long battle. If cornered, they would either wait in a neutral port for German victory or sink the ship and go into captivity. Rheinberg would prefer to be able to break through back to Germany to avoid this rather shameful fate. Ultimately, this was a decision that would be made by von Krautz.

Rheinberg didn't envy him.

After leaving the English Channel, he relaxed a bit. On the faces of the other men he saw the same feeling. Only von Klasewitz had pretended as if he didn't care at all. No one took this seriously, not even the captain, and the second officer was smart enough not to exaggerate. The *Saarbrücken* won the open sea and was free from the French coast, which longer was visible, and the illusion of freedom relaxed Rheinberg to an extent that he was soon back to his normal routine.

The days passed, and the two groups of men on board got used to one another. The congested and difficult conditions made frictions inevitable, and Rheinberg and Becker therefore developed a drill to disturb the normal routine on board and to make sure that everyone was always busy. During free times, everyone usually fell tired into their hammocks soonly during meals remained an opportunity to share animosity. In addition, Chief Petty Officer Köhler had become friends with Sergeant Behrens, and many problematic issues that would otherwise have drawn the attention of the officers were resolved at that level. Rheinberg and Becker were both aware of this and happy with it as long as the veteran NCOs had the situation under control, and they obviously had.

On the evening of the tenth day, about fourteen hours before their scheduled arrival in Portugal, Captain von Krautz held a staffdinner in the wardroom. Except for those on duty – the third officer First Lieutenant Joergensen, and two division chiefs – all the remaining 15 officers of the *Saarbrücken* were present, as well as Captain Becker and his deputy, Lieutenant Roger von Geeren. The new lord of the machines, Marine Chief Engineer Johann Dahms, joined them also. Rheinberg had not yet had a chance to sit in peace to talk to Dahms, for his night shifts had meant that the engineer was asleep when Rheinberg was active. Rheinberg knew Dahms' deputy pretty well, though, and had talked to him briefly about the new boss, and it appeared that Dahms knew his job in the engine room and ruled with a steady hand. The duty below deck was murderous, the heat often nearly unbearable, and the shifts like hell. The mechanics were a close-knit community, if their superior officer succeeded in forging them into a team. That was not easy because crewmen there had in the past shown to be particularly vulnerable to social democratic infiltration. Dahms, however, seemed to be aware of his responsibility.

The officers' mess wasn't a big room, and was dominated by the dining table. Residing at the head, von Krautz quietly conversed with Dahms, as Rheinberg finally walked into the room and started to salute. One glance was already enough to make it clear that the captain didn't put too much value on formalities that night and by waving he asked Rheinberg to simply take a seat and to wait for the steward to serve the food. There was fish, potatoes and white wine, nothing special, but as always of good quality. After the captain had offered the toast to the Emperor and all raised their glasses, everyone started eating, and a conversation began to sway back and forth.

"I think that there can be no doubt," Rheinberg heard the slightly arrogant voice of von Klasewitz while still shoveling a fork of boiled potatoes into his mouth.

The general attention was directed to the second officer, not so much because the man had said something, but more because Captain Becker stared at his plate with a reddened face and chewed with very mechanical movements. Rheinberg knew Becker well enough by now to realize that he fought for his composure and was obviously angry. Klasewitz didn't seem to notice or he didn't care. He continued undaunted, and it quickly became clear why Becker preferred to grind on the fish instead of saying something.

"Our Majesty has said on several occasions, and in no uncertain terms, that the Navy is enjoying the highest favor and appreciation and remains preferable to the other parts of the armed forces," von Klasewitz continued. "Yes, it is of particular importance for the Emperor to expect the greatest and most excellent progress of the navy and its officers."

Klasewitz spoke like a communique, and he did so with a degree of complacency that wasn't received well by everyone. Rheinberg felt with Becker. Of course the second officer wasn't totally wrong; Emperor Wilhelm II was known to give the navy his fullest attention and to a far greater extent than to other military branches. But for someone like von Klasewitz, this seemed to become something like a hierarchy defined by natural law and to emphasize this in the presence of an army officer was more than just rude – it was close to insulting.

Rheinberg restrained himself. He looked up and his eyes met those of Dahms staring at von Klasewitz with visible disgust. Rheinberg knew that the naval engineers were almost all from the middle classes without any nobility, and this special blend of arrogance and bonhomie with which the noble naval officers sometimes despised the "lower" class of officer attracted very little sympathy among them. Dahms looked just as pissed as Becker, but both were silent, for it was not up to them to respond.

Von Krautz cleared his throat. "Klasewitz, we are all aware of the special grace of Her Majesty, but I think that we as professional officers know all very well that every victory depends on the fact that it is equally won at sea as on land. It would be shortsighted to deny this, and the mere fact that we were ordered to bring the captain and his men to Cameroon shows us that they have to accomplish something there that this cruiser cannot."

The tone of the captain had been blaming, albeit quietly, but with a distinct undertone. Von Klasewitz seemed unimpressed.

"Negro control, holding wild natives in check. Maybe for this task a man of the army is necessary, but nothing of real significance." He grunted disapprovingly.

"What is significant in your view?" asked Neumann. The ship's doctor didn't seem to be overly impressed either.

Von Klasewitz looked at him as if he had asked the stupidest question since the beginning of human history. He sighed and replied in a tone as if speaking to a naughty child. "Doctor, that should be self-explanatory. Fly the German flag on the oceans, and in case of war to clear the water from our enemies, and thus to provide wealth to the Empire as a global naval power – this is likely to be much more important than to patrol villages of Negroes."

"Indeed," muttered Neumann. "And for what purpose do we control the waters exactly?"

"What a question! For glory and power ..."

"This means that we have acquired the colonies in order to increase power and glory?" persisted Neumann.

"Certainly!"

"Not because of the raw materials or due to strategic considerations?"

Von Klasewitz made a face as if he had bitten into a sour apple. "Well, yes, well ..."

"And what will happen to our so magnificently protected sea lanes if the colonies do not produce goods that would be transported on such routes?"

"I think ..."

"And what happens if the colonial troops were not doing their job? Do you think that the Africans actually are full of happiness and enthusiasm in regard to the foreign domination of the German Emperor? Maybe they might rather come to the conclusion that it would be better to establish their own government."

Von Klasewitz laughed. "Government? They are savages! There never was any government in Africa worthy of the name!"

Neumann frowned. "The reports of German researchers have been talking a different language. May I remind you of the Congo kingdom, well researched by our scientists? In any case, it is clear and undeniable that without the presence of the army in the colonies, our duty at sea would be pointless since there would be nothing to protect."

"So it is!" agreed von Krautz and threw Klasewitz of a warning look.

Slowly the second officer began to realize that he was fighting a losing battle. With a red face and without even thinking about such a thing as an excuse to Becker, he devoted himself to his plate. The infantry captain had calmed visibly, but in Dahms' face there was still a deep, unrelenting disgust.

Rheinberg made a mental note to keep an eye on that.

The conversation died down and then turned to other things, much less suitable to raising a dispute. Finally, after the meal, Becker, Neumann and Rheinberg assembled half an hour later on the front deck, again near the bow. The sea was calm and the evening air cool, but not too chilly. All three men puffed on cigars from the storage of the captain, which he had liberally distributed. For a few minutes, the three officers gazed at the starry night, each occupied with his own thoughts.

Becker cleared his throat. "I want to thank you, Doctor."

"Hans?"

Becker smiled. "Jonas." He offered Neumann his hand which he casually grabbed and shook.

"There is nothing to thank me for," the doctor said. "Men like von Klasewitz are a problem for the whole fleet. They believe themselves to be the most precious of them all; they flay the crew and think NCOs are their personal slaves, look down on the Marine Engineers, and think their origin alone would give them every right to trample on others. Klasewitz is a classic example of the civil failures that have unfortunately spread among the fleet because of our Most High Majesty's opinion that the nobility should have precedence in holding the posts of officers and this therefore gives them preference in recruitment. Tirpitz is signing on to this without prompting."

"Tirpitz has his strengths and weaknesses," said Rheinberg, inhaling the pleasant smell of his cigar. "His weaknesses include that he thinks it is good to cement the cleavages within the officer's corps. Men like Dahms have received a longer and harder training than I did, and yet certain privileges are denied to him and his comrades. What a struggle it was until the Navy engineers had been allowed to carry a sword! That is silly."

Neumann nodded silently. Becker declined to comment on the delicate mechanisms of navy politics.

"When it comes to war, Jonas, how do you rate the chances of your men?" Rheinberg asked.

Becker's immediate reaction was a sigh. "Bad. Not against the natives, although I'm absolutely of the opinion that they would take the opportunity to rise against us, if it offers itself. I remember the Herero uprising in the Southwest. That was a nasty affair. A massacre. I will honestly say that I never understood what brought us to that place under the sun. That's a waste of money. Colonies will sooner or later become a burden to everyone."

Becker stood on thin ice, and he knew that political discussions among the officers were not welcome. But a quick look at the faces of Rheinberg and Neumann showed him they understood his complaints very well.

"But to answer your question," he continued, "the French and the British colonial troops are plentiful and have the strategic advantage. Our colonies are scattered across the continent. If it comes to war, we will lose Africa at least initially, there is no doubt, and permanently so, if we lose in Europe as well."

Again only confirming glances. Neumann and Rheinberg shared this assessment. A war would be disastrous for Becker as an individual just as for the crew of the *Saarbrücken*: imprisonment or death. And unlike the cruiser, Becker had not even the distant hope of being able to break through and flee to home. Someone like von Klasewitz wouldn't consider this.

"We pick you up once the war is over," Rheinberg said and put a hand on Becker's shoulder. "Just try not to get captured by the French."

"I'll do my best," replied the soldier casually, but in his voice was a silent sorrow and the doubt that this would be enough.

The three men exchanged no further words, waited until the cigars were smoldering stumps, which afterwards flew in a high arc into the sea. Portugal was before them, and then Douala.

3

"That's a little strange," muttered Becker, trying not to appear too anxious. Seeking help, he glanced at Rheinberg and von Krautz, who stood beside him on the bridge. Both had their eyes armed with binoculars and looked intently at the horizon. Quartermaster Börnsen seemed as confused as Becker, and as their eyes met, the man shrugged. If even the experienced helmsman who had sailed the seas of the world seemed irritated, Becker could hardly be blamed for not understanding.

It had begun in the early morning when the *Saarbrücken* had gotten into a fog bank of impressive density. The proverbial "cannot see the hand in front of your eyes" had materialized in a way Becker has not encountered before. Everyone's visual perspective didn't reach further than a few meters; each crewmember walked on the decks like a blind man, and an unnatural, disturbing silence had fallen over the cruiser. Von Krautz had ordered quarter speed and both the foghorn as well as the ship's bell announced the existence of the ship as it slowly sailed toward the Portuguese coast. Becker saw it on the faces of the two naval officers that even for them the murderously thick fog was a rather rare experience. As the sun had risen fully – discerned through the appearance of general brightness because the sun itself was not even recognizable as a diffuse luminous body – it fortunately didn't take long before the *Saarbrücken* finally left the fog and ventured on a completely calm and silent surface in bright sunshine cruising under a blue sky. The outside temperature suddenly jumped within ten minutes from very moderate to quite warm, the sky was cloudless, and the division chiefs had to allow the men to take off coats and jackets, as all were quickly sweating.

Yet, the coast could not be seen. Although once the fog had lifted von Krautz commanded the ship to accelerate to half speed and the muffled vibration of the powerful expansion engines shook the whole ship, nothing of the coastline was even remotely visible. That was also the reason why Rheinberg and the captain continuously kept their binoculars on their eyes while the *Saarbrücken* moved forward with a gentle bow wave, itself absolutely undisturbed by any movement of the surface. The cruiser was on course, there was no doubt. The sea hadn't been too bad during the last few days; a little gusty wind had prevailed, all in all acceptable weather conditions. Nothing had happened to the cruiser that would have veered it massively off course.

And yet, and yet ...

Becker's discomfort arose not because of his lack of confidence in the navigational abilities of his comrades – he estimated that, as far as he could tell, Rheinberg and von Krautz were experienced sailors who knew their craft – but from the insecurity and lack of understanding on the faces of all those experienced men. He knew even less about what was going on, and they seemed to offer nothing more substantial than speculation.

"A second bank of fog ahead," Rheinberg reported.

The captain lowered his glass and nodded. Becker squinted and stared in the direction indicated. Rheinberg had observed the situation correctly, and even with the naked eye the infantryman could make out a fine, whitish line of haze that was rapidly growing.

"Slowspeed," the first officer ordered, and the order was repeated and executed. The vibration of the machine diminished and the forward movement of the *Saarbrücken* became immediately slower.

"Very strange," Rheinberg whispered and set the binoculars down. The approaching fog bank was clearly visible, and it didn't touch the water, as the bright sunlight still reflected on the quiet surface. But increasingly, the visibility became more and more restricted.

"The fog horn every 30 seconds," commanded von Krautz. "We have to abide to our course, otherwise we will never get out of this ... situation." Silent approval on the bridge, and then, as the cruiser slid again into the mist, every utterance from the mouths of the soldiers sounded like their heads were wrapped in cotton wool. A strange pressure weighed on Becker's head, and he instinctively shook it as if he could get rid of the feeling that way. But the deeper the *Saarbrücken* drove into the fog bank, the more burdensome was the feeling. A glance around confirmed that he was not alone in this. Slowly the pressure grew into real distress. Börnsen uttered a low cry of pain and suddenly clung to the helm, Becker's head started to feel like exploding, and he began to wobble, stumbling directly on the mate's falling body. Rheinberg's last clear thought was that more was at work than just the fog.

He tried to stay awake but had no chance. Darkness and dizziness took both pain and consciousness away from him and he slumped in a final, semi-controlled movement alongside the others to the ground before darkness engulfed him.

Silence fell over the leaderless *Saarbrücken*, as the cruiser rode with slow speed onwards and slipped through the fog.

* * *

Marcus Necius looked thoughtfully into the dancing waves. He should have preferred to pay attention to what his twelve-year-old son Marcellus did at the stern of the small fishing boat, because for sure the boy had other things in mind than to control the fishing net that the small boat with its single mast pulled lazily through the water. But Marcus had other worries. Due to the adverse weather conditions, fishing in front of the Italian west coast has become increasingly difficult, and only last week his brother Drusus wrote a letter in which he asked him again to finally immigrate to Sicily. Drusus had had luck – he'd married a rich woman, and fathered many sons, inherited a fleet of 30 fishing boats that did all the work for him. Marcus remained in the vicinity of Rome, had married a simple but hard-working and loving wife, had one son, Marcellus, and toiled for him and his future. Drusus offered Marcus to join his business as a supervisor of the small fishing fleet and Marcellus would probably have his own boat in no time. But Sicily was quite far away from Rome, and even further away from Ravenna. Marcus had great plans for his son, and those plans went beyond the command of a fishing boat. He could read and write and had taught his son all this through hard work, and this year he had saved enough money to send him to the school to become a rhetor, at least for a year. Who knows? Marcellus could prove to be talented, he might get a scholarship, either from Marcus' patron, Senator Virilius, or even from Drusus, who might respond to the suggestions of his brother and put Marcellus in the care of his sister in Rome – if only for his son to escape the misery of being a fisherman and get a chance to become something else, maybe enter the administrative service of the Empire. With a little money, one also could ensure that the legal obligation for a son had to take his father's profession was implemented ... less restrictively. His wife, Emilia, supported him, and for that he was grateful as Drusus' constant insistence had become annoying. Marcus guessed that behind the seemingly generous offer something else lurked: Drusus, who had become fat and lazy and had for years held no rudder in his hands, wanted someone who did all the paperwork, grappled with the crews on the various ships and their demands, organized the sale on the market, saw to it that the necessary repairs were carried out, and so on – so that Drusus himself could retire permanently to his beautiful patch of land, which he had bought in order to drink, eat, and in the absence of his strict spouse to indulge in the pleasures of his female slaves.

Marcus loved his brother; he was, next to his sister Letitia, the only of the former eight siblings still alive. His other brother, Arcellus, had gone to the Legion and had made it to decurion, after which he had died in Germania against the barbarians. That was three years ago, and although Marcus was a devout Christian, he prayed secretly at every of Arcellus' birthdays to the ancestors and asked them to be gracious to the dead soldier. Arcellus always protected him and Drusus in their youth, and although Marcus was now just over 30 himself he often longed back to those times, especially when he lacked everything and felt the burden of life resting heavily on his shoulders.

No, Marcellus should not endure this. A job as a writer perhaps, maybe for a senator. He could praise a patron and write eulogies or work as an assistant to a curator or censor – a place in the imperial administration, so low it might be, was a better place to create income than on a ramshackle boat, sailing through the waves of the Mare Internum and catching fewer and fewer fish. Or to run a rented boat for a playboy like Drusus, doing his dirty work. Marcus loved Drusus, but he also knew what would become of his gracious offers once his son would aspire for more – Drusus' business was undoubtedly a dead end and he was just looking for someone who relieved him of tiresome work.

Not his only son.

His attention was now completely focused on his boy, who knew nothing about the thoughts of his father, sitting comfortably in the sun wiggling his bare toes. Next to him was an already half-empty tube with diluted wine and in the wicker basket an already heavily gnawed loaf of bread could be seen, which has been packed for her men by Emilia in the morning. She earned a little extra money as a baker and baked bread for a small booth on the street. But one loaf was always available for them when they went to sea early, and every time Marcus saw the silent sorrow in her eyes, because often enough fishermen never returned to shore. They were victims of the waves, or of one of the sea monsters the rumors talked about. Gracious nymphs who protected the fishermen had never been seen in his time.

They existed, of course. No one doubted it. Like all sailors, Marcus was superstitious to the bone. It was this belief in the strange creatures of the sea, the good and the resentful, which made him to calculate the risk to go out into the water with his boat every morning.

For the moment, there seemed to be no danger. Yes, it was too calm, because the sea was very silent and the boat had lost any momentum provided by the winds. The sail hung limply on the single mast. Marcus frowned. A trawling net did not provide anything if it couldn't be trawled and he cast a glance over the now cloudless sky from which the sun increasingly burned down mercilessly. The alternative was rowing, and that was not only laborious and sweaty it was also dangerous because if they spent too much time in this weather and the doldrums remained, they might finally be too weak to return to port.

"Marcellus!"

The boy woke up from his daydream and looked guiltily at his father. Almost automatically he groped for the nodes to which the trawl at the stern of the boat was moored and found them tight and intact. Noticeable relief crossed his face and he relaxed.

"Yes, Father?"

"The wind."

Marcellus took a hard look at the sail and nodded. This was his third year at sea, and he knew everything almost as well as his father, or so he claimed. The prospect of grueling rowing was clear to even the untrained eye, and now the bitter expectation of tormenting work showed on the boy's face. He sat up on his bench and looked behind him into the water, but the net lay low and there was no telling how far and if at all it was already filled. Then he looked up and squinted. He seemed to be surprised.

The boy had better eyes than his father, Marcus was ready to admit at any time, and so he drew near and put a hand on his son's shoulder. "What is it?"

Pirates were not rare here – the power of the Imperial Navy had waned considerably in recent years and only the grain ships from northern Africa still had significant escorts. Small fishing boats usually were not the preferred prey of brigands, but one never knew.

Marcus followed the gaze of his son to the horizon and could account for a tiny black dot, albeit blurry.

"A galley?"

Marcellus shook his head. "From the size, it could fit to a grain ship ... but ... no, I see no oars rowing and they should in this weather."

"Is it coming closer?"

"Yes. And it seems to be burning. Smoke is rising into the sky."

"A fire?"

Marcus' interest was piqued. A merchant ship could use some help with problems, and the captains were, at least in his experience, quite a thankful and generous lot and proved it with hard cash. A bag of coins would sweeten all the rowing and afterwards maybe a trip in the wake of a galley, without further effort, and all for a little help. It would not be the first time in Marcus's seafaring life that something like this happened.

"I cannot see the details, Father. But it's coming toward us!"

"Bring the net in," Marcus said. His son set to work without any ado and within minutes the net was in the boat. The yield was pathetic enough. What fidgeted there was hardly worth the trip to the open sea. But perhaps today's fate still turned out well.

Now he could see what his son had made out with his better eyes. A ship, and a big one indeed. But the shape ... and the color ... the clearer the picture became, the more the hopes of the fisherman vanished and fear spread through him.

Marcellus was quiet. Very quiet. His eyes were wide, his mouth open. He clung to the side and wiped his hand twice over his forehead, as if to dispel an illusion. Marcus couldn't blame him.

This was something he had never seen before. He'd never heard of anything like it. Even the wildest stories in the pubs had never spoken of such a ship. This couldn't be real. This couldn't possibly exist. God had his fun with him and for a moment Marcus forgot his good Christian sentiment and asked Neptune why he allowed himself to joke with this poor sailor.

But Neptune kept his silence. Meanwhile, the ship had come within about 200 *passus* of Marcus' fishing boat. It was big, bigger than a grain transport, but it felt more powerful, more threatening. It seemed made entirely of iron, and though it had masts, Marcus saw no sail. There were long metal tubes sticking out of the middle of the hull, and from this dark, regular plumes drifted in the windless sky. The ship did not burn, Marcus decided immediately with unerring intuition. The fire burned possibly within the huge trunk, but this was intentional, no threat, and help was not needed here.

Or was it?

Marcus squinted. He couldn't see anyone from the crew. Not a soul moved on the deck of that monster, which was already so close that Marcus could hardly see anything up on the planks anyway. Again fear took possession of him. Was it a ghost ship, a messenger of the underworld, a curse that plagued sailors at sea and tried to lure them into the darkness?

"Father, there is someone!"

The strange tone of his son's voice – he seemed to be less frightened than curious – disturbed his brooding thoughts. He looked closer. The distance was reduced more and more. Yes, Marcellus had been right: The crew was there – at least he now saw two men leaning on a railing, motionless, as if dead, and he saw a few more, as if they had fallen in the middle of the movement, struck by a sudden enemy. But nowhere the signs of a struggle were evident, no damage, no weapons or arrows – nothing indicated an attack.

"Father, what should we do?"

Marcus looked his son in the eye and concern for his only child threatened to overwhelm him. But then cool calculation prevailed. For a fisherman, life normally wasn't filled with too many opportunities. Whether this was divine providence or the smile of Fortuna, he couldn't simply row away. He felt a strange fascination that emanated from this mighty ship, and as the sailors on the deck were dead or asleep, he didn't have any real sense of danger.

Finally, curiosity won out. And greed. It was basically the same. The decision was obvious.

"We row over, my son," ordered Marcus. "Look there, a rope hanging down to the waterline. Dare you to climb up to it?"

Marcellus nodded eagerly.

"And there, that looks like a rope ladder, rolled up and ready." Marcus pointed at a different area of the railing. "If it is really a ladder, you can let it fall, and I'll tie our boat to it and come on board. Then we can look at what we've got here."

"Yes, father," his son agreed, remarkably obediently and eager. The fascination of the new and unfamiliar had wiped out any fear or doubt from his consciousness.

They went as planned. Soon the fishing boat had reached the rope and Marcellus' slender body, full of power nurtured by his hard work at sea, climbed the rope like lightning. Quickly he had reached the railing, then paused, admiring the strange and inexplicable structures on the big ship, and for a moment seemed to have completely forgotten his waiting father. Marcus called him finally and Marcellus rushed to the rope ladder, threw it down and let it rattle to the waters.

In less than five minutes, Marcus stood next to his son on the planks – which were no planks, but more sheets of iron – aboard the strange vessel and both were amazed in silent harmony. Truly, this was a miracle, and it seemed that it was a man-made miracle, because the sailors lying on the deck were just normal people, dressed in strange clothes that reminded of the uniform clothing of soldiers, and all quite remarkably large – but men, living and breathing ...

Living and breathing!

Marcus bent over one of the fallen. Indeed! The man's eyes were closed peacefully, but he breathed and the fisherman could feel the beat of his heart. He examined another, then a third. All lived. Some had swellings, often on the head, as they had fallen on something that had inflicted superficial injury, but no one looked to be seriously harmed. There was in fact no sign of a struggle.

"You know what that means, my son," Marcus muttered, while he looked at a metal structure from which stretched a long iron pipe, which made him somehow afraid. "If these men sleep, they will wake up soon."

"What kind of misfortune has affected that they all fell into unconsciousness?" asked his son.

"I do not know. But maybe they'll show their gratitude when they wake up and realize that we've helped them."

Marcellus saw his father full of energy. "What do we do?"

Marcus looked around.

"Those are resting in direct sunlight, which will do them no good. We pull them into the shade. Do you see that cloth? We span a sunscreen. There is bleeding from a head wound. We pull some of his white clothes and bandage his skull. There, those two are dangerously close to the railing. We pull them into a safe position. Those fell on each other. We free the one underneath. There is much to do. Let's show them that we were willing!"

Marcellus didn't try to discuss his father's decision but rather set out with zeal to implement them. Silently father and son toiled and cared for all on deck who they had found in a precarious position.

"More will be inside the hull," Marcellus postulated. A sudden fear took hold of his father, as he thought about the prospect to probably descend into the interior of the iron monster. What might await him down there?

It was once again divine intervention – or Fortuna's smile – which relieved him of a decision. A distinct groan resounded from the throat of one of the men, followed by an unconscious movement.

It had begun.

The sleepers awoke.

There was nothing more to do. Now they had only to hope for the grace and gratitude of these strangers. Marcus sent a prayer to heaven.

He had done what he could. Now it would be proven whether he had acted wisely or foolishly.

Father and son stood at the railing. They kept close to the ladder still swinging from the iron hull and tied to the fishing boat. But if it would be possible to flee in time, if it should prove necessary – Marcus had his doubts. Involuntarily, his hand sought his son's, and his fingers clasped those of Marcellus with almost painful reassurance.

One of the men opened his eyes.

Another swore something in an unknown language.

A third moaned, groaned, spat and muttered to himself.

Other voices joined them. Muffled groans became language, although incomprehensible to Marcus, and after curses he heard exclamations, and the tone of it, however, he knew quite well: commands.

And then someone saw them and commotion started. Marcus and his son were immediately surrounded by large, powerful, wild-looking men and strange, metallic things were targeted in their general direction – not swords, also not bows and axes, rather dark tubes that were wider at one end and had all kinds of hooks and whose function could not be explained by Marcus. He accepted, however, that these were weapons, because the men targeted the mouths of the tubes in a clearly threatening move on them. It was probably only a total lack of any threat emanating from the fishermen that prevented the strangers from rushing at them. Or there was something else. The hoarse, barking language of some other men, dressed in blue robes, close to the body and oddly shaped. Two approached the couple and the semicircle of men parted as they arrived. Then another command, and the tubes were lowered. Just another word in that foreign language, and most of the strangers turned away, though not without throwing the fishermen enigmatic glances.

Finally one stepped in front of them, a wiry man of impressive size and with brown eyes and short cropped hair. He looked inquisitively at the two fishermen, but without any threat, just curious. He talked to his companion, a stocky, somewhat slovenly guy, also dressed in blue, who was of comparatively advanced age.

A first question was addressed to Marcus, formulated in the incomprehensible language. For a moment it seemed to the fisherman that he heard a familiar term, but before he could grab it, it disappeared in the concert of foreign words, and their diversity covered the brief flash of understanding immediately.

Marcus knew nothing else but to respond in the language of the empire.

"My name is Marcus Necius, and this is my son Marcellus. We are simple fishermen and intend no harm!"

The response was amazing. Both men exchanged surprised looks, as if they hadn't expected that Marcus could speak at all. Both conversed again in their barking language. They seemed perplexed, puzzled. Marcus took that as a good sign. Maybe he and his son would survive this encounter unscathed.

He decided to speak again. "We've discovered your ship floating on the sea. Your men seemed to feel quite unwell, without consciousness. We came on board and helped!" Marcus pointed to the tarp that he and his son had stretched as sun protection. Many of the formerly unconscious men under it were already awake. He raised his hands. "We wanted to help. We haven't stolen anything. You can search us and our boat!" He pointed over the railing.

The eyes of the two men followed the hand and when they saw the bobbing fishing boat, they talked again with very astonished tone, gesticulating, scratched their heads. Marcus still didn't understand a word, but gestures and facial expressions left no doubt.

Finally, the first man coughed. He exchanged a final glance with his companion, then came a step closer to Marcus, hands outstretched. "My name is Jan Rheinberg. I'm the second in command of this ship."

The Latin of the man sounded strange, as strange as his name. But Marcus understood him and he felt very relieved. This meant his statements had been understood, and that there was a high probability that Fortuna had smiled for a third time. No, surely the Lord was with him, Marcus corrected himself immediately. He smiled broadly. "I greet you ... noble captain. Welcome to the waters of Rome."

Rheinberg looked at Marcus with searching eyes. "Explain something to me, Marcus," he begged cumbersomely.

The fisherman nodded eagerly and motioned for the man to ask his question right away.

Rheinberg paused. He shrugged, half apologetically, as he finally brought forth his question: “Why for God’s sake are you speaking Latin?”

4

"Why for God's sake is he speaking Latin?"

The wardroom was full. In addition to Neumann, Rheinberg, von Klasewitz, the captain and Dahms, twelve other key officers of the *Saarbrücken* heeded the call of the commander. The others were busy keeping the troubled crew under control. The two ragged fishermen Rheinberg had decided to send to the galley. Becker, who also joined the meeting, had ordered a reliable sergeant to keep an eye on the two, but until now they had behaved perfectly harmless.

"Because they claim to be Roman," Rheinberg answered the captain's question. "His name is Marcus Necius, and the boy is his son, Marcellus. They are both fishermen from Ravenna and have found our ship drifting in their fishing grounds, have come on board, and, as Neumann here confirms, helped our unconscious men as far as possible. Now they probably expect a reward." Rheinberg coughed. "And this is not completely unwarranted, I might add."

"Filth," came the outburst from von Klasewitz. "Underlings and liars. I take none of it seriously, Captain!"

Von Krautz raised a hand to silence the second officer.

"What else, Rheinberg?"

"Not much more. They are simple people. I interviewed them several times. My Latin is passable, but I basically learned only to read and write, never to speak. Neumann here can confirm that I have made reasonable efforts."

"That is correct," said the doctor. "For being only passable, the first officer made himself understandable quite well, and I had the impression that Marcus got the gist of things. And I think that I understood his answers as Rheinberg did. He says he is a fisherman from Ravenna." He sighed. "Welcome to the Roman Empire."

"Completely absurd," von Krautz exclaimed. "First this strange lull, then the entire crew thrown into unconsciousness and now ... now we are where?"

"If Marcus' information is correct, about 23 nautical miles southeast of Ravenna, in the Mediterranean," said Rheinberg.

"When we fell asleep, we were close to Portugal! To the West! In the Atlantic," von Krautz said. He shook his head. With enough space he would have restlessly walked up and down, but now he was left with nothing but drumming his fingers on the tabletop. "That's absurd."

"Lies!" said von Klasewitz then winced immediately, as the commander sent him another reproachful look.

"Condition of the engines?"

"Everything is fine, Captain," Dahms reported in a cool voice. It had been his very first act to scrutinize his machines after waking up from unconsciousness. "There is no visible damage to the ship. We have examined all the important sections and conducted a leak check. We haven't found anything."

"Injuries?" The question was directed at Neumann.

"A few bruises," Neumann said. "A cracked ankle from falling awkwardly is the worst. A few have gotten a little bit too much sun. That would have been worse if our guests would not have helped. But all are doing well so far. That is ..."

"Yes? Out with it, Doctor?"

Neumann sighed. "Physically, all are fine. But there is great unrest on board. Rumors going the rounds. A few of the cadets have listened and some of them also had Latin in secondary school. They might have passed quickly what our guests have told us. It will be necessary to speak to the crew soon. Or at least keep them busy somehow."

"But what to tell them?" asked von Krautz gloomily. "We don't know anything!"

"Right, Captain," said Rheinberg.

Before he could add to it, a signalman knocked and entered. He hesitated, but the first officer waved encouragingly and held out his hand.

"What's wrong?" Rheinberg said.

"Commander, Ensign Volkert reports that the nautical yearbook is incorrect."

"Excuse me?"

The man swallowed.

"Ensign Volkert reports that the information in the nautical yearbook does not match the measurements done by sextant. He thinks that it's not possible to have an exact positioning of the *Saarbrücken* using the data laid down in the yearbook."

"This is crazy," Becker blurted. He also knew that every year the German Hydrographic Institute in Hamburg published this book containing accurate information about the positions of the sun, moon and stars, which were essential for exact celestial navigation, in detail broken down by date and hour. It was re-calculated for each year and was the central foundation for navigation at sea.

Rheinberg sighed. "Mate, you relate my sincere sympathy to the ensign." The general chuckle broke the tense atmosphere somewhat. "Then take a look at the sky and tell the helmsman to stop the engines for a noon measurement. Very soon, we'll have the right time. We should be able to learn from it."

"Yes, Commander!"

With luck, this would define the navigational positioning. The noon calibration was only possible at the highest level of the midday sun, in order to give at least approximate information about their location.

For a moment, stunned silence fell over the assembly before a pandemonium broke out. The captain allowed his officers to discuss the issue for a few minutes so the tension could deflate before he commanded peace.

He had an ashen face when he finally spoke again. "Irrespective of all possible explanations, we cannot sit here and do nothing. We will go under steam and turn West. This fishing boat didn't have a long journey to come here. We can verify the story of Marcus without much effort."

"We were under steam all the time," Dahms responded.

Von Krautz squinted. "Explain."

"When we lost consciousness, the *Saarbrücken* has made little speed. Then the slack and the fog bank ... and, well, nothing more. When we woke up, the engine was still on little speed. So we came across the fishing boat."

"Wait. With little speed and an unconscious crew we traveled from Portugal to Italy? That sounds even more incredible."

Dahms shook his head. "Nothing like that, sir. We have consumed coal for only a short time; the boilers started to lose pressure slowly – but that's about it. We have not completed 20 miles, let alone drive around Gibraltar and sailed around the southern tip of Italy. Completely impossible. The bunkers are full, and no one was able to shovel coal. The cruiser was rudderless. No. That means either the Klabautermann has been in charge or else – the *Saarbrücken* wasn't under any control and didn't travel for long."

No one could dispute Dahms' conclusions.

"Then this Marcus must lie," insisted von Klasewitz.

"That may be it. But what kind of Portuguese fisherman speaks Latin and gives us his welcome in the Roman Empire?" objected Rheinberg. "No one would make such a joke with a foreign warship."

"Then the man is mad," the second officer said.

"Neither he nor his son give this impression," Neumann said quietly. He had examined both of them thoroughly.

"We ..."

Von Krautz was disturbed again. This time the soldier entering was Lieutenant Langenhagen, a young man who was already on his second trip on the *Saarbrücken.* He saluted half-heartedly because he knew now that neither the captain nor the first officer put too much value on formalities when things were urgent. Von Klasewitz he conveniently ignored. The nobleman would still insist on standing at attention when the *Saarbrücken* was on fire and the crew jumped into the water.

"Captain, I've searched the fisherman's boat as ordered." He heaved a big bag on the table. "You have to look at this, Captain."

Without waiting for a command, he emptied the bag on the table. All eyes were turned on the items displayed. Rheinberg leaned forward and took the items one by one in his hands. He could feel that the others were looking at him. Everyone, even Captain von Krautz, expected him to come up with an explanation.

He lifted a brass plate into the air.

"This is an astrolabe."

"I've read about it," muttered von Krautz and took it gently.

"I didn't," Becker said.

Some naval officers grinned. Rheinberg nodded sympathetically to the infantryman. "An astrolabe is basically an ancient predecessor to the sextant, which was used until the last century – that is, our last century. The position of the visible stars of the northern hemisphere is registered in planar projection on a brass plate and in a coordinate system. Connected to it is a second plate with an oval area, representing the horizon and being rotatable around the center. At the edge of both discs you see scales engraved, on the bottom the date and on the top a time scale. If the upper disc now rotates in such a way that the current time on the top scale on the actual date of the full scale come to rest, you can recognize the stars visible at this time if you look at the oval section of the upper disk. To determine the exact position of the those stars, there are those little hands, which we use on a scale declination ..."

"Well, thank you," interrupted Becker. "This will be boring for everyone else. I understand. It's the predecessor of the sextant."

"Developed by the Greeks – and also most commonly used in the Roman Empire to determine the position in maritime navigation," von Krautz said then put the metal plate back on the table.

Rheinberg took another item. "A wineskin." He sniffed it and made a face.

"Ropes and fishing net are in the boat," Langenhagen added. Rheinberg nodded. He held a leather sheath in his hand, which he carefully opened. A bundle of parchments appeared, which he began to open up almost reverently.

He took a long look at the writing on the parchment, frowned, looked distracted, then he smiled. He read aloud: "Of bodies change'd into various forms, I sing: Ye Gods, from whom these miracles did spring, Inspire my numbers with coelestial heat; 'Till I my long laborious work compleat: And add perpetual tenour to my rhimes, Deduc'd from Nature's birth, to Caesar's times." He raised his head and looked invitingly into the round. "Well?"

Neumann grinned.

"Yes, doctor?"

"P. Ovid Naso, if I'm not mistaken."

"Who?" said Dahms.

"Ovid. 'The Metamorphoses.' I have suffered through this in school and remember it only too well."

Some of the officers nodded understandingly. Neumann enjoyed the sympathy of most of them.

Rheinberg went through the papers. "The first book, if I am not mistaken. Just the right stuff for his son in order to learn how to read after he has already mastered 'The Gallic Wars' by Caesar. We have here a fisherman who insists on a proper education."

Silence greeted his remark. The scrolls looked very real. Rheinberg dug back into the pile. The remaining items were not very impressive. A bag of olives. A few simple tools. A fishing rod with a fishhook. A bunch of carefully wrapped simple clothes, apparently intended in case they needed to change. Everything looked like the real thing in the sense that it made a very ancient impression, not what one would expect to find on a 20th century fishing boat. Rheinberg saw that the doubt in the eyes of the officers made way to growing amazement.

Once again von Krautz allowed discussion for some time. Rheinberg quickly realized why. Noon arrived and passed, and shortly thereafter a mate entered. He didn't get into the trouble to announce himself formally, just immediately handed Rheinberg a paper and left. Rheinberg read and passed it to von Krautz.

"Compliments from Ensign Volkert," he said. "As far as possible, he has been able to confirm the position of the ship and therefore to verify the information given by Marcus. We are definitely in the Eastern Mediterranean, east of Ravenna, and not too far from the coast of Italy. There is no doubt that the fisherman's claims are correct in this regard."

A murmur went through the officers.

"That said, Marcus seems not to be a liar," stated Rheinberg. He already had been convinced that this theory had been only one of many possible explanations, and not the most likely one. Von Klasewitz pressed his lips on each other and said nothing.

"But that's still insane," said Dahms. "What does it mean? That we actually somehow, God knows how, have traveled through time and arrived in the past? That's ... it sounds like someone has read too much of that French –"

"Jules Verne," Becker helped.

"Whoever. Or the pulp fiction about that advanced dirigible Langenhagen always reads. Do we really want to accept this as an explanation?"

"Presently we don't have any explanation," said Rheinberg. "But you might want to remember one thing, Dahms: If the current nautical yearbook does not help us to identify our correct position with the sextant – and Volkert definitely knows how to handle the instrument – then that means that the data contained in the yearbook are simply not valid because we are not in the timeline we are supposed to be."

"Or the ensign did indeed make a mistake," said von Klasewitz.

"Feel free to go to the bridge and try again," von Krautz growled. "And then ask Volkert, as well, how it is that his noon measurement, without using the data in the yearbook, confirms the statements of our fishermen."

"Maybe a conspiracy," surmised von Klasewitz, who apparently ran out of ideas. "The two are in cahoots and it is an insidious plan of the enemy to kidnap the *Saarbrücken*! A sleeping pill in our food and a subsequent change of course!"

"And then they send a fisherman with a crazy story we can verify simply by sailing to the next port – rather than boarding us with a company of British Royal Marines?" Rheinberg objected. "And what, by God, should our enemy gain by 'kidnapping' the old *Saarbrücken* which doesn't contain anything more valuable than some recently refurbished old machines?" Although he tried to deliver his words in a calm tone it became clear that the second officer walked on his nerves.

"What do I know? The war is coming. Our fleet is strong, the British are afraid of us. One who is scared does strange things."

Rheinberg wanted to reply but saw in the corner of his eyes that von Krautz raised his hand and so he kept his quiet. Such discussion led nowhere anyway. Still, thoughts whirled in his head. It was hard for him to preserve his inner peace, given the importance of what now appeared so obvious. While the men around him expressed to their emotions in different ways – by anger, by rejection, by fatalism, by bordering on hysteria, nervousness – Rheinberg felt simply confused, as if someone had pulled the rug from under his feet. A journey through time? Who could blame someone like von Klausewitz for not believing it? Rheinberg himself couldn't grasp the thought in its entirety. And the reactions of other men showed that they felt likewise.

And the crew ...

What should he ... They had to speak to the men very quickly now! They had to give some answers to questions, and had to relay this completely unbelievable story. They had to read the mood and react. Discipline alone might not be sufficient to alleviate the problem.

Rheinberg felt a bit dizzy. The excited conversations around him made him even more confused. He looked around and realized that beside him only three other men kept silently to themselves: Dahms, Neumann and the captain.

Then Langenhagen smiled broadly. These crazy books he always read had to be gone to his head. He seemed to actually enjoy the situation.

Any further discussion came to an abrupt end, as mate stormed back into the rooms, red-faced and out of breath. "Vessels," he blurted without prompting.

"Announce your message properly!" barked von Krautz and rose.

The mate instinctively came to attention. "Ensign Volkert reports a flotilla of strange vessels with a direct path toward the *Saarbrücken*, from south-southwest. He asks the captain to appear on the bridge."

Von Krautz was already on his way, closely followed by Rheinberg. None of the other officers needed any orders, and they hurried to their stations.

When the captain, Rheinberg and von Klasewitz entered the bridge, they immediately seized their binoculars and looked in the same direction as Volkert. For a moment, silence prevailed. Led by their NCOs, the crew was very busy. Volkert had apparently commanded combat readiness, and rightly so.

"What is it?" von Krautz asked, and it was clear that he directed it primarily to Rheinberg.

He looked very carefully a second time before he answered. "Triremes."

"Sorry?"

"Triremes. Oared galleys with auxiliary sails. Pretty big pots. On the front there are ram bows, not unlike the one carried by the *Saarbrücken*, but less decorative. And if I'm not mistaken, the ships are full of armed men."

"In fact," muttered von Krautz now. "I see the rows and the sails – and the soldiers."

"We should verify this," muttered Rheinberg. "Mate, bring our Roman guests to the bridge!"

"Yes, Commander!"

"No matter if soldiers or pirates," the captain went on softly, "I slowly have to reconcile with the idea that this is indeed no sick trick the British have been playing on us – because they surely wouldn't go so far. But that doesn't really improve our situation. If it is true – and I still stress the 'if' – that we have traveled to the past, then the question remains, how we got here and how we can return to our time?"

Rheinberg lowered his glass and nodded gravely. In the corner of his eyes he saw von Klasewitz opening his mouth with astonishment and disbelief, still staring through his eyepiece. That should convince even the old conspiracy theorist, Rheinberg thought a bit amused.

"Captain, I agree with you," von Klasewitz said. "But I am afraid that we have a more pressing concern. I counted two triremes, each loaded with soldiers to the fullest. And it doesn't look like they want to pay us a friendly visit. I highly recommend to prepare the guns for battle."

Von Krautz was about to open his mouth when the mate entered with Marcus and his son. Rheinberg talked to the fisherman, who was visibly intimidated. He smiled kindly. "Marcus, we need your help."

"I like to help, sir!"

"Take this. This device allows you to see things in the distance closer than they are. It is completely safe, and I want you to take a look in this direction."

Marcus hesitantly took the binoculars and turned them in his hands. Then Rheinberg showed him how to use them. Finally, the fishermen held them to his eyes, anxiously watched by his son, who then, as von Krautz handed his glasses to the boy, stared through it with sudden eagerness. It didn't take ten seconds and Marcus lowered his binoculars again, looking pale and agitated.

"Well?"

"Imperial Navy," the fisherman exclaimed. "They don't do many patrols in these waters anymore, but this must be one of their occasional efforts."

He himself seemed not to know whether to be happy or distressed about this encounter. "We may get lucky and meet someone who asks first and then attacks. But given your ship and ..."

Rheinberg knew what the man wanted to say, as he stopped talking just in time. For him the *Saarbrücken* and its crew would have to be more than just "strange."

"Fighting us won't be quite that easy," Rheinberg said soothingly. He looked questioningly to von Krautz.

"I've seen enough," replied the captain to the silent question and turned around. Orders were barked. Combat readiness achieved, the 15-cm guns were moved into position. The triremes approached at considerable speed.

"Dahms," von Krautz shouted into the mouthpiece, which linked him to the engine room, "I want full steam!"

"Full steam, yes!" The voice sounded faint. Down below, deep in the body of the cruiser, the men shoveled the coal into the combustion chambers of the engine. Rheinberg felt almost immediately the return of the usual vibrations. The cruiser became alive!

5

Aurelius Africanus has been captain of the *Scipio* for five years and though he loved his job at least as much as the sea, he boiled with deep dissatisfaction. It might have to do with the fact that since the Roman Mediterranean fleet had been moved to be stationed in Constantinople – with only two squadrons remaining in Ravenna – the presence and significance of a posting there was falling very short of how it had been before in the Classis Ravenna. At those times, a command in the fleet in Ravenna would have been only slightly minor to one in the Classis Misenesis, and the prospects for an able officer's career would have been excellent. This career was not simply what his family had always hoped for him. It was, ultimately, the goal of his grandfather, who had at that time, still bearing the name of his Nubian ancestors, entered the fleet as part of the Egyptian contingent and had ended his career as proreta, the assistant of the gubernator, the helmsman. It was quite a career for a farm boy from the African hinterland. His son, Aurelius' father, with his name already romanized, followed in the footsteps of his grandfather and had risen to the position of the secutor, responsible for discipline on board and being the direct voice of the captain, the trierarch. And here Aurelius stood on the bow of the *Scipio* staring over the mirror-like surface of the coastal waters alongside his proreta Lucius, the quiet sea quite atypical for the Mediterranean with its usually strong winds. He had made his father happy by achieving the rank of a trierarch, commanding a mighty trireme of the Roman Empire, and he would, if he survived his 26 years of service, bring honor and respect back to his home village. But he wanted more, had dreamed of a significantly higher position than even his father had wished for him and had worked hard on himself, achieving his current post in his early years. But now Constantinople was far, and only there he could really make a career, rising to the staff of the prefect, find his ear, give expert advice, and then after a few years hope for a promotion to navarch, the rank of squadron commander, the place to which Aurelius Africanus really belonged.

Others said that the Grand Fleet was lying largely rotting in the harbor of the capital of Eastern Rome and that it was better to have two fairly intact squadrons in Ravenna than to have a large fleet of wrecks in Constantinople ... or even commanding one.

But Aurelius still aspired for an additional challenge and felt that he could only achieve his aspiration where the center of power had moved quite some time ago: to the east.

But how to achieve this? For eight years he had been trierarch, and for eight years his career had not moved a step forward. He was stuck. Everyone on board knew about the frustration of their commander, and especially Sepidus, the old gubernator. The helmsman held his office for almost ten years, being perfectly content with his position, and without doubt one of the best helmsmen in the fleet. Sure, the two squadrons were located near the seat of government of the Western Roman Empire, but it wasn't necessary to be a senator, a courtier, a magister militium, the supreme military commander, nor a navarch or prefect, to see how the power of Rome had moved to Constantinople. The relocation of the entire Mediterranean fleet at the time of Emperor Constantine was only an indication, and everyone knew how important it was that the Emperor of Eastern Rome formally recognized the emperor of Western Rome and supported him – while conversely, no one in Constantinople could possibly give a shit about what the one in Ravenna, Trier or wherever the Western Roman emperor resided, was thinking about them. And all that was true, unfortunately, for the frustrated trierarch of the *Scipio*, and he had to seriously restrain himself, especially his bad temper, in order not to make his men suffer from it and to be able to zealously perform his duty.

Not that there was much to do. From below, from the helm deck, he heard the sounds of the symphoniacus, who by playing his flute gave the rhythm of the beat frequency for the oarsmen, always under the supervision of the pausarius, who was responsible for the correct work on the thwarts. Aurelius had once sat there himself during the first two years of his military service, had been, like any other recruit, initially not more or less than a rower. Roman law never allowed slaves to be used in the defense of the realm, and although many freedmen were in the ranks of the armed forces, never anyone unfree. Those who wanted a career in the fleet and had no connections to nobility began where the hardest and worst paid jobs were available: on the thwarts. Sometimes, if Aurelius was in the mood, he sat with his men and rowed an hour or two, and this did good for his massive biceps and muscular chest. Anyone down there sweating and lurching the mighty *Scipio* against wind and waves felt what it was like to be a Roman citizen. He sat with those from Pannonia and Africa, from Spain and Gaul, on the bench and the tangle of curses from different languages reflected the origins of the seafarers. Eventually they were all Romans, also former Nubians like Aurelius Africanus, though he wore his origin in his name, perhaps more than any other.

Today only a little rowing has been necessary. The *Scipio* had been in no hurry.

Aurelius looked to port, where he could identify, during the fine mist of the horizon, the east coast of Italy. No galley ever voluntarily left the protective area near the coast, and only the remarkable calm weather of the day had induced the trierarch to dare leaving the vicinity of the shores to such an extent that the coast had diminished to a fine, dark line. Closer, about a mile landward, the vague silhouette of the *Augustus*, the sister ship of the *Scipio*, was discernible. Today it was on patrol with them and on board her trierarch, Africanus' old friend Vicius Dacians, who was not quite as keen to go further away from the coast than absolutely necessary. As impressive as ships like the *Scipio* were, they were a disaster in rough water, didn't cope well under high waves, and had the nasty tendency to break apart under heavy weather.

Unlike many of his comrades, Aurelius knew how to swim. And he knew he could make it from here to the coast, especially when he got hold on a piece of driftwood. But they were in no danger at all: Such a lull like this he had never encountered, the water was smooth as glass, and was only ruffled by the slow, almost deliberate stroke of the oars, which pushed the *Scipio* forward sluggishly.

"Sir ..."

Aurelius looked thoughtfully on the calm sea. He had obviously not heard Lucius. The proreta cast a helpless glance across the *Scipio's* elongated deck. Sepidus, who stood behind the rudders, twitched his shoulders and made a characteristic movement with the right leg. "Kick him in the ass!" the veteran said, but Lucius was sure that it wasn't wise to take this advice literally. Unlike the old gubernator, who had 24 years of service at sea under his belt, the younger Lucius still wanted to become someone, and if you had aspirations, it was advisable not to kick one's trierarch ...

"My Lord!"

"Yes?" The somewhat more pressing undertone woke Aurelius from his thoughts. "What is it?"

"A ship, seaward, perhaps ten miles!"

The eyes of the trierarch followed the outstretched hand of his proreta. He narrowed his eyes. Seaward it was a bit hazy, like a fog which just cleared away. The weather was crazy today.

But Lucius as proreta of a ship had to have remarkably sharp eyes, because he was the lookout directing the helmsman. It was his job, from the bow of the ship, to watch the way the galley sailed and to provide the gubernator with guidance for the course of the ship. He was rarely wrong, and he was never wrong when it affected his powers of observation. Aurelius might be a frustrated trierarch, but he knew exactly why he had promoted every man in his crew to a particular position.

Aurelius' eyes were not as good as those of Lucius, but could recognize the black dot with a little bit of concentration.

"What is it?"

"A single ship. But big. A trireme – or larger."

"A grain transport?" The massive freighters transporting grain from Africa to Italy were the largest ships the world has known. Against these giants even a quinquereme seemed small, and quinqueremes were impressive warships. They were stationed in Constantinople, so Aurelius Africanus hardly saw any. But a grain-ship this far east?

"I'm not sure. It moves slowly."

"What do you see?"

"Smoke rises to the sky."

"A fire?"

Two disasters could befall ships outside the vicinity of the safe shores, even in this quiet weather – a fire could have broken out on board and be consuming the ship, or it could have been attacked by pirates, looted and set afire. Both would explain the smoke plume that Lucius had seen.

Aurelius gathered himself. Whatever it was, there was something to do. He cast a searching look at the bright blue, totally cloudless sky, turned and hurried to the rear deck, where Sepidus already looked at him expectantly.

"Sir?"

"Expect directions from Lucius. We head toward the alien ship."

Sepidus nodded. He gave his men at the two powerful rudders clear orders, and the *Scipio* turned gently in the right direction.

"Increase the number of strokes. Secutor, wine for the rowers. Flavius!"

Flavius Calvinus, the ship's centurion, appeared out of nowhere and approached the trierarch. He was formally the same rank as Aurelius, but at sea a subordinate. He was not a sailor but commanded the small group of infantrymen the *Scipio* had on board – and in boarding combat he was in charge of the entire crew of the trireme, because as soon as the fight began, all rowers turned immediately into marines, seized their swords, and belonged to Calvinus. This also applied to any necessary land expeditions.

"Trierarch!"

"Flavius, prepare your men. Prepare the bridge. I want to use it immediately if needed. Get the best archers of the thwarts. I want them to stand ready and await my command!"

The centurion had no need to hear the commands twice. Even as he turned away, he called for his optio. The deck shook as the soldiers moved into position. The crew was excited but not in an uproar. The secutor had a watchful eye on every move. The Roman fleet was a disciplined fleet, and the *Scipio* one of the best ships.

"Sepidus, you care about the course. I go back to the bow. Watch for my sign!"

The gray-bearded sailor nodded.

Metus, the nauphylax or armorer of the *Scipio*, entered the deck. He had heard the centurion giving his orders, and together with his assistant he carried the weapons to be issued to the rowers. The bows were kept ready for those who Flavius would choose immediately to perform as archers; swords and spears he lined up for the event that more rowers would be reassigned and armed. Flavius had already gathered a dozen Marines in full armor at the bow next to the bridge entrance, and held them in readiness. He carefully made sure that they didn't cover the line of eye contact between the proreta and the helmsman Sepidus, because Lucius was the one who had to give exact orders for the course to the rear.

The trierarch joined Flavius, having armed himself along the way. The short sword hung at his side. He stood next to Lucius and saw the excitement in the face of the young man.

"What do you make of it?"

"I don't know, sir. I really don't know."

Lucius' confusion and perplexity were so obvious that it involuntarily filled his captain with worry. The proreta knew every class of ship, any wooden silhouette on the Mediterranean, and no one could delude him. The fact that he couldn't give a definite answer to the question spoke for itself. Aurelius leaned forward, eyes narrowed. The flute playing on the rowing deck had become more hectic, the beat rate had increased. Water splashed up as the oars dipped in faster and the mighty *Scipio* drove ahead. On port, the *Augustus* was signaled. With luck, she would follow her sister with increased speed.

With each passing second, the exact image of the alien ship became more visible. With each passing second Aurelius began to understand the perplexity of his proreta more and more. Whatever kind of vessel it was now approached with constant speed; he had never seen such a thing in his life. An excited murmur rose on the *Scipio*, the Marines looked at each other and pointed forward, the sharp-eyed began to report in a whisper what the short-sighted didn't see properly. Aurelius allowed this lapse in discipline for a few seconds, as he was also almost stunned by the strangeness and menace emanating from the alien ship, the anguish which appeared with every stroke to become larger.

But he was the trierarch.

He turned around and threw the secutor, who was himself standing at the railing and staring forward, a distinct look. The man got the message and immediately barked sharp commands across the deck. Discipline returned, and Flavius ordered his soldiers to remain silent. It was like the calm before the storm, but this time there was a danger that was inexplicable.

From the coming ships stubby masts, smoke billowed as if from chimneys. It had to be made of metal, of iron or bronze, as some shimmered in the sun, and it had a powerful battering ram, of such great force that Aurelius was absolutely sure that the *Scipio* would be broken by this monster in a single attack. He resolved to deny the adversary this opportunity and called commands, heard the cries of confirmation by Sepidus, saw the nod of his proreta, who understood the tactics of his trierarch. The trireme then gave the other ship less exposure by turning front directly to the side of the metallic body, which was now more and more visible to all of them. The ship was moving slowly, but with no visible rudder or sail, and Lucius shouted more instructions. The *Scipio* would reach the enemy amidships, bow forward, her own battering ram directly pointed toward the body of the alien vehicle. Soon it would be too late for the metal monstrosity to turn and bring its own spur into position.

And now one could see people on deck. No demons or sea monster, as some had cursed under their breath, no diabolical figures, but men, tall, many dressed in white or gray or blue cloth, which stood and watched as the men of the *Scipio.* Whoever commanded this ship and from wherever it came from, the crew was not made of metal but of flesh and blood, and the encouraging comments of the marines became louder. Bows and arrows were at the ready, because a well-aimed arrow would kill these sailors just like everybody else.

That was good news. Aurelius felt the fear disappear a bit. However, he didn't waste a minute thinking to make peaceful contact with this monstrosity – it looked every bit as threatening, very alien, very ... wrong. It was almost like a reflex, and a look into the faces of his men showed that it wasn't only him who felt that way. Whatever this ship was, it could only be a danger, a threat to the *Scipio* and Rome, and therefore it was their duty to engage that threat.

Excitement became visible over there. Aurelius smiled faintly as he watched the chaos on the deck of the stranger. Roman discipline was something those men could still learn. And Roman tactics as well: Instead of turning their ship quickly in order to align the battering ram in the direction of the *Scipio* so to be able to attack if their enemy would make an error, they continued to present his highly vulnerable broadside. Only small houses with long tubes protracting from it turned slowly toward the trireme.

Men stood at the railing of the giant. They waved and shouted in an incomprehensible language. Aurelius could identify a man who differed significantly from the odd stranger: He almost looked like a simple Roman fisherman.

He gesticulated and shouted, too. The sea carried off his words. Beside him, silently, stood two men, clothed in dark blue, wearing white hats and golden ornaments flashing in the sun. There could be no doubt that the fisherman was either a prisoner or a traitor. In both cases, Aurelius was obliged to attack.

He raised his hand. The agreed upon signal. While the crews on the rear thwarts now sunk the rows quickly into the water under the increasingly hectic play of symphoniacus, the crews of the front benches broke away and rushed to the upper deck and, quite disciplined under the watchful eye of the secutor, to stern. On the way, they passed Maltus and his assistant, took the weapons provided, then they gathered silently close to the helmsman, who guided the glorious *Scipio* steadfastly toward the body of the metal vessel. The more the weight was concentrated at the rear, the more the battering ram lifted out of the water, until it gently glided over the surface, in an exact, perfect angle, ready to slit the belly of the enemy.

Aurelius threw Lucius a look. The centurion had been waiting. He gave an order.

The archers, a dozen of the best aboard the *Scipio*, raised their bows.

6

"I can't believe this!"

Von Krautz, standing alongside Rheinberg and the fishermen, stared stunned across the sea, and saw a museum piece moving toward the *Saarbrücken*, becoming significantly faster, the battering ram easily lifting out of the water, with the clear, unambiguous intent to ram them.

A timber ship was about to ram an armored light cruiser!

Absolutely crazy! The ship would burst in the middle. The spur, severed by the hull of the cruiser, would split at best, and at worst drive backwards into the galley and cause the already weak enough looking design to fold into itself. The crew of the vessel was substantial, the upper deck of the attacker full of sailors and ...

"Legionaries," gasped von Krautz, as if he could only now fully understand, as he had never truly believed the words of the fisherman, as he had to see it with his own eyes first.

"Captain, we should commence fire!" Rheinberg said.

Von Krautz turned to Rheinberg and looked at him with total disbelief in his eyes. "Fire? One shot, and this rowing boat sinks or goes up in flames!"

"It attacks."

"It's a rowboat!" von Krautz almost cried indignantly.

"It's a warship. A trireme. Those soldiers are trained killers. We must defend ourselves!"

The captain threw up his hands as in comic despair and turned speechless toward the rapidly approaching opponent, as if to move him with a mere gesture to give up his senseless endeavor. Rheinberg was not sure if von Krautz had seen it as well, but the twelve muscular men leaning over the wooden railing of the trireme had donned their bows, and with the confidence of years of practice and knowledge about their own abilities, targeted twelve lean, fast projectiles toward the cruiser. Rheinberg knew intuitively who would be the target once they shot up.

He dropped, quickly pulled the fisherman standing beside him to the ground, and grabbed the legs of the captain to unbalance him as opening his mouth to yell a warning.

But he was left to see that two arrows suddenly grew from the chest of von Krautz, long, feathered wooden projectiles, and his dark blue uniform jacket became soaked red, dark red, and the blood spread fast.

Von Krautz slumped silently to the deck, one hand clutched in vain around the shaft of the arrows, the other seeking for support, and in falling he met the eyes of Rheinberg, still full of incomprehension, and then they broke, even before he finally touched the planks.

More men cried, all hit by arrows. A second volley went over the deck, fired with the speed of thought. Now the Germans realized the danger and took cover, though too late for many.

Too late for von Krautz.

For a moment, time stood still and nothing and no one moved.

Rheinberg stared at the body of his captain, suddenly completely aware that whatever might happen now, he himself was from now on the commanding officer of the *Saarbrücken* – he, Jan Rheinberg, who had always dreamed of a command.

What a cold thought, given this sudden death, shooting through his head.

And his command was still under attack.

That was the reason for his lack of emotion. Focus. He needed to focus.

And then the trireme crashed with furious force into the side of his ship.

The cruiser shuddered slightly; a gentle swaying transited the ship's body, and at the same time came the crunch of decomposing, splintering wood, and surprised, horrified screams from the trireme. Rheinberg straightened and saw how one of the 10.5-cm quick-loading cannons on the starboard side targeted the already mortally wounded galley gaining distance from the cruiser and fired a single shot.

The shot tore the rear, full of sailors, like paper. Splinters flew through the air, one penetrated his arm painfully, and Rheinberg protectively covered his face. Cries of pain, a deafening chaos of sounds, and a staccato of terror filled the air. Shots rang out, the infantrymen of Becker's company aimed at the few Romans who still held at the rapidly sinking wreck of their ship.

"Cease fire! Cease fire!" came finally the commanding voice of Becker and the banging ebbed. Rheinberg got up, spun around, let go of the hand of Marcus and headed for the bridge. Blood ran down his arms from where they had caught bigger wood splinters, but he ignored the pain. Breathless, he rushed to the bridge.

"The captain – where is Neumann?"

"On his way," Volkert said, who was on the bridge and apparently gave the command for the cannon to shoot the trireme.

"Men in the boats. Arm everyone. I want all the survivors fished out of the water."

The ensign didn't ask and gave the orders immediately. A medic stormed onto the bridge, saw Rheinberg's blood-soaked uniform and opened his suitcase.

"Not now, these are just scratches. The captain ..."

"... is dead."

That was Neumann's voice. He had climbed the stairs to the bridge, and the way he spoke everyone could see that his statement was without doubt. "He was killed instantly. An arrow caught him right in the heart. Dead right there."

Rheinberg stared at him, surely made a terrible impression on his friend, looking confused and exhausted and overwhelmed. Neumann wanted to say something, but Rheinberg interrupted him.

"Who else? Injured? Dead?"

Neumann shook his head. "We have some good news. Most men have either crouched or stood relatively protected." He sighed. "Another dead. Dr. Sommer."

Rheinberg sighed deeply. He had met the clergyman, who had been one of the newcomers on board, only briefly, and judged him to be a very silent, humble man, who was always more willing to listen than to say his mind – a very pleasant change compared to some other crew members. He didn't know him well enough to say more, but he felt that he would feel the loss to be very painful in the future – especially in this difficult situation.

"Two slightly injured by arrows," continued Neumann. "The rest are okay. No third salvo from the archers as young Volkert responded quickly."

"No, the shooters were standing at the bow. As the trireme rammed us, they have been incapable to further their attack. The lucky ones were thrown into the water. They only got von Krautz and the priest." Rheinberg gasped for air, ignoring the pain in the arms and legs. "Only those two."

"Jan," Neumann mumbled so quietly that only he could hear. "Pull yourself together. Don't limp. Remember: If you are not commanding, the highest ranking officer is von Klasewitz. Consider."

Rheinberg wiped his forehead. His already bloodied hands left a dirty red trace on the skin. Of course. With the death of von Krautz, all bridge officers had slipped a position upwards. Rheinberg was now the captain – and von Klasewitz was first officer. It could hardly be worse.

Volkert's firm voice jerked Rheinberg from his thoughts. "Captain! A second galley, Captain. Approaches with ... well, as fast as they can, I guess."

Rheinberg grabbed the binoculars, pointed them at the second trireme, coming closer with a fast beat.

"I set the gunners ..."

"No shot without my expressed command," barked Rheinberg. He was still shocked at the effect that a single shot from a small cannon had, despite it had been his own proposal to open fire.

Then the oars went up, the trireme turned. The captain of the ship now surely considered the chaos that had been caused upon his sister ship by the *Saarbrücken*. Rheinberg in his place would ...

"They leave," Volkert announced unnecessarily. Everyone saw it. The oars were lowered into the water. In fast, desperate cycles, the oars pushed the second galley away of the *Saarbrücken*. An intelligent man, this captain. Report back home rather than to feed himself to the fish.

"He will seek help!"

"There is nothing that can stand against us here," came the suddenly confident, even arrogant voice of von Klasewitz, who entered the bridge and looked around, reflecting his new and absolute power. When he realized that Rheinberg was present, he grimaced and faked compassion. "You need to go to the infirmary!"

"I am fit for duty," growled Rheinberg. "And yes, there is no one here who could effectively fight us. That's why von Krautz is dead – because he was invulnerable. And we are alone in ... in a time that is not ours and if we cannot get coal, if we have to stop greasing the machines, and if we run out of the spare parts and ammunition, we're still invulnerable – invulnerable time travelers in a metal coffin. Don't be too confident, Klasewitz. We have, if our luck doesn't turn, just made ourselves an enemy of the Roman Empire." He sighed. He recalled his own spontaneous reaction and felt confused, dizzy and sick. "And that's not a good thing," he added weakly.

"They attacked us," the noble returned.

"Don't be so shortsighted," Rheinberg replied angrily. "It doesn't matter who is to blame. This trireme will report to Rome that here is a metal monster ship that sinks imperial war galleys in the Mediterranean. Do you seriously believe that the question of who shot first has any relevance?"

"Then after them and sink them, too!"

"That will only delay the inevitable. We cannot hide forever."

Von Klasewitz kept silent. Even he seemed to realize it.

Rheinberg sat down hard and allowed Neumann to remove the wet uniform, to open his case, and to tender the fortunately only superficial wounds. Someone handed the newly minted captain a small metal cup of schnapps, which he took and swallowed gratefully. The burning sensation in the stomach revived his senses, and he anxiously waited for news, for Neumann to finish caring about his wounds, and for developing any idea how to get out of this mess.

When he got up, the excitement had somewhat abated. The second galley was hardly visible in the distance. The wounded were cared for, and his boy had brought a fresh uniform. Rheinberg left the bridge, was careful to take both Neumann and von Klasewitz along and appeared on the rear deck, where the men had gathered the fish caught from the shipwreck. The rescuers in the boats had done a quick and effective work and gathered the Romans floating in the water. There had been no problems, not least because apparently only very few of the castaways were able to swim.

Köhler's massive figure stood in front of Rheinberg as he saluted and reported as if the veteran wanted to demonstrate to Rheinberg that he knew and respected the new captain on board. Rheinberg stretched, replied the salute. Everyone should see it. All had to see it.

"How many, Köhler?"

"Forty-three survivors. Twelve of them injured. Two serious."

Neumann needed no further invitation. He knelt beside his medics who already cared for two men lying quietly. One had burns, the other gunshot wounds. Rheinberg focused on the rest. He looked up, straightened as a dark-skinned, muscular man approached. His clothes were torn but seemed to be more expensive than those of many of the other survivors. Rheinberg tried to find a clue but only as Marcus, uninjured, joined him and whispered him a word, he knew who he was dealing with.

"Trierarch," had been the breathy note.

The captain of the destroyed ship.

Rheinberg was stumped. The comparatively tall man, apparently originating from Africa, reached only his chin. They stared at each other, then Rheinberg saluted, slow, precise, carefully considering to avoid any too embarrassing eye contact. His opponent recognized the gesture apparently, nodded, but didn't produce his own salute. He stared constantly at Rheinberg, as if looking for something specific in the man's face. He didn't seem to find it.

"I'm Jan Rheinberg, trierarch of this ship." He searched for the right words. "Trierarch of the *Saravica*," he added finally.

The bumpy Latin seemed not to disturb the man. He had probably learned to know more than people who mastered this language only inadequately.

"I'm Aurelius Africanus, trierarch of the *Scipio*." For a moment he seemed to pause, as he remembered, and bowed his head. "I was trierarch of *Scipio*. You have destroyed my ship."

"You attacked my ship and without reason."

"You broke my trireme like a twig. That's reason enough for me to accept that you are a danger to Rome. The *Augustus* will report. Soon the news will spread like wildfire and reach Treveri. Then you will see how it is to have the Roman Empire as an enemy."

Rheinberg nodded. "I don't want to be an enemy of the Roman Empire."

"This is not your will. It is that of the Emperor."

A sudden thought crept into Rheinberg, a question that he had wanted to ask Marcus, but had not been able to pose because of the attack – namely, to ask for the name of the reigning emperor. The reference to Treveri – or Trier – had already helped him: They must have arrived sometime after the transfer of the capital of the Western Empire from Rome – and before the transfer of the seat of government to Milan and later even Ravenna, the city, from where Aurelius Africanus had most likely set off from on his fateful journey. That limited the time period a bit, although Rheinberg was unable to remember the exact dates. But the name of the Emperor ...

"Who rules in Treveri, Trierarch?"

The man made a surprised face. "You come from a faraway land if you don't know who rules the empire. Where exactly do you come from?"

"Who rules in Treveri?" repeated Rheinberg. Currently, he was not in the mood to provide explanations. Aurelius again seemed not to want to insist.

"Gratian, son of Valentinian, rules the West. His residence is Treveri. Valens, brother of Valentinian, rules the East. His residence is Constantinople."

Rheinberg's mind raced. Something stirred in his memory. Historical events tumbled around in his head. Aurelius seemed to notice his dismay turned with a quizzical look to the other survivors of his ship. Some of those had joined him, including a gray-bearded veteran who looked like the Roman equivalent to Köhler. Nobody seemed threatening; everyone seemed to become more curious about the strange ship and its strange crew.

"Köhler, make sure that the prisoners receive sufficient food and drink. I want them to be treated well."

"Yes."

Rheinberg turned away, rushed along the railing, vanished inside the

Saarbrücken and arrived, panting, his cabin. He finally realized that Neumann and Becker had followed him, when he had already taken a heavy tome on hand. The two men didn't bother to ask for what he was looking for but glanced encouragingly at Rheinberg after he had browsed for a few minutes and read quietly.

"Ah hell," exclaimed Rheinberg.

"Out with it," urged Becker.

"Gratianius Flavius, son of Valentinian I, had his residence in Trier, until the year 378. His uncle and co-emperor Valens died in the year 378 in a battle against the invading Goths, the first prominent victim of what historians call the *Völkerwanderung*. So we have arrived sometime in the later fourth century. Let's see ... in 365 Valens was Valentinian's ... stepbrother, to be exact ... and named co-regent. So we are somewhere between these two years ..."

"We can still find out more details," Neumann said. The three of them rushed back to the rear deck, the thick book with them. Among the suspicious glances of von Klasewitz, the Romans had apparently gathered for a meeting, which was dissolved as Rheinberg unerringly headed for Aurelius again.

"Trierarch, you might perceive my questions as very confusing, but I beg you to answer them."

Aurelius looked at Rheinberg as if he would take him to be a little crazy. Still, he seemed to willingly expect those questions.

"Where is Emperor Gratian currently?"

"He rides against the Alemanni."

"His campaign is crowned with success?"

Aurelius didn't know, that much was clear, but he wouldn't admit it. "The Emperor wins because God is on his side."

"Without a doubt." Rheinberg flipped a page and said in German, addressing Neumann and Becker: "Gratian led a campaign against the invading Alemans in 378. Associated with this has been a big victory in Colmar, the last historical record of a Rhine crossing by a Roman emperor. Then he took residence at Sirmium; later he moved to Milan."

"And?" said Becker. Rheinberg looked at him.

"This means the end of the Western Roman Empire has begun. Rome is from now on only on the defensive. Gratian will appoint Theodosius co-regent after the death of Valens, and after the death of Gratian, he will die in the battle against an usurper, Theodosius will be the last ruler of the entire empire. Eighty years later, Western Rome collapses and Eastern Rome becomes the Byzantine Empire."

"Ah," made Becker, obviously not too impressed.

"Aurelius ..." Rheinberg turned back to the trierarch who followed the German conversation with incomprehension. "... where is the Emperor Valens at the moment?"

"I don't know. Some say he wants to quash the uprising of Fritigern. Here, we receive news from the east rather late." Before Rheinberg could say anything, the trierarch hastily added, "He will be victorious as well!"

"Of course," confirmed Rheinberg and turned away. He stuck his head together with Becker and Neumann and waved von Klasewitz.

"Gentlemen, I'm now pretty sure that we are at some point in the year 378, more in the summer according to the temperatures we encounter. In the West rules Emperor Gratian, who fights against the Alemans, and he will be victorious indeed. He still officially resides in Trier. In the east rules Valens, who will be defeated in August this year by the Goths at Adrianople, where he himself also dies."

"He was defeated," corrected Neumann.

Rheinberg sighed. "Don't confuse me. Valens will die – or died – and Gratian, as the new emperor of all, will give Eastern Rome to Theodosius, the son of a victorious commander of the same name, and that shortly thereafter because he felt overwhelmed with the government of the whole empire. *Völkerwanderung* has begun."

Von Klasewitz jerked his thumb at the prisoners.

"And this one?"

"Roman navy, and in all probability from Ravenna."

"What does all this mean for us?" asked Becker.

Rheinberg pondered the question. He himself had no clear answer.

"We will have to discuss this. But it is clear now that this is not a dream, not a trick and not a delusion. We are in the year 378. We have traveled through time."

Rheinberg let the words sink for a moment. Even Klasewitz was no longer able to hide from the truth. And he looked almost happy about the fact that only von Krautz had been killed and not Rheinberg, so that he didn't have to answer any difficult questions like those of Becker.

Rheinberg suddenly felt a weakness consuming his body. All the excitement, the rush of the attack, the unnecessary death of the captain, the knowledge about their situation, the new responsibility and, not least, the slight but painful injuries had their impact at once. Rheinberg sighed and crouched down, tried to fend off Neumann's supporting hands, but lacked the strength.

"Captain, you need to rest," insisted the doctor. "The first crisis is over and we cannot afford an exhausted commander on the edge of his powers."

Becker nodded. Von Klasewitz looked rather confused as he realized that he was the master of the *Saarbrücken* while Rheinberg rested, and this seemed to bring him some discomfort. Rheinberg couldn't refute Neumann's argument. He felt exhausted, and thoughts tumbled in his head now that the first tension subsided. His wounds ached, and the death of the captain lay like a demon upon his consciousness. He pulled himself together, rose with Neumann's help. "I will rest. Six hours. In the meantime, these are my commands."

He summarized clear instructions, and one could see the relief in von Klasewitz' eyes, a relief greater than his displeasure about the fact that these orders were given to him by Rheinberg. "The prisoners will be well cared for. The corpse of the captain will be cleaned and prepared for burial. We will do that tomorrow at dawn. We change course to the east, away from the coast, because no galley will follow us there. Slow speed; we do not have a specific course yet, we just have to win some time. The quartermaster will create a complete list of supplies on board, including all that has been brought by the infantry. We may soon have to ration certain items. After the funeral of the captain, there will be an officer's meeting, to define our common strategy. I expect proposals. Did you understand everything?"

With emphatic clarity, von Klasewitz repeated the commands. He was aware of the presence of Becker, Neumann and Köhler all too well and Rheinberg was somewhat reassured that the new first officer wouldn't start issuing unauthorized orders.

At least not yet.

He finally was helped by Neumann to his cabin, got rid of his uniform jacket and sat on the edge of his bunk. Neumann was silent, helped him to undress the pants and then swung the legs of the captain on the white linen. With pain did his chest finally come to rest on the thin mattress and Rheinberg looked at the gray-white painted ceiling above him.

"In six hours," he muttered.

"Don't worry. Go to sleep." And then Neumann disappeared from the cabin, closing the door behind him.

Rheinberg stared for some minutes at the ceiling trying to displace the swirling images of the shattered galley, the dying captain, and the knowledge about what has happened from his mind – but without success.

They were in the past. They had traveled almost 1500 years through time by some freak of nature.

What, for God's sake, he asked himself, should he do now?

7

"Lord, Nannienus and Malobaudes ask for an audience!"

Flavius Gratian, the Western Roman Emperor, looked up from his papers. It was already dark, and the torch and oil lamps spread an unsteady light. It seemed to carve deep furrows in the face of the emperor, even though he was only 19 years old. For three years, he has been master of the Western Roman Empire, and for three years he had not come to rest. On the shoulders of the one person ruling a vast empire sat a great responsibility, and the fact that he was not in Trier, but resided in the camp of his legions in Argentovaria was a sign of the kind of challenges he had to face.

Gratian sighed. Not that he would have had his rest in Trier. Many forces tugged at him. The constant submissions of Senator Symmachus craved for his attention as well as those of Bishop Ambrosius, and it was in times like these that the young man desired the advice of his old teacher, Ausonius, who had already supported his father Valentinian. But Ausonius was Prefect of Gaul and helping the emperor by protecting his back, so that he could lead the war. And there was his young wife, Constantia, whom he married when she was thirteen, and who hadn't bore him a son yet. Nevertheless, the young emperor had to admit, there hadn't been that much time to try. Constantia had taken a liking to the ritual pomp and ceremonies of the court and therefore refused to accompany her husband to the camp, where these ceremonies were much less important. And there was always a war to fight these days.

This war was the very reason why two men, ushered by Gratian's manservant Elevius, entered the emperor's tent. Their breastplates, meticulously polished, threw back the flickering light of the torches. Gratian got up, set his pen to the side and motioned the two men to sit around a table.

"Elevius – wine, bread and cheese!"

Nannienus wanted to throw up his hands defensively, but Gratian charged him with a gesture to stop. "While we're discussing things that have to do with killing, we should ensure that we stay alive!"

He eyed the two Franks, men who could hardly be any different. Both stood in the service of Rome for many years, and had worked their way up in the military hierarchy. From Frankish nobility, Malobaudes even being a Frankish king, but proud Roman citizens, the strenuous service at the border had made the two generals' faces hard-edged. But where Nannienus was thin, almost gaunt, and seemed to nearly disappear behind his metal breastplate, Malobaudes' shape was wide and expansive. Where Nannienus seemed silent and reserved, you could hear his comrade often blustering loudly, laughing and striding through the camp, wanting to be close to the simple legionaries. Common to both was a sharp mind, a great tactical understanding, that they knew the border regions and, what was at the moment the most important issue, the Alemanni. They knew King Priarius, the Lord of Lentiensians, and they had followed his path throughout the year. In February, the enemies had invaded the empire across the frozen Upper Rhine, just as Gratian wanted to march his men to the East, to his uncle Valens, the emperor of Eastern Rome, to stand against the Goths of Fritigern. The border troops had been assembled otherwise, and Priarius, who was among the most rowdy of the Alemanni, had collected his warriors and had advanced with more than 40,000 men into the Alsace. And now that they were at Argentaria, Gratian stood before them, and his hopes rested on these two Franks to lead them to victory. Valens' situation in the east was still difficult, and his uncle could use any support – but as long as Gratian was bound here, the East was alone in his fight against the Goths.

"So, generals, how are things?" the Emperor began.

The two older men exchanged glances. Both had learned not to underestimate the young emperor. Gratian had already been made Augustus in 367, still a child, but the comprehensive training bestowed by his teacher Ausianus and the fact that Gratian was forced to grow up very fast had left their mark. Both generals felt the threat, the danger that hung over the empire. The Goths in the East had asked for settlement areas because they had given way to an even bigger, almost unimaginable threat. Something was going on there in the far east, far away from the borders of Rome, and yet closer than anyone wanted to admit. Both were convinced that what happened here, at Argentaria, was just a first taste of things to come. They expected that the young Emperor saw this threat as seriously as they did.

But now it was necessary to devote to the actual danger.

"Priarius is a bully, and he is a fool," Nannienus opened the discussion and saw from the corner of his eye that Malobaudes nodded approvingly. "He is thus both an easy target as well as a great danger to himself."

Gratian said nothing.

"He positioned his troops like a wild bunch, and I'm a bit surprised. I know that among his subordinates are a number of Roman veterans, and I also know that these have a fairly accurate idea of how to place troops in a proper formation and discipline them. But Priarius doesn't like to listen much to his advisers, and therefore he is doomed."

"How many men follow his orders?"

Malobaudes spoke. "We estimate about 45,000, Sire. Some more are around, but those are the women and children and the traders. The warriors – I'd say 45,000. Because he does allow such a chaos in his camp, the scouts can hardly make out details, but we have the usual collaborators and they have given us a very realistic picture."

"Our own final strength?"

"Eight legions each with 3,500 soldiers, sir. Some auxiliary troops, a lot of lightly armed cavalry and infantry. All in all, we come to almost exactly 32,000 men."

Gratian slipped back and forth on his stool. Military decisions made him uneasy. No, he corrected himself immediately: To be dependent on the experience of old generals made him nervous. There were moments in which the small number of his years meant more burden than pleasure.

"That will be enough?"

"If Priarius is the fool we believe him to be, he will run into our trap," Nannienus replied confidently.

"And the tribes he persuaded to join him? They are all still loyal?"

asked Gratian. With this question, he moved back into familiar territory – politics.

"The deserters report that the nobles still follow the king – although his last defeat didn't go down well," said Malobaudes. "One additional disaster, and they will run away from him and we can deal with them individually."

"Rather, the frontier garrisons," added his companion. "Direct involvement of your person won't be necessary anymore."

The Alemans, like the Goths, didn't have as firmly established a state as the Romans, and their loyalties and hierarchy were often difficult to comprehend. A lot had to do with prestige, with corruption, and with the prospect of booty. Constant intrigues were common, and they could easily lead to murder.

Not that the Alemans would differ so fundamentally from Rome in regard to the latter point, thought Gratian bitterly. Nevertheless, Rome just functioned better, and the emperor wanted to use this advantage as long as he was able to.

"You're so confident?" he said.

The generals nodded in unison. "Lord, the victory will be ours if Priarius is not suddenly overwhelmed by reason and tactical understanding," added Malobaudes. "Our troops are well equipped, trained and disciplined."

"We have Alemans amongst our men," stated Gratian.

"And they become more, not less, because the number of defectors increases with each hour. This is a problem for the Lentiensians, less for us. There are certainly a few spies among them, but they will see nothing Priarius doesn't know already. He knows our positions and our strength; all border peoples pretty much know the Roman garrisons. The problem of Priarius is not that he lacks knowledge about his enemy; his problem is that he is a reckless ruffian, surely of great bravery, but not a general."

Gratian lowered his head, played with the jug of wine in his hand for a moment. "Does he have a general?"

"He would have candidates. He doesn't want one. He needs the prestige of leading the fight, as he wants to transform a victory into political power. If he gives the command to a subordinate or listens too much to the advice of his veterans, who definitely know better, he will have to share a victory. For the Alemans, this means that a shift within the internal power structure could occur. Priarius definitely wants to avoid that. So he does it his way."

Malobaudes looked very pleased. "It can't come any better, my lord."

"Very well." The Emperor rose, stretching the muscles, felt the fatigue of a long day and the incessant camp life. "Now the last question: We attack or do we wait for his first move?"

"I advocate offering Priarius battle at dawn," said Nannienus. "He will reject us maybe once, maybe twice, but then his people will become restless."

"An additional factor is that he sits on a hill," added his companion. "He will regard this as an advantage and won't turn down the offer."

"Isn't it an advantage?" persisted Gratian.

"It only seems. It surely gives the fierce attack of the warriors more impetus. And it will be harder for them to escape when they realize that they have run into our trap. When the first waves are broken by our men and they start to run away, they will run up the onrushing comrades and uphill. A glorious mess." Full of anticipation, Malobaudes beamed, and Gratian could hardly suppress a smile in view of this vivid description.

Nannienus nodded. His comrade had said everything.

"Then it's decided. Gentlemen, I'm not a king of the Alemanni, I am the emperor of Rome. You lead this battle and make all tactical decisions. I'll be constantly informed, but I won't intrude." Gratian paused. "I'm going to learn. Be victorious teachers, so that the instruction is worthwhile not only for me but also for Rome."

Gratian saw the proud glint in the eyes of the generals, as they formally bid him farewell and left the tent. He saw that he was alone, sat down on his nearby bed, and yawned openly. Elevius scurried in, cleared away the barely touched food, and took one quick look at his master, staring pensively at the flickering light of the torches and oil lamps. Gratian was not one of those who appreciated any help in getting ready for sleep and preferred to undress by himself. Nevertheless ...

Once again, the young emperor had to think about what it meant to be the son of the great Valentinian. His father had been declared emperor by the army and had crowned, against all good advice, his stepbrother Valens as ruler of the East – and in fact, Gratian's uncle had been found to be a procrastinator. Valentinian had been famous for his military prowess. Gratian's father had saved Britain from being overrun by the barbarians, had crushed a revolt in Africa, and repulsed an earlier invasion of the Alemans behind the Rhine. Eventually it wasn't astonishing that the powerful and active emperor had been killed by a stroke after a fit of fury during negotiations with a stubborn German envoy, leaving his young son to the throne. And so everyone spoke of the example of his father, whom he had hardly known, and whose power was Gratian's only legitimacy if he failed to gain his own.

Ultimately, the young emperor thought, his own position was not so different from that of Priarius, only that the Romans had covered everything with a shell of civilization and rules that crumbled quickly when any legion in any province decided to appoint its own emperor. Gratian hoped he would never have to face such a rebellion, as those had already cost too many "legitimate" emperors their life.

"Sir, any wish?"

"Oh yeah, Elevius."

"What can I bring?"

Gratian raised his head and looked unspeakably tired. "A few more years of life, Elevius. Bring me only five or eight more years of life, so that I finally know what I have to do."

Elevius returned the gaze of his emperor and put a hand on his shoulder. He served Gratian since he was a boy, and was able to afford this kind of confidentiality. "You're doing all right, sir."

"I doubt sometimes."

"I do not."

Gratian saw his servant with gratitude and sighed. "I go to sleep. Tomorrow I want to learn how to defeat barbarians."

Elevius smiled. "You will be an excellent student, and in the not too distant future be a master among the masters yourself."

Gratian pursed his lips. "Do you know what is the worst thing about being an emperor?"

"You will surely allow me to participate in your wisdom immediately, my Lord!"

Gratian grinned. "It is so difficult to distinguish between genuine praise and flattery."

The servant bowed. "You are a man of great insight, oh my Emperor."

"Elevius."

"Sir?"

"Go to sleep as well."

8

"Well, gentlemen, this is the situation. I'd like to hear your suggestions."

Jan Rheinberg leaned back and looked expectantly at the others. Neumann had let him sleep a whole of seven hours instead of the prescribed six and had declared him fit for duty after a further examination, the replacement of the bandages, and a hearty breakfast. Rheinberg had accepted the administrations of the doctor half-grudgingly and half-grateful.

The meeting of the top officers of the *Saarbrücken* had begun with a long account given by the quartermaster and the chief engineer, who had both prepared a thorough inventory of perishables and consumption forecasts. Within the next four weeks, lack of certain provisions would emerge, depending on the way the cruiser and its crew would be used. Coal was the most pressing problem, but also food, especially now that the *Saarbrücken* was overstaffed, with the infantry and the prisoners of war, as they were now called – although Rheinberg rejected this notion. He didn't want to start a war with anyone. The cruiser couldn't survive in the long run. There had to be another way.

"In addition to the coal we will soon experience lack of other consumables," Dahms explained further. "Oils and fats are the next problem. Then all sorts of parts wear, depending on how much we will test the machines. The good news is that our storages were filled to the maximum upon our departure. The question is how to refill."

Rheinberg's gaze fell into the void. About the facts, there was no doubt. The discussion about the stocks hadn't left much room for interpretation. With strict rationing and avoiding all wearing exercise for man and machine, they would be able to operate the *Saarbrücken* for a few weeks without problems. After that, the lack of this or that would be painfully noticeable.

"We need to establish a base," Neumann said.

Von Klasewitz nodded eagerly. "Very good. We are in a time where our weapons will not meet any resistance. We capture a port and force the residents to subjection."

"To achieve what?" asked Rheinberg quietly. He knew that the newly appointed executive officer was not the only one on board who was playing with fantasies of power and wealth. For many, the naïve notion of plentiful female slaves played a part as well. This had to be discussed.

"Well, it would be a start ..." Klasewitz' sentence trailed off.

"It wouldn't," Dahms intervened. He still hadn't developed any sympathy for the new first officer. "We need coal. Technology. Except for food, we can't expect much, and the *Saarbrücken* will be like a metal corpse in an enemy port. Finally, once the ammunition is finished and the Romans or whoever learn about that ... I don't know much about military history, but I can hardly imagine how we ... with our sabers and bayonets against a well-organized and professional body of ... I don't know the proper name for such a unit."

"A cohort would be sufficient to attack us," helped Rheinberg.

"A cohort then," Dahms said. "Sure, before that we would be able to inflict one or another massacre, but as soon as someone realizes that we are out of ammunition – and I don't assume for a moment that we are dealing with idiots here – we're history." He bared his teeth. "In the truest sense of the word."

Rheinberg said nothing, didn't want to widen the gulf between himself and von Klasewitz, but he could only agree with the navy-engineer. Dahms had analyzed the situation in short and clear words and very aptly.

"Captain, you are obviously the best expert," said Langenhagen. "Can we keep the *Saarbrücken* alive at all – I mean, at this time?"

Rheinberg paused for effect, before he answered. "Well, certainly not by conquering a port and exploiting the population." He could not resist now and looked past von Klasewitz' deeply red face. "I can't answer this question in a simple way. Coal may be the least of the problems – the *Saarbrücken* can be fired, although with diminished effectiveness, with wood or charcoal, and in this time exposed coal seams were known in some areas of the empire. We can certainly produce charcoal by ourselves. For this we need more than just one port, of course; we must have access to the facilities and roads of the Roman Empire. It becomes more difficult in regard to fats and oils, but I guess that we can identify practical substitutes that will help us for some more months. The spare parts will be very difficult. There are without any doubt many skilled craftsmen in this time, and we have a well-equipped workshop with many well-trained people in our crew. But it lacks the tools to build the tools with which we can produce even most necessary spare parts." Rheinberg nodded to Dahms, who was very thoughtful. "Ammunition is another problem. Here, too, we lack the industrial base. We will have to be very carefully and use it sparingly. The technical problems are endless. We can't produce steel easily, especially in necessary quantities, so we have to resort to inferior metals or alloys. The consequence for us is therefore quite clear." Rheinberg sighed, looked into his coffee cup and sighed again. "Coffee, gentlemen, should also be rationed, as it has been completely unknown in the Roman Empire."

A suppressed "Damn!" made the rounds on the table. For some men, this was as serious a problem as the spare parts. Rheinberg decided to leave the wider crew ignorant of these little details until further notice, especially keeping in mind that the local beer would unlikely meet the quality expectations of the Germans, and spirits were largely unknown as well.

Rheinberg put his hands flat on the polished ebony finish of the table.

"Either we try to manage as long as possible, and then somehow abandon the *Saarbrücken* and survive otherwise. We won't be able to keep the crew together, our technology base will be lost, and eventually everyone will have to take care of himself on his own."

A look around showed that this alternative was not received enthusiastically.

"Or we can align ourselves with the Roman Empire, became part of and help the imperial state, use the resources of the Empire, transfer our knowledge and create a stable basis in order to keep the ship functional as long as possible, maybe on a lower level. We can keep the crew together and establish a power-base, but not against the Empire, but for and with it. So we have a chance for survival – and for a meaningful survival, exploiting our potentials and opportunities effectively and efficiently."

Their faces brightened. Only Klasewitz looked distraught. Rheinberg looked at him invitingly.

"With all due respect, Captain," he said, "but we are Germans! If it is really true that we are lost in the here and now, shouldn't we travel home and offer our own people, the Germans, the services of the *Saarbrücken*?"

"The question is valid, indeed," replied Rheinberg to von Klasewitz' recognizable astonishment. "But whom do we want the ship to support? Franconians? Alemans? Burgundians? Vandals? Tervingians? Greuthungians? Or one of the many smaller tribes? In the area of Wilhelmshaven, the Frisians rule, if I'm not mistaken. And then, if we go to war, we do fight against the Germans who are in Rome's services? Against the numerous German generals and German legionaries? And what kind of technological base do you expect from our ancestors, Lieutenant Commander? Which state are we talking about? Which great German port exactly should be the home of the *Saarbrücken*?"

Von Klasewitz said nothing, pursed his lips, was alternately red and pale when Rheinberg fired his questions calmly and persistently.

"No, that's absurd. It's pointless. We would demise fast. The ship would be a wreck shortly. We would not even survive before our supplies are running low. In this time the Germans – the Germans outside the boundaries of the Roman Empire, I mean! – have nothing to offer us. On the contrary. We may have to fight them. They are the barbarians."

"Fight?" echoed Becker.

"Yes. It is the time of the *Völkerwanderung*, the great migration of the peoples. If we want to survive, we must keep the Roman Empire alive. So we have to help the most sophisticated civilization, and it is here where we find it."

"One issue should be raised," said Neumann. "What about our efforts to return to our own time?"

Approving nods came everywhere, and then the eyes turned to Rheinberg.

He raised his hands in a gesture of despair. "I'm all for it. But how do we do that?"

"Let's go exactly the same way back from where we came," suggested Becker.

"We've already done that when I gave the order to increase the distance from the coast. We can't know exactly because we have been unconscious, but the waters and the weather has returned to normal, no fog, now quite a strong wind – and we can't look for that strange phenomenon forever."

As if to confirm, the *Saarbrücken* bowed slightly in the waves and everyone was automatically gripping their cups.

"It can be of our advantage when we work together with the Roman Empire in this case as well. When we receive reports by the Roman ships about a similar phenomenon, they might encounter, we can search specifically. Until then, we grope around in the dark."

"So what are our next steps?"

Rheinberg scratched his head. He knew that this was the crucial question, and for him there was only one possible answer to it. "We are heading for the nearest port – which is probably Ravenna – and return our prisoners of war. We contact the government. We prove our worth."

"We're doing what?"

"We have to prove ourselves. Valens will fall. He'll be dead before we can make a difference. Gratian will make Theodosius Emperor of the East, and that one will be the last Roman Emperor ruling all of it, for Gratian will soon die, victim of an usurper. We must prevent that. Indeed, we must prevent Theodosius, if we want to save the Roman Empire. He may have been a legendary figure, but he has made too many mistakes." Rheinberg looked around, looked at faces full of incomprehension. "Gentlemen, Rome is facing a desperate situation. The nation is forced to ask for exorbitant taxes to maintain the army. There is a massive shortage of labor. The Empire is under threat at four or five border areas. A civil war is imminent. The schism and fanaticism of many bishops consumes energies that should be focused on far more urgent tasks."

The captain paused. Most of the officers looked at him with polite interest. He suddenly realized that these "details" were of limited interest for many. They expected that Rheinberg kept their lives and the ship operational. Was it necessary to start a revolution, a struggle for power? That was the job of the captain.

Rheinberg closed his mouth. His eyes met with those of Becker and Neumann. Here were the only men at this table, with whom he could possibly discuss the political and economic consequences of their decision. More he could not expect.

The captain felt a great desire to delve into his books. He needed to know more about this period, evoke memories of books he already read. The burden of responsibility weighed heavily on his shoulders, and he knew that he would cause upheaval once he'd start to serve the Roman Empire. Once he started to make history. To change history.

Rheinberg rose. "Set course to Ravenna," he said softly. "Small speed ahead. I'm in my cabin. Double crew on lookout. I want two men ready with binoculars. Immediate combat readiness, if something is seen. Oh yes ... and no shots without my expressed command. I expect absolute discipline."

He looked around. No doubt in their eyes, no contradiction. Even von Klasewitz seemed content for the moment.

So far, so good.

9

It was warm that morning and sunny. Gratian looked from the back of his horse across the troops, who filled the plain before him. The center of the Roman legions, organized by cohorts, had taken a roughly rectangular area in the middle. The lines looked like they were drawn with a ruler. Officers rode along the front, shouting commands if one unit was still not a hundred percent in formation. The center contained the elite troops of the Roman West, comitatenses, fast moving legions of the field army. These were supplemented by limitanei, the border troops, and too many of them, as Gratian was painfully aware of. For each new campaign he led against invading barbarians, more troops had to withdraw from the garrisons, to compensate for the high death toll of eternally recurring battles. One day the carefully planned and elaborate border security system with troops located in staggered frontier fortresses, which Diocletian had once built, would crumble simply due to a lack of personnel.

The auxiliary troops were a little bit distanced at the left and right of the center line-up, including Gratian's preferred unit, the Alan cavalry, with which he himself had tried his abilities in fighting games again and again. Then there were archers and the quotas of *laeti*, tribes living in the boundaries of Rome who, due to their own fighting style and weaponry, were specific units. This was reflected by a less rigid formation than in the center, but one could be mistaken: The officers of the auxiliary troops knew exactly what was at stake and which plan to follow, and they knew the value of discipline. There would be no individual action, no anarchy in the Roman army.

The left block of the auxiliary troops was a little further from the center than the right. The generals had a good reason to choose these tactics for this battle.

Further ahead, Priarius has gathered the rubble of the opposing forces. It was an impressive amount of warriors who shouted themselves hoarse to gather courage. Their sheer quantity seemed overwhelming as they surged over the hill and threatened to sweep away the compact formations of outnumbered Roman troops at any time. But Gratian had seen this many times before. At 15, his father had taken him along on his campaigns and taught him what he could before he himself had unexpectedly died. Barbarians were always in the majority. But the soldiers of Rome were well-trained professionals – a majority of them also barbaric, often of German origin – but here quality won over quantity, and the Emperor was sure that this principle would also remain valid this time.

They were also much more spearmen and archers on the Roman side. The men of Priarius might be all brave warriors – Gratian was always ready to bear witness to this, since his own army consisted largely of soldiers recruited from barbarians – but their way of fighting had a preference for direct confrontation with the sword, where physical strength and endurance would be put to use to the fullest advantage. The Roman legions were quite willing to avoid putting a valuable fighter in danger when a continuous shower of arrows and spears could carry chaos and death to the enemies, with no one on the Roman side hurt.

About fifty *passus* before Gratian and his bodyguard rode the two Roman Frankish generals, accompanied by messengers and signalmen, which were prepared with trumpets and drums to relate the commands to the legions. The whole parade already took an hour, and the men of Priarius stood idly by. Sure, it meant more prestige for the barbarian prince to beat a fully established Roman army – but even a notorious ruffian like Priarius couldn't be so stupid as to wait until the Romans were fully prepared for battle.

On the other hand, who was Gratian to unnecessarily muse on a happy coincidence? He might be a committed Christian, but he felt nothing wrong by sending a secret thank you to Fortuna. And the multitude of gods that were worshiped by his soldiers down there would receive numerous messages as well.

Horns sounded. Gratian's eyes narrowed. Priarius had called for the attack, and a roaring, surging mass of people rushed down the hill. Then all of a sudden a cloud of missiles covered the sky, as archers fired their arrows. The roar of the attacking warriors mingled with the cries of pain by the wounded, but the barbarians were not impressed and stormed on. A second cloud soared toward the attackers; this time it was the spears thrown with force. Screams rang out again, then more whoops and cries. Gratian saw with pride that the legions remained completely motionless and seemingly ignorant of the onrushing warriors, absolute discipline ensured by the centurions, whose plumes clearly loomed within the formations. No one would dance out. Even the most timid recruit knew that his chances of survival were much higher in the lineup than with a meaningless escape, which also would likely to end up with his execution. The comrades and their cooperation was the best insurance for survival in a battle like this.

Then again, the horns were blown. The slightly removed positioned left phalanx of legionaries began to march forward, raised their shields, swords ready, stomping with smooth, controlled steps. The center and the right flank halted. The further the Legionaries advanced, the more they oppressed the onrushing wave of barbarians. War cries grew louder when the barbarians broke against the shields of the legionaries, their bodies impaled with the blade protruding, and chopped down in the methodical strikes. Centurions brandishing their swords on the bodies of the barbarians, fighting on the front line, next to them the carriers of the cohort's banner, symbolic figures of each century, whose protection was the most honorable task of each legionnaire.

A good hour passed in this way until Gratian saw how the left flank drilled into the mass of warriors and recoiled in a slight angle toward the center.

The hoped-for effect ensued, and the storming hordes were pushed against the waiting center. The barbarians fought desperately, visibly unable to react coherently in face of tactical maneuvers. Some time passed, then the horns sounded again. The right flank marched forward, slowly closing the trap. When the barbarians saw that they were squeezed into the valley simultaneously from three sides, the first tried to escape the established funnel – only to find that the cavalry and archers had been waiting for such an escape. The men running uphill or laterally along the slope were easy prey for the waiting archery or zooming Alans and Moorish cavalrymen who dispatched the fleeing warriors in short time. Few opponents managed to escape from the encirclement. The war cries of the barbarians turned increasingly into panicked shrieks, spiced with the angry roar of the chiefs and war leaders who were desperately trying to organize their disintegrating force. But all efforts were in vain. Half an hour of battle passed, and when the Roman legions had been combined into a single unit, entrenched and slowly forming a marching front up the hill, wave after wave of barbarians had disintegrated into a wild-roaming bunch, some still doggedly fighting, others seeking their safety in flight.

Gratian nodded approvingly. The day belonged to the Roman Empire. Priarius was beaten, no matter how long the remaining fighting would drag on now. The Roman Emperor threw a searching glance at the sky. It was close to noon. The battle, as effectively and efficiently it developed, lasted around three hours, a period that passed in a flash for the young emperor. He had learned and both Malobaudes and Nannienus had proved to be worthy teachers.

He turned around when he saw one of the generals approaching him. It was Malobaudes, almost cheerfully swinging his sword.

"The victory is ours, noble Augustus," he shouted from afar. Gratian waved to him. "Priarius has fallen! The enemy is in disarray!"

"Priarius is dead?"

"He is and was a roughneck, Augustus! His bravery has become his undoing. Too close to the fighting, he turned to flee when an arrow hit him in the back. His men are running."

"I see. You have lived up to your good reputation, General. The Emperor is thankful."

Puffing Malobaudes came to a stop next to the emperor. His horse shook with the effort. The general was not spared in the effort of this battle and had traversed the battlefield from left to right, shouted commands, sent messengers, accompanied by the bugler, who had converted his instructions immediately into signals. The carefully lubricated machinery of the Roman legions was working perfectly. "Now they run like rabbits. Your orders?"

"Whoever gives up should be spared. Those who fight will be killed. We won't follow the refugees, because there are more pressing things to do. I want accurate figures about our losses, General. My uncle fights in the East against the Goths, and he needs help. Once I'm sure that the barbarians here leave us alone, we must turn to the East!"

Malobaudes tilted his massive head. "As you command, Augustus. The camp ..."

"Allow plunder by our men. They should take the women as they wish. All valuables should be distributed fairly. Tomorrow night, I will muster the troops. Summon the centurions and legates and collect reports about the brave ones, those we have to consider for promotion or commendation. I liked the third century on the left flank, Malobaudes. An optio there seemed particularly eager."

"Ah, young Telmachus. One of my best!"

"See if you can make him a centurion."

Malobaudes grimaced. "Telmachus appointed to become an officer? Who's then left to do the real work?"

Gratian grinned at the General. "This is the fate of the successful, my friend."

Malobaudes bowed in the saddle, jerked the reins and rode back to his troops. The battlefield was finally lost in chaos. Chasing the fleeing barbarian was now left for the cavalry. Horns sounded signals, then the soldiers made their way to the camp of Priarius to collect their reward.

Gratian hoped Priarius had left enough to loot.

Nothing was more dangerous than a disgruntled soldier. In the past, one or the other Telmachus had been decorated with the purple by his men, because he had promised them more pay and booty than what had been offered by the Emperor.

This, Gratian knew, had to be avoided.

"Elevius!"

"Lord!"

"Back to the camp. We're done here."

Cries were heard from the battlefield. The soldiers had begun to redeem the seriously injured among the barbarians from their suffering.

10

"No one would have been more worthy, and I recognize with great pleasure that our Emperor has given this high office to someone who is known as a man of good will and great skills like you. I hope that you will soon thereafter have the opportunity to return back to a proper private life, because just as no one can be prevented to hold an honorable office, no one should be prevented to leave again. I write this so that you realize one thing. Much as we thank the Emperor for having you to receive this honor, we thank him in the same way, if he declines to give you another one."

Quintus Aurelius Symmachus paused for a moment and read the last few lines for a second, then a third time. He lowered the pen, nodded, dipped it in the ink again and expanded the letter with a few more sentences, a farewell formula and a signature. Then he let the feather fall and laid the paper aside. It was always a joyful burden to maintain the friendship with his senatorial colleagues; it was a necessary part of dealing with equals of the same cultural refinement. Amicitia has firmly established rules of courtesy, respect to all social differences in status, and the principle of complete and unswerving focus on the care of relations. It was part of his life, and he admitted to himself that writing these letters were to him both joy as well as a burden.

The senator rose from his desk and looked through the window into the atrium of his villa in Rome. He hated the city, the confrontation with the mass of its people, and avoided them when he could. Normally he preferred to dwell on one of his estates, or in his house at the lake, away from the crowds and chaos of big cities, let alone such a massive metropolis as Rome. But every now and then he could not help but walk this behemoth, especially when the Senate convened. Symmachus was a senator with conviction and passion, and in contrast to the old senatorial families who usually made up the power among themselves; in his case, it has been only two generations since his family arrived at this exalted rank. It was not his more humble origin that made Symmachus' work so hard – it was the fact that he along with his supporters, led by his father's friend Pretextatus, had to defend their values against the growing influence of the Christian senators. The latest rumor caused him particular concern: Cheered on by the fanatical Bishop of Milan, Ambrosius – tacitly supported by Ausonius, the teacher of the emperor – the Christians pressed the Emperor to order the removal of Victoria altar from the Senate, the traditional symbol of Roman power and at least formal supremacy of the Senate in all state affairs. Symmachus did not consider himself a Republican – even when he had to, as a Senator actually, at least pretend to be – and he recognized that Gratian had, after the death of his father, started to improve the relationship between the throne and the Senate. But young Gratian, not least just under the influence of Ausonius, a devout Christian, seemed to succumb increasingly to the bishop's whisperings.

Symmachus sighed. He knew for a long time that the time of the ancient religions drew to a close. The charismatic preachers of the Christians surpassed each other in order to increase their influence, as well as they rushed to pounce on each other at every opportunity. Arians, Manicheans – and how all these trends were called, each claimed to know the only truth, and they were always ready to shed the blood of their own as well as the blood of followers of other faiths. They only agreed in their opposition to the old religions, those gods who had made Rome great and to whom Symmachus was still praying. As much as the attraction of the old gods disappeared, the senator didn't acknowledge that he should give up the fight, at least the fight for a certain role of ancient cults and the preservation of the ancient temples. No one had ever taught him how to give up.

The senator rolled the paper with his letter to a fellow senator, who had just been awarded a vicariate by the Emperor in Gaul, and sealed it. Tomorrow, he would fill a second sheet, this time with the juicy details and political news from Rome that he would really like to address.

"Sir, a visitor!"

Harich, his majordomo, had approached almost silently. Although the slave stood for more than ten years in the service of the senator, he had never been able to present the same level of obsequious devotion showed by other servants. His quiet announcement sounded more casually interested. Symmachus had appointed the stocky man, who had come as a sold prisoner of war to his house, nonetheless as the manager of this property very quickly. Harich, who had held high office at the court of a German leader before his capture, showed great skill in the organization of the other servants, and had a knack for trading, an unmistakable sense for exotic flavors in food and the ability to discern the right time to purchase them on the markets of Rome.

"Who is it?"

"His Excellency, Senator Marcus Gaius Michellus."

Symmachus frowned. Michellus was an example for the fact that there were Christian senators, who could endure a man of his status and with his pagan inclinations, if they otherwise met the social and political obligations of senatorial rank. He wouldn't count Michellus among his closest friends, but he also belonged to a family that had only achieved senatorial dignity a few generations ago, and like Symmachus' ancestors, his family called from the provinces. This common fate, especially the way how long-established Roman families sometimes regarded the upstarts, had something quite connecting. Apart from that, Michellus was a rigidly conservative senator who didn't like the way many Christian Senate colleagues lived. And he was a friend of literature, just as Symmachus. There was more that bound than separated them.

"Tell him to come in."

Michellus soon entered the room. He looked a little sweaty and exhausted. Symmachus realized immediately that the senator had not come to discuss current literary developments. The corpulent man with the beginnings of balding – and he had just turned 45! – sat down without being asked. Symmachus didn't blame him. It was clear that his friend was upset.

"Harich – let's bring wine."

"Yes, yes," exclaimed Michellus. "Wine. This is really a good idea." He groaned and sighed. A bit too theatrical for Symmachus' taste, but it served its purpose: The visitor had the undivided attention of the host.

“My friend, my friend, how are your sons?” began Michellus after the wine had been served and the slaves had withdrawn.

“Very well. I assume that they will continue to make their way. And your daughters?” asked Symmachus.

Michellus grimaced. Now it was the host who controlled himself so as not to sigh openly. It was again about his daughters. *No, not quite right*, the senator corrected himself. It definitely was about a certain daughter.

“My Drusilla is the star of my life,” Michellus opened his speech with the inevitable conclusion, “full of grace and obedience, as befits a daughter. She recognizes me as the Lord of the family without restriction. Pious, and she cultivates good manners. She will soon be married to a young man. I'm still looking, but yes, some are on the shortlist. I've had offers by suitors of elevated standing.”

Symmachus nodded. His sons didn't belong to the applicants, as both were already married, and with two daughters from esteemed families. Children didn't generally get a chance to make that decision themselves, and daughters even less than sons. Offspring were a tool for the senatorial families to cement social relationships and mutual obligations. Symmachus couldn't find anything wrong with that. Michellus neither. Julia on the other hand ...

“Julia, however ...” His guest sighed now, casting a reproachful look at the sky. “... Julia, however told me today that she wouldn't marry Julius Aenius under any circumstances. ‘Over my dead body’, she said. Rather she would eviscerate. We yelled, Symmachus. My daughter yelled at me, her father! I may kill her for that!”

Symmachus smiled understandingly. As *pater familiae*, Michellus indeed was free to do so. The biggest problem was that Julia, like her sister Drusilla, was charming, impressing everyone with her beauty. Her beleaguered father was therefore burdened with a 17-year-old daughter, who in addition to an extremely attractive appearance also had an extremely stubborn mind he couldn't cope with. The problem was compounded by the fact that the senator's noble wedded wife, Lucia by name, behaved in matters of family like she was in charge, so that the poor Michellus was blessed with two women who claimed to have to think for him. Symmachus didn't envy his colleague for this problem, and of course he always felt something like glee when he listened to the complaints of his friend.

"What have I done that the Lord strikes me with such a daughter?" Michellus asked half rhetorically. Symmachus grunted politely and made a gesture of ignorance. "I don't know how to find a husband for this girl! Anyone who asks for her hand must be completely insane!"

"Maybe you should dress her up as a man, and send her to the Legion," joked Symmachus. "After what you have told me, she might make a good tribune."

"Oh yes," replied his host with a tired twinkle in his eyes. "If Julia would've been born a man, I would've a glorious, heroic son who contributes to the family's honor. Instead, I have a permanent offense sitting on my back."

Michellus sank into brooding silence. Symmachus knew the routine. He would break into loud swearing a couple of times, then drink another cup of wine and leave for home, somewhat reassured, but surely just as desperate. The central reason why he appeared regularly with this matter at Symmachus' doorstep was not due to their particularly close relationship, but the simple fact that Michellus' town house was not twenty yards away on the other side of the street and his colleague therefore offered an easy escape route.

Symmachus suspected that aside from that, the well-known and excellent wine cellar of his house also radiated a certain attraction, especially as Michellus' complaints were dampened somewhat through consumption of the fine grape juice. On the other hand, who would seriously believe that Michellus came only to have a drink in peace?

"Why, o my friend, why am I punished in such a way?" The lamentation of Michellus began again, and he turned the empty cup in his hands. "Why, Symmachus, tell me!"

"I'm not an expert for your God," he replied, raising his carafe.

"More wine, my friend?"

Michellus handed him the cup.

11

In retrospect, Rheinberg didn't really know what he had expected. Panic? Horror? A desperate assault? Perhaps he had simply done the right thing: As the Italian coast appeared in the distance, he had asked Aurelius Africanus to be on the bridge. Meanwhile, his men had been given food and the still bewildered trierarch had watched with obvious appreciation as Neumann and his helpers had saved the most severely injured survivors' life and thereby also some limbs. The Roman's good mood increased furthermore because of his continuing amazement at the technological marvel that the *Saarbrücken* constituted. After a short tour of the engine room, Africanus had proved, after showing utter astonishment, a stunning technical understanding. When he made a reference to Archimedes at one or two places during the tour, Rheinberg had definitively concluded that this man had a remarkable educational background and was definitely more able than just to command an oversized rowboat.

The only thing he hadn't shown the trierarch were the guns. Africanus had experienced at firsthand what these powerful weapons were able to do. Rheinberg wanted to impress but not frighten him. The man was his ambassador, and he had apparently believed the assurance that Rheinberg would free him and his men in Ravenna immediately after their arrival. The captain of the *Saarbrücken* had considered it absolutely necessary to show confidence. The *Saarbrücken* needed the Roman Empire more than he had told his officers.

"From here, trierarch, I command my ship," Rheinberg said. Africanus glanced at the wheel. Along with him a gray-bearded man with a weathered face had appeared on the bridge. Africanus had introduced him as his helmsman Sepidus. The older man with the wide scar on his right arm had the word "veteran" virtually tattooed on his forehead. He might come from a time in which the *Saarbrücken* was an inexplicable miracle, and his ship might have never presented a serious threat, but as he entered the bridge and looked around, standing steadfast with both feet on the slightly swaying deck, the significantly younger Rheinberg could feel the same aura of authority that surrounded Köhler as well.

"This is the helm. It is connected by a mechanism to the rudder of the ship. This allows the control to be built at any location of the ship, and it only takes one to serve it," Rheinberg explained and saw the quartermaster exchange a furtive glance with his guest. Börnsen was now a good ten years at sea and far from being a rookie, but he felt the personality of the gray-bearded Roman as much as Rheinberg.

"Börnsen, how is your Latin?"

"No way, sir. I left school in the upper sixth, Captain."

"Show it to him anyway."

Rheinberg gestured and the helmsman took half a step aside. Sepidus gripped the helm first awkwardly then noticeably more confidently, and Börnsen led his movements.

"Request for permission to be allowed to demonstrate a bow," Börnsen asked now self-conscious.

"Permission granted, Börnsen. Let him do it."

"Passing control as ordered."

Sepidus held the spokes a bit too tight, but after the German showed him how to turn the well-oiled wheel with gentle pressure, the Romans realized how elegant the *Saarbrücken* followed the order of the rudder, and soon he didn't need any more assistance. The face of the Roman showed an enthusiastic smile that flashed through the thick, wild beard. Some of the enthusiasm seemed to transfer to Africanus. As the *Saarbrücken* had driven a complete circle and lay on the old course, the trierarch told Sepidus to return the helm gain, and Sepidus let go reluctantly.

Whatever the old veteran thought about the strange foreign crew, he was thrilled by their vessel recognizably.

Aurelius Africanus turned to Rheinberg. "Soon my squadron will be on us, because the *Augustus* will have informed headquarters by now. May I ask you not to attack them?"

"I won't, if they behave peacefully," Rheinberg replied.

"They will, if I can talk to them."

"I'll make sure you get the opportunity."

"If we enter Ravenna, there are various ways to contact the government," continued Aurelius. First he had reacted with disbelief to Rheinberg's suggestion not to continue the fight but instead to initiate official contact with the Empire. Afterwards, he started to take the idea seriously. Finally he agreed to be, as far as he could, a moderating influence on any hotheads and therefore making it easier to communicate – should Rheinberg fulfill his promise to release him and his crew.

"The first contact will surely be with the Navarch who commands the naval contingent in Ravenna. His name is Marcus Flovius Renna, my immediate superior. The port is under his command in all military matters, and he is a very assertive man. He will surely report to the city administration, but I'm assuming that he will immediately send messengers to the imperial court as well. All this is too important for our pay-grade."

Rheinberg had found some time to refresh his knowledge of the Roman Empire and its management in his books. Since the reforms of Diocletian, civil and military authorities were strictly separated. The arrival of the *Saarbrücken*, it was assumed, was viewed as primarily a military matter. Before any higher-ranking officer was present, Renna would be the man who would have to deal with Rheinberg.

"What's Renna like?"

Africanus thought about it for a moment, as if he had to choose his words carefully. "He is a career soldier who worked his way up from humble background. He married into one of the senatorial families. Everyone says that he might have a prospect for a position at court, may probably withdraw from military service and take a civilian office. Perhaps as a prefect in the troubled provinces where military experience might come handy for a civil servant. He is an impeccable superior."

Rheinberg nodded. He had not expected that Africanus would wash dirty laundry. But even if only a portion of what he just had been told was true, there was a good chance that one would be able to talk sensibly with Navarch Renna.

Navarch, the captain recalled, corresponded to the rank of admiral or at least a squadron commodore. Renna wasn't his peer but ranked much higher. Rheinberg felt his palms getting damp. Diplomacy was not one of his strengths but a skill he needed to acquire quickly.

Africanus apparently had a good eye. "Renna also makes me nervous," he said softly. "He's one of those few who hold the Empire together. This includes the right degree of harshness and cruelty. I once watched as he personally decapitated a deserter. The Navarch stood there, covered in blood, raised the sword and looked at the men, everyone in full attention, and then radiated a silent and very urgent threat. He is not easily impressed." Africanus made a wide gesture. "But I'm confident that this ship will put his composure to the test."

"I'd like to impress him but without threat," Rheinberg said frankly.

"A big challenge."

"You have to help me."

"I'll do what I can. But I'm just a trierarch."

Rheinberg had to smile a bit listening to the somewhat thickly applied modesty, but then wasn't so sure whether Africanus was really modest or very realistic. Rheinberg didn't know so many important things about this time, and like the historian he had to conjecture somewhat. It was something completely different to read a book and get an idea about the distant past on the one hand and having this experience personally on the other. Rheinberg repeatedly had the surreal feeling that this was just a dream and that he'd wake up soon, very soon. Only that this awakening didn't happen and he started to get used to the idea that ultimately it was all very real.

"Captain, three ships, ten degrees starboard!"

The voice of Langenhagen tore Rheinberg from his thoughts. In the indicated direction three triremes were peeling from the afternoon haze. The land line was clearly visible now, and just as clearly the port of Ravenna was discernible in the distance.

"Little speed!" commanded Rheinberg.

"Little speed!" confirmed Langenhagen. A tense calm settled over the bridge, as more and more ships became visible. Besides the three war galleys, sailing ships of all kinds appeared on the waters – massive ships with big sails as well as small fishing boats. The closer they got to the port, the denser was the boat traffic, but the civil units apparently spun as soon as possible, as their mates recognized the approaching

Saarbrücken. The three triremes held unswervingly toward the cruiser, however.

"They have courage," muttered Rheinberg. Aurelius looked at the captain, and he had certainly not understood him but seemed to gather the meaning.

"They will fight, even if they suspect that they will lose," said the trierarch in Latin. "The *Augustus* is among them!"

"Langenhagen, the megaphone for the trierarch."

Soon Africanus had the funnel-shaped metal in his hands and led the mouthpiece to his lips intuitively.

"Over there," Rheinberg pointed the way. "We go outside! Langenhagen, all machines stop."

He didn't hear the confirmation of the command anymore. Together with Africanus he stood at the railing, where they were joined by Becker and Neumann. Rheinberg looked around. Everywhere the men were in position, the assault rifles were ready to shoot. The lateral 5-cm gun had fixed her mouth on the approaching triremes. Rheinberg's men had been repeatedly enjoined not to fire without the expressed command. A massacre among the Romans would destroy their chances of establishing more friendly relations.

Africanus used the megaphone. "*Augustus*, this is Aurelius Africanus," his voice echoed over to the galleys. "Vicius! Do not attack! Listen to me! No attacking! You wouldn't survive it! The strangers want to negotiate!"

Rheinberg squinted.

First it seemed as if nothing had happened, but then he saw with relief that the foremost of the three galleys began to heave by. A man stood on the upper deck and waved to Aurelius.

"How are you?" He shouted across with strong, unamplified voice.

"I'm fine!" was the answer back from the metal funnel. "Accompany us into the harbor. There will be no fighting! Are you listening? No fighting! Inform the Navarch! Let's isolate the pier from the public! There is no fight! They want to negotiate!"

The man on the trireme waved back and shouted something unintelligible. All three triremes turned in, maneuvered around the *Saarbrücken* and took them into their midst.

Africanus turned to Rheinberg, a smile on his lips. "They will not attack."

"Good." Rheinberg turned to the bridge. "Langenhagen."

"Captain!"

"We go slowly. Stay within the convoy's protection. Keep your distance! Follow into the harbor!"

"Little speed and following, yes," it echoed back. The gentle, rhythmic pounding of the machines was again more noticeable as the *Saarbrücken* cautiously gained conceivable speed. The rowers of the triremes put in everything they had. With great difficulty they could keep up with the cruiser.

Rheinberg watched the legionaries on the triremes. They looked grim and ready for battle, all armed and a large number of archers were ready. It seemed as Navarch Renna made tactical decisions based on the reports of the *Augustus*, and they were not the dumbest. The triremes were hopelessly inferior to the cruiser in all respects, but the death of Captain Krautz had proved that a well-placed arrow could find his target even on an armored marvel of engineering. Renna rose in Rheinberg's professional judgment by a few more degrees. He made the right decision in refraining from any confrontation.

The port of Ravenna was finally in sight. All on board the *Saarbrücken* took the magnificent panorama in. Until a few decades ago, before the whole Roman fleet was moved to Constantinople – with the exception of Africanus' squadron – Ravenna had been one of the two main naval ports of the Empire. The great buildings which could be seen from the sea signified the wealth and influence of the city. Rheinberg saw extensive port facilities with numerous piers, and a variety of moored vessels. Further back, more buildings were to be seen, the ancient temples lined with Christian churches and palatial mansions as well as administrative buildings. Everything in Rheinberg urged him to plunge into this city to adore the ancient architecture, whose colors stood out clearly from the monotony of the ruins that remained in his time. On the harbor walls were the citizens of the city, marveling at the ship which sailed into its waters. Rheinberg could sense open excitement, but no panic, and the legionaries, who had taken position on the walls seemed rather confident and calm and less anxious. None of these people had ever seen the *Saarbrücken* in action, and the ship was surrounded by three triremes – the audience had to feel relatively safe. Renna surely had kept the report of the captain of the *Augustus* under lock and thus avoided rumors and panic. A smart man, without any doubt.

The seagulls shrieked as the *Saarbrücken* glided over the harbor's calm waters. Although the city had lost its importance as a naval base, Rheinberg knew that her true heyday was still approaching: As the capital of the Western Roman Empire she would be the last witness of the collapse of the empire under the pressure of *Völkerwanderung.* From here Galla Placidia would govern through her son Valentinian III, from here the last great general of Western Rome, Flavius Aetius, would head out to ally himself with the Burgundians on the Katalaunian fields in order to fight Attila, just to be murdered a few years later, also in this city, and by the hands of his own emperor.

All of which Rheinberg sought to prevent. The death of Aetius had initiated the final demise of the Western Roman Empire, and exactly this development could be halted. When he got the chance to.

If this man over there gave him the chance. The triremes led the *Saarbrücken* to a completely closed-off pier, swarming with soldiers. And on the quay, in a flowing cape, stood a tall, lean man with a remarkable hooked nose and all the trappings of a Roman officer, surrounded by archers and spearmen. Rheinberg registered that two large onagers were driven onto the quay. Renna had taken all precautions he could think of. Smart, again.

Rheinberg took a deep breath and sighed.

"What shall we do?" He turned back to Africanus. "Let him on board or ask for permission to leave the ship?"

"Let him decide," was the trierarch's laconic reply. He obviously had no intention to try to read the thoughts of his superior.

Rheinberg could hardly blame him.

As the *Saarbrücken* closed to the pier and the crew threw ropes that would be fixed by soldiers to the bollards, Rheinberg felt a strange mixture of relief and excitement – relief because it was good to be in a harbor and tension because he didn't know if Ravenna could become a new home port for the *Saarbrücken.* As the gangway touched the pier, the lean man who had been identified by Africanus as Navarch Renna went without further hesitation and without accompaniment on board.

The gray eyes of the naval officer narrowed as he let his gaze wander over the width and length of the cruiser. The motionless face of the navarch didn't show what he thought or felt, whether and to what extent he was impressed. As Rheinberg approached him and saluted according to the custom of the German Navy, he nodded curtly and turned directly to Africanus.

"How are you, trierarch?"

"My ship is lost, like the majority of my crew. The survivors are on board here. They are well cared for."

"Are you a prisoner of the foreign barbarians?"

"I am, but my freedom upon arrival in Ravenna was assured."

Renna's eyes went to Rheinberg, who had said nothing and stared at him.

"I'm Marcus Flovius Renna, navarch of the empire."

"I'm Jan Rheinberg, trierarch of the *Saravica*."

Renna made an expansive gesture. "This is the *Saravica*? It's the name of a village in Germania."

"It's my ship."

"Who is your king?"

"We hope to serve the Emperor of Rome."

Renna frowned, exchanged glances with Africanus, who nodded at him. "You wish to submit yourself to the command of the emperor?"

Rheinberg hesitated. "I want to reach an agreement with him that will be beneficial for both of us."

Renna seemed to understand this language. "But my question was not answered. Which king did you serve before?"

"An emperor, far from Rome. We cannot return there, and need a new home."

"Refugees? In such a powerful and strange vessel? Are there more of it around?"

"My former Lord commands many."

Renna looked alarmed. Rheinberg hastened to add, "The land of my former king is out of our reach. We are alone." He hesitated. "We need help."

"Help? Trierarch Daker told me that the *Scipio* had no chance against your ship."

The navarch made this statement calmly and objectively, without reproach in his voice. Rheinberg took some courage. "A misunderstanding. The *Scipio* attacked our ship in the assumption that we are a threat. We fought back."

"And? Are you a threat?" Renna finally asked the most important question.

"I don't want to be one. We will leave our guns to be silent as long as we are not attacked, and we shall be ready to use them for the sake of the Empire if we reach an agreement with the Emperor."

Renna said nothing. He turned back to Africanus. "Take your men and leave the ship."

"Sir!"

Rheinberg waved. Köhler had been waiting for the sign. He called a few commands, then the POWs trotted from aboard, the wounded in the lead on stretchers, carried by their comrades. Finally only Africanus and his helmsman Sepidus remained.

"I have sent messengers to the prefect and to Treveri," Renna said. The easy handling of the prisoner issue seemed to fill him with obvious satisfaction. "I expect a reply soon. Until then, your ship should be moored. No one is leaving without permission, and I promise my men will not try to come on board."

"I agree."

"Your weapons remain silent."

"Like your own."

"Then so be it."

Renna fixed Africanus with his sharp eyes. "Trierarch, you will remain on board as my ambassador. Keep Sepidus with you. You report to me every day. Is that acceptable?"

The last question was again addressed to Rheinberg.

"Yes," he hastened to answer. "The trierarch is welcome aboard."

Renna showed something like a smile for the first time as he turned abruptly and left the ship behind the prisoners. He walked onto the pier and disappeared among his soldiers who joined the guard line at the pier in front of the *Saarbrücken* behind him.

Now wait.

"I'm happy," Rheinberg muttered in Latin.

"Happy?" asked Africanus.

Rheinberg rubbed his neck.

"My head is still sitting on the neck."

The trierarch grinned. "Renna had a good day. Don't ever rely on it."

12

"Richomer, you are a pessimist! The oracle cannot be wrong! Victory is certainly ours!"

"We should wait until the reinforcements arrive, my Emperor. Then we can be sure that we will gain the upper hand!"

Valens, Emperor of Eastern Rome, looked suspiciously at the general. The muscular man with his polished armor made an imposing appearance – more imposing than the plump emperor in his toga, who walked up and down in the general's tent.

"Are you for me, Richomer, or against me?"

"My Lord, you know the answer. I have always served Rome faithfully!"

Valens snorted. He stopped abruptly, threw up his arms. "The oracle told me otherwise. I know that conspiracies are underway. I don't know who is behind it, but I swear that I will find out soon enough."

Richomer tried to hide his displeasure. "Noble Majesty, your nephew has asked me personally to support you in your preparations for the battle as well as my humble abilities allow me to. My loyalty is beyond any doubt. My career is clear from any stain, and I'm an officer because I've proven myself."

That was the maximum someone like Richomer could afford as gentle criticism. Valens was a man who became increasingly erratic. The older step-uncle of Gratian, elevated by Valentinian to his office, now became more manic in his paranoid suspicions, his confidence in the oracle, and an ever growing fear of conspiracies. It was not megalomania to which he succumbed – Valens was, despite his craziness, no Commodus or Nero – but he had already gone a long way toward lunacy. The victory against the Goths a few years ago, where the Eastern Roman Emperor had in fact distinguished himself as a general and earned the loyal following of the military, had apparently risen to his head. Since then he had allowed the Goths to cross the Danube. After his underlings exploited refugees brutally and harassed them, Fritigern and Alaric were on the campaign against Rome, and although they didn't manage to take fortified cities, they plundered the rural areas and avoided any pitched battle so far.

The eternal curse of Rome. Of course, the harassment had not been made by order of Valens, who had a vested interest to direct the onslaught of Goths into peaceful channels. But you couldn't rely on all subjects, and this was true for both the civilian and the military administration. Thus, the Goths had gathered and started a war. And they were under the leadership of their kings, Alaric and Fritigern, who refused to act stupid, and that was probably the major problem.

Here, before Adrianople, Valens wanted to force a decision. He had mustered all his troops, but the Goths were many.

Very many.

As some thought, carefully, quietly, too many.

Richomer and the other generals had implored Valens to wait for the arrival of the Western Roman legions under Gratian in order to jointly fight against the barbarians. But Valens envied the young Western Roman Emperor, who seemed in many ways to follow into the footsteps of his famous and adored father with his military successes. So Valens went with the idea that he alone would be able to beat the Goths in order to gain all the glory – and to show his perceived or real enemies that he still held the reins in Eastern Rome.

"We have assembled the largest Eastern army that has existed in years," exclaimed Valens. "The scouts have reported that the Goths are much fewer than expected! We will scatter them to the four winds and overwhelm them for good!"

"Noble sir, the scouts' reports seem to be inaccurate, and the Goths are distributed over a wide area! We cannot be sure!"

"Coward!" snapped Valens, pulled his toga up and stood right in front Richomer, who was a head taller. "Coward! Since Sebastianus has won his last victory against Fritigern, the Goths are weak and on the run! We have driven them before us like cattle!"

Richomer pondered what to say. Valens' interpretation of the truth was as wrong as his imperial delusions could go. They had shadowed the

Goths as they wandered looting across the country, and yes, General Sebastianus had led a successful attack against a part of those hordes, but it by no means caused the damage Valens claimed. Fritigern was no fool. He had lost to Sebastian because he had spread his troops too far. This time he has been wiser and took care to assemble the bulk of his soldiers massed against the Romans ... Richomer literally smelled the disaster that had to follow inevitably.

But this was Valens, the emperor of the East, brother of Valentinian. And he was Richomer, an officer of Gratian, and he knew when to stop provoking an emperor.

He bowed. Richomer had been given command of the advance guard by Gratian and he was a capable Comes, and could allow himself to talk more frankly to Valens than his own generals, because he owed obedience and service foremost to Gratian. But even for him at some point a certain limit was reached, and Valens had executed quite a few critical spirits in his ever-increasing irrationality, not least with the all too quickly expressed allegation of a conspiracy.

Valens waved.

"You will serve me, Richomer, and ask Sebastianus where your place in battle should be!"

Richomer could only obey. Eventually he was allowed to leave the tent and entered the August summer heat, shading his eyes with one hand. Before him lay the entrenched camp of the Eastern troops, all veterans and professionals. The Western Roman officer had no doubt about that. But there were too few of them. And aside from the critical parts of the officer corps, most of the soldiers who had gathered here were at least as convinced about their invincibility as their emperor. A dangerous hubris, as Richomer thought.

From the shadow of the neighboring tent approached another officer. Richomer recognized the older man immediately; it was Victor, the Magister Equitum of the East, and thus the second-highest military commander behind Sebastianus. An experienced general who had served three emperors, he had been an ally of those trying to convince the sovereign not to initiate any battle too hasty. A look at Richomer's face told him everything he needed to know.

"You have tried and failed," Victor whispered to him out of earshot of the guards and after they had gone a few steps together.

Richomer sighed. "He is quite insane, more or less. To me, he seems torn between his desire for fame and the envy of Gratian's victories on the one hand and the rationality of the experienced general he basically is, on the other."

"The one he once was," Victor corrected with a worried expression. "Since the death of his brother, he listens only to Modestus, and if he even makes his own decision, then more often than not a stupid one." Modestus was the pretorian prefect and member of the Consistory of the East. He wasn't incompetent, and quite a deliberate politician but hadn't understood that one couldn't leave Valens alone on his campaigns. If Modestus would be present, there would still be a chance to achieve something, Richomer was sure of it. But the prefect was in Constantinople, and Sebastianus, drunken with victory, wanted the glory of a quick and decisive victory as badly as Valens. And, here, beyond the moderating influence of the Consistory, Valens was also completely addicted to the oracle interpreters and astrologers that made him even more crazy with all sorts of insinuations. They swarmed around him with their runes and drawings, and Valens heard their counsel more than that of his experienced officers.

"We must make the best of it," Victor finally sighed. "I'm very scared about the emperor himself. Stay close with your men; I want to make sure that we are not separated in battle. Sebastianus isn't a bad general, but he underestimates the value of the cavalry – both for attack and for retreat. You have cavalry along with your troops?"

"Moorish and Aleman cavalrymen," confirmed Richomer. "Fast as the wind, that's why we were the advance guard. Gratian's troops must already be on the way. If we were to wait only a few weeks ..."

Flavius Victor snorted. "Forget it. Stay close to me. Maybe we can turn the situation!" Victor's confidence sounded forced, but Richomer didn't contradict him. It was better than nothing.

At the other end of the camp, Sebastianus inspected his troops. One could hear his jokes and laughter. Sebastian had a contagiously friendly way with the soldiers, which made it very difficult to disagree with him. He was among the ordinary legionaries as popular as with the auxiliary troops and the officers, and he made sure that the wages were paid regularly and everyone got his rations. Richomer would serve with pleasure under his command, if not for this nagging doubt that made him anything but enthusiastic. Regardless of how much Gratian would order forced marches – and whether he had the Alemanni under control Richomer didn't know either – it would still take many days for the two field armies to coordinate, to take common action against the Goths.

"Not that there would be no more major problems even if we are victorious," the Western Roman growled.

Victor nodded. "I know what you mean, my friend. There is a reason behind the fact that the Goths came to us and asked for settlement areas."

Both looked at each with other meaningful glances. When the Goths had fled to the borders of the empire, it hadn't looked like a military invasion at all. They had started negotiations, asking for settlement, and they promised to serve the Empire. For Rome, there were only advantages: There was plenty of land that was significantly under-populated, and the shortage of capable men for the armed forces had become dire to the point that any slave who reported a deserter gained his immediate freedom. Every son of a soldier was legally obligated to join the army and had no other choice. The Empire was attacked from many sides ... Alemans, Goths, the Persian Empire gaining strength ... too many holes, with only a limited amount of flexible troops who were not put into the frontier garrisons. Had the officers in charge of the Goths not been incompetent managers and had they not totally botched their crossing of the Danube and the care of the refugees, Richomer wouldn't be here, and there would be no need to discuss gloomy forecasts with Victor.

"The Goths themselves report terrible things about what is taking place to the east," said Victor now. "I don't know what of it is truth or rumor, but if hordes fell upon them, they must have been huge."

"True enough to move an entire people to flee," Richomer commented dryly. They had reached the tents where the officers slept. "I fear the battle against the Goths is only the beginning. And that's one more reason not to risk our own forces in a futile search for quick fame, but rather fight well planned and on the basis of a realistic assessment."

"I won't contradict you."

Victor held out his hand. "I have to go to my men. See you, my friend."

Richomer looked after him. The feeling of helplessness that overwhelmed him he wasn't used to. He shaded his eyes and looked into the summer sky.

None of this wouldn't go well, of that he was quite sure.

13

"Sit down, Aurelius!"

Navarch Renna pointed to a stool then looked at the large wall map showing the Roman Empire in its current borders – or at least the borders everyone assumed to be valid at that point of time. One could never really be sure.

Africanus accepted the invitation and sat down. On a small table stood a carafe of wine and a bowl of fruit. The trierarch ignored both.

"Tell me, Aurelius," Renna said. "Have we a serious threat to our security in our harbor? The bishop said yesterday behind closed doors that the ship was the work of demons and one should consider an exorcism."

"The bishop himself talks like a demon," said Aurelius. "The foreigners are strange, I admit. They are powerful, and they are surely are a threat to our security, because if we do offend them, they alone can put Ravenna in ruins with the power of their weapons. But they are alone, that I understand clearly, looking for a home, just like the Goths in the East. They are no demons. All are Christians, as I was able to learn myself. They had a church service in their strange tongue, but the meaning wasn't to be denied. Demons are not like that, Navarch. I would say ... they are an opportunity."

Renna looked his subordinates directly in the face. "An opportunity for what?"

Aurelius seemed to hesitate. Renna waited a moment, then sighed. He stood next to the captain, put a hand on his shoulder and leaned toward him. "Speak to me openly, trierarch. Whatever you have to say, it will not leave these four walls. We've so far dealt openly with each other. You are one of my best men, with a clear view of the reality of a situation. If I wouldn't listen to you, let you tell me what you want, to whom should I listen instead?"

Aurelius pulled himself together. "We are facing major problems. The tax burden sucks the last bit of blood out of the people. Only the super-rich are spared due to political reasons. My sons are not free, and even as Roman citizens, they need to become soldiers like me without anyone asking them for their preference. The coins that are given to us as pay are becoming worthless; silver is not silver anymore, and gold is not gold. Each year, new barbarians push against the border, and every year we lose more legionaries who we cannot replace. The senators and landowners cram their pockets while the once free peasants become tenants of the affluent. Corruption is everywhere. Those who can afford it buy themselves free of all obligations. The Church, God be merciful to me, is exempt from all taxes and sows unrest throughout the Empire by its constant internal struggles. I don't know how long it will take, and I don't know what will be the final straw, but I'm no fool. My father sent me to school, and although I knew I was going to the navy, I studied hard. And I suspect that sooner or later the Empire is doomed unless something happens. The army cannot forever hold the pieces together. Something has to change."

Renna snorted. "Diocletian said that. He has adopted the relevant laws."

"He has also divided the empire into four parts and begotten incompetent sons," Aurelius replied fearlessly. "If we want to endure, we must find new ways. We need more power where our number dwindles. I have seen what these strangers are capable of. By God, I don't care where they come from. They have sunk my ship! Friends of mine died in the sea! But if we can just win them for us, if the Lord Emperor recognizes the opportunities that they bring – then I want to forget it and forgive them."

Renna nodded in a measured way. He let go of Africanus and walked for a few minutes thoughtfully through the room. Then he stopped in front of the large wall map and looked at it as if the studies would give him new insights. Finally, he turned back to the trierarch, which had waited patiently. One didn't push a man like Renna.

"I've had similar thoughts," the navarch said softly. "But you see the danger. What the bishop whispers silently to me could go through the priests like wildfire. You know how they are. When their zeal is roused, they burn everything down, start to destroy and kill in the name of God, and are willing to sacrifice their own lives, regardless of their faith. Still they wait for the emperor to finally prohibit the ancient religions, so they can tear down the temples and kill or drive out the priests."

Aurelius said nothing. He was a Christian, an Arian, something one didn't say too loudly here in the West. Renna was known to be a follower of Mithras, as there were still many in the armed forces, whether openly or concealed. Religion was an issue that bothered both of them repeatedly, and both distrusted the church authorities in the West, although for different reasons. Both were well aware of the danger of religious conflict.

"I think that we need to avoid one thing: that the foreigners are mad demons," Renna said. "If the people are incited by the zealots, I can post my whole port watch in front of the pier, and it wouldn't suffice."

The trierarch nodded.

"How do we want to prevent that?" he asked.

Aurelius felt that Renna connected similar hopes with the appearance of the strange ship like he himself. Maybe the tour through the iron vessel that Trierarch Rheinberg had given him yesterday helped him to recognize the potential of the visitor. Whatever the reason, the navarch had realized that they had to keep control of the situation, no matter what. And if they succeeded, they might succeed also to seize the opportunities of this strange coincidence.

"I sent messengers. Gratian marches to the east, and I don't think he will turn to Ravenna just because of this ship. I have sent a message to the prefect of Rome. And I have sent an invitation to a few selected senators."

Aurelius nodded. He had always known that Renna was an active man, and this only confirmed the impression.

"May I assume to whom, navarch? Moderate senators of high reputation and personal integrity? Christians as well as others? Men who are respected by all, and who even the biggest fanatics couldn't simply discard as heretics? Men who enjoy the confidence of the Emperor?"

Renna smiled thinly. "You should be a senator. Or, better yet, see that you're promoted to navarch soon. Diocletian may have separated civil administration and the military, but believe me, without a hand in politics you won't go far as a high-ranking officer. You seem to have a talent."

"I learn from a great master," said Aurelius, and lowered his head submissively.

"The art of fake submission you have mastered as well!" Renna laughed. "Well, listen up: You're right in everything. Once I have an equal number of curious and bored dignitaries in the city, I will meet with the senate of Ravenna to organize a treat in the villa of Urianus. Which is a great and pleasant place and his cooks are the best. We will invite them all – including a delegation of the strange foreigners. They should learn to know them, chat with them, share in the wine, watch the dancers – and note that the visitors are a little strange but in the end terribly normal men, whom nobody has to fear. The news will spread quickly and stab our suspicious zealots in the back. What do you think?"

"That sounds sensible. I'm with you! But I have to add: Whether that will really cause an urge for peace and understanding among the fanatics, I sincerely doubt."

"You're even invited. Contribute! The trierarch whose ship was destroyed by the strangers getting pissed with them. A convincing performance."

"Then I thank you for the great honor! Yes, I will come and drink a toast to my dead comrades. Or two."

Renna grabbed Aurelius at his shoulders. "I understand your bitterness, Africanus. But nothing will bring those men back to life. I'm more interested in preventing further unnecessary deaths. Head back to the ship of the strangers and prepare them for their own invitation. I'll have to send dress makers, so they get all the appropriate clothing. They shouldn't only act as normal men, they should also look like them. Make sure it works. We might have a chance to fulfill your dreams of a different Rome, my friend."

14

It was cold and rainy despite being summer. There were various reasons why Magnus Maximus, Comes Britanniarum, more than just hated the territory over which he ruled. He stood on the parapet of the fortified garrison and stared through the haze to Hadrian's Wall, whose imposing line was almost in sight. For three weeks now the British military commander rode from one frontier fortress to the next, met his officers, praised the men, visited the families. He had himself invited to dinner and brought fresh wine. He carried mail from Rome as far as it had arrived in London, he gave comfort to the injured and listened to the heroic stories of veterans at the campfire. Three weeks and another two months still lied ahead of him, because his goal was to visit every garrison personally, no matter how remote and small, in order to increase the morale of his men.

As much as he appreciated the respect of his soldiers and did everything to expand their loyalty, as much he hated Britain, why this island had once been conquered – or at least the southern part – no one knew for sure anymore. The times of Roman expansion were over since the great Traianus, already more than 200 years ago. Britain had never had anything that was necessary or helpful for the Empire. There were few natural resources, but there were many highly recalcitrant barbarians who showed little willingness to make friends with Roman civilization and way of life. The climate was harsh and wet and uncomfortable in every way. Hadrian's Wall was built in order to pour the surrender of the Empire before the hordes of the North in stone and wood, and since then the Roman troops did nothing more than to defend themselves against the barbarians' growing pressure. There was nothing of value for Rome but the prestige, and besides what the long Roman conquest finally had been able to establish, especially the provincial capital itself, that definitely was the only place on this inhospitable island which represented a hint of what Maximus and his men understood as Roman civilization.

Britain was a depressing place, and the men who served there tended to express this frustration. Desertions had increased before the arrival of Maximus, and morale was down. He had been appointed Comes by Valentinian in order to keep Britain for the Empire, and the situation since had improved recognizably. Maximus cherished his men, showed personal courage in numerous skirmishes with barbarian hordes and dispensed generous commendations and promotions. He was popular with his legions, for he had brought them hope in a dreary and gloomy situation.

The fine drizzle that had prevailed all morning was intense. Maximus pulled the cloak tighter around his shoulders and turned when he heard someone joining him on the balustrade. He knew the steps of his closest confidant, and he could distinguish them from those of thousand others. General Andragathius, Master Equitum, one of his highest officers, preferred to fight from horseback since an injury damaged his right leg slightly but permanently. The elderly man, whose gray beard was already well moisturized, joined his leader and looked like him toward the remote, dark stripes of the wall.

"It's all quiet, Comes," he said in a deep voice. "Since the last attack the barbarians have probably had enough. We have concluded agreements with some chiefs, and it looks like they want to keep this at least for a while."

"We still need a few years," Maximus reminded him and turned to his companion. "The preparations are not yet complete. And I will give Gratian the chance to redeem his mistake."

Andragathius let out a snort. "The Emperor leaves the men in the mold. Since Valentinian has secured the border, I haven't noticed any significant imperial attention anymore. Gratian cares about the heartland and has long forgotten Britain – and those who defend it."

Maximus couldn't disagree. Not only that, his own career since the death of Valentinian was no longer developing with the expected speed, at least not with the speed he deserved in his view, and the general discontent in the remote provinces far from Trier was almost tangible.

"I have spoken with some of the tribunes yesterday," Andragathius continued. "Casually, with wine and at the fire. It was late. They had drunk more than me."

"And?"

"They would like you to take the purple immediately."

"It's too soon, my friend. We need the support of all officers and all British legions. Only then can we realistically enter Gaul and dare to speak out against Gratian."

"Merobaudes sends his greetings. Yesterday came a chest with fabrics and new boots from Milan."

Maximus was silent. Merobaudes had been one of the most successful generals of the late Valentinian, showered with the highest honors. Since Valentinian's son Gratian was emperor, the old general had been resigned to a minor role. Among the men he continued to enjoy great popularity, though. If he would be able to pull him to his side, Gratian's position would be weakened – he would eventually have no chance to defend himself effectively. Maximus' grip on the throne would be crowned with success, as with so many emperors who had been elevated likewise by their armies. There were many like Merobaudes, just waiting for the right candidate.

And more often than enough those emperors quickly fell again. There were good reasons why Maximus spend his time and a lot of energy to generate loyalty among his troops. He would need it.

"What's with Gildo?" asked the General.

"He is using his contacts already. We have very positive results. The fact that Gratian has been so successful against the Alemans on the battlefield helps us a lot. The joy about the victories of the Emperor is somewhat restrained."

"He will help us?"

"More than expected. He thinks he'll make troops available and that he would use his connections to the mainland in order to ensure that the Alemannic sub-tribes will join us as soon as we are set to Gaul. He also promised to keep things controlled here in Britain once the majority of border troops are with us. I think we can rely on him – for some time."

"He was settled with his people here by Gratian's father," Andragathius pointed out. "Valentinian is held in high regard!"

"He is also in my high regard," growled Maximus. "It is his son, whom with I have an issue here. I intend to continue the work of the great Valentinian."

"Will Valens recognize you as emperor once Gratian is overthrown?"

"He will probably have no other choice. He has his hands full trying to defend the eastern part against the Goths and the Persians. If he sees that in the West a man of action has been raised through his popularity with the troops, and that he has sufficient experience of doing what needs to be done, he will accept the inevitable. Valens is weak. The consistory will vote against a civil war. Gratian has no children."

"Valens has none as well."

"I have no ambitions in the east. I will make that clear immediately and in no uncertain terms. I'm not a revolutionary, and megalomania hasn't overwhelmed me. I'm a man of principle, and I will make the west strong. I will especially strengthen the neglected provinces, and I will ensure that the wars against all those Alemans who help us will end. This will contribute more to border security than any battle won."

The rain stopped. Like following an order, the clouds tore and a promising ray of sunshine danced on their side of Hadrian's Wall.

Andragathius and Maximus took the symbolism of the moment in with all their senses. Silently they stood side by side, both busy with their visions of the empire, and their respective role in the events that have already materialized themselves in their secret and careful preparations.

They had patience. The right moment would come. And when it was there, no one would be able to counter the legions of Maximus and prevent his ascent to the throne.

There was no doubt about it.

15

"I cannot, and I will not wear this."

"We can, and you will."

"This is outrageous! Silly! I look like a ..."

"... a male Roman of high rank, who accepts an invitation to which you cannot say no."

Von Klasewitz stared down at himself.

The two tailors hadn't understood a word but gathered from the tone of their customers that their enthusiasm was somewhat limited and had withdrawn to the background after the first outbreak of open disgust.

"I'm not saying that we shouldn't go," murmured von Klasewitz. "I say we wear our dress uniforms! What is good enough for the German Emperor is good enough for the Romans!"

Rheinberg tried not to show his impatience as well as the way how the first officer strained his nerves too obviously. The invitation sent on behalf of Navarch Renna by Africanus was a terrific opportunity. Rheinberg had considered for a tiny moment of leaving Klasewitz behind with the command of the *Saarbrücken*, but quickly decided against it. For one, he just couldn't bring himself to trust his first officer enough. For another, he knew that von Klasewitz loved such events. He had probably underestimated that he especially liked it because he could make a good impression with the female guests in the admittedly very chic navy dress uniform.

However, in the toga, which his tailor had just knocked over, he could not have this effect. Under the edge, his pale and scrawny legs were visible. Rheinberg had difficulty adjusting to this kind of clothing to as well, but he never intended to dupe his hosts by refusing this kind gesture. Becker, Neumann and Ensign Volkert – the delegation appointed by him from the *Saarbrücken* – had accepted the new dress code with jokes but were completely willing to wear it. Rheinberg should have known that only von Klasewitz would object.

And he had no desire for lengthy discussions. The celebration took place in four days, and there were guests of honor from Rome – senators, specifically – as Africanus had indicated. The name of Symmachus had slipped, and therefore this would be the first time Rheinberg would know a person of real, albeit tragic historical importance.

"I order you to cease complaining," Rheinberg finally growled. "You put this on. Stop it."

"Sir ..."

"Stop it!"

Rheinberg nodded to the two tailors. "We're ready now. Let's continue, please," he said in Latin. Then he spoke again to von Klasewitz and changed the subject. "Have we made progress with the study-roster?"

"Good progress," the first officer said. "You are teaching the first hour. I have divided Neumann and Volkert. They've mastered both ancient Greek and Latin, at least that's their own confession. I have flagged myself for Greek."

Rheinberg nodded. Von Klasewitz had obviously not been paying attention in Latin class, but his Greek was passable, which secretly had surprised him. As of today, the schedules were adjusted so that each morning would begin with a two-hour language course for NCOs and enlisted men. Moreover, something had been scheduled for every Sunday, a course Rheinberg called "Roman Geography." It should provide a general historical, geographical and political overview of the time – if Rheinberg's memory and his modest private library could provide sufficient information. Obviously, they were still too few teachers, and should their general status improve in the course of time, tutors from Ravenna should complement the work. But he didn't want to wait. They had to work with what they had.

"Yesterday's battle drill?" Rheinberg asked.

"Results were not bad," said his first officer, who looked with disfavor at the tailor dealing with him again until the toga was falling reasonably correct. "Becker's men at least know how to follow orders, and they have sea legs by now. They do us no good on deck, but if it should ever come to fighting against boarding attacks, they know now where they should be and where not."

"Good, very good," praised Rheinberg. The plan for the drills was indeed developed by Becker and Köhler, but it didn't matter if one paid tribute and give some recognition to von Klasewitz now and again. Not that von Klasewitz was the kind of man who took notice of praise and used it draw the right conclusions. But Rheinberg didn't want anyone to hold it against him that he hadn't tried his best. And he had to admit, since they had reached Ravenna, the first officer hadn't consistently acted like an asshole. Conceivably the smell of the city and the prospect of enjoying the company of Roman nobility had beneficial effects on him.

Rheinberg was distracted from his thoughts when he heard excited shouts from outside. He shooed the tailor to the side, jumped down from the stool on which he had stood, and hurried through the door of the cabin. In a fluttering toga, he ran outside and held on to the railing. Beside him were many other men and everyone looked into the harbor. The calls did not come from his people, but from pathetic looking men on a large sailboat whose sails, partially lacerated, hung on the mast and only a lucky current and a very appropriate wind had helped the vessel to make any progress. Numerous smaller boats came up to the damaged ship, and there was excitement on the wharf. A rope was thrown, and the rowing boats began to pull the stricken ship to a free space.

"What do they shout? That's a terrible whining!" asked one of the men and looked at Rheinberg without regard to his strange appearance. Rheinberg listened closely. A word was repeated again and again.

"Pirates!" he translated for the others. "Pirates! They have been attacked by pirates." He stepped aside as Africanus approached him, his eyes full of serious concern.

"Trierarch Rheinberg?"

"That was an attack by pirates?"

Africanus nodded sadly. "They are getting bolder. Two ships of my squadron have just received the order to leave. It's an emergency."

"This vessel?"

"No, a second one. It would be bad enough as it is, but the other has the young son of the prefect of Rome on board, a senator of high rank as well, who had visited his relatives in Sicily and was supposed to go to school here. He has been kidnapped. We fear a very high ransom. And all this casts a large shadow on our squadron. That this was possible, will bring a lot of problems for Renna. We need to stop these people before they are gone."

In Rheinberg's mind appeared a sudden thought full of clarity and logic. He touched Africanus' shoulders. "Get Renna. Ask him and a bodyguard to come on board! And get us permission to sail! We will deal with these pirates for you – and thus prove our honorable intentions."

Joy drove doubt and apprehension from the features of the trierarch. Without another word, he turned and ran toward the gangway.

Rheinberg waved to the bridge where Langenhagen was on his duty station. "Lieutenant!" he bellowed.

"Captain!"

"Machines under steam! Clear ship to sail!"

"Clear ship to sail!" Langenhagen yelled back. Seconds later, the boatswain whistle shrilled through the deck. Commands echoed across. Well-organized and trained activity broke out. It helped that their present situation made landfall impossible and therefore all crew was on board. Everyone was bored – and they were more than ready to finally do something meaningful.

Rheinberg looked down at himself, at his bare feet in the braided sandals.

It was probably better to get changed.

Ten minutes later, he was in uniform on the bridge of *Saarbrücken*, watching the tailors flee from the suddenly active ship. As Dahms reported steam in the boilers, it was already an hour later, and that was also only possible because the engineer had never completely allowed the machines to become cold.

Another thirty minutes later, Renna, accompanied by twelve legionaries and Africanus, arrived. The navarch knew the way now and joined Rheinberg next to the bridge. No sooner had the Romans entered the cruiser, and it was already cast off.

"How is the situation, navarch?" asked Rheinberg straight away.

"The culprits are the ships of Claderius," the gaunt man replied. "He's famous and infamous, and he's getting bolder. We suspect that he has his base in Sicily, but so far he has always escaped us. He commands many small and very fast ships and attacks his prey with a pack mentality. He usually doesn't take hostages, but this time he has probably noticed what kind of fish he had on the hook and couldn't resist. The boy is worth his weight in gold, or more. Claderius is old; maybe he wants to retire."

"How do you usually respond to such an incident?"

"We go to sea immediately, but in the wind the sailing ships are far superior to the triremes. We often search in vain. When we come anywhere close to the southern tip, he has vanished with his people to safety for a long time. Once we have seen his masts on the horizon, that was our biggest success so far."

Renna gave a snort.

"He impresses senators and prefects. They have for so long kept a protective hand over him as many have been involved with him. But that was before taking a son of a prefect as hostage. He went too far. To plunder merchants and fishermen, that's fine. Now they will cry for his head."

Renna looked hopefully at Rheinberg. "This is important, Trierarch Rheinberg. You have a fair chance to prove your worthiness. A failure is also a serious flaw, of which you will hardly be able to clean yourself."

"I know. But I've made the decision. And we are faster than a trireme or a sailing ship. We will take southern course. In this clear weather, and if we take some of the surviving sailors on board to help us, we should succeed. When in doubt, we head to Sicily."

Renna looked half-incredulous, half-expectantly at Rheinberg. Then he roared his own instructions into the harbor. A few minutes later, sailors rowed from the wreck toward the cruiser. They stared at the German ship with big eyes but put their trust in it when they saw the navarch.

As Renna felt that the *Saarbrücken* pushed progressively further from the pier and then slowly gathered speed, he stopped and looked around. The cruiser pulled away from the dock and won open sea. Even the pirates were operating near the coast, and the raid had taken place close to Ravenna. The wind was light and blowing from the east. If the pirates wanted to escape, they had to cross into the wind, which was nearly impossible with the kind of rigging used in these times – ideal conditions for a successful pursuit.

Renna and Africanus clung involuntarily to the railing as Rheinberg gave the order to follow the coastline southwards in full speed. White foam formed before the mighty bow of the cruiser and the pounding of the machines let the body of the vessel tremble. Renna and Africanus admired with wide eyes as the coastline began to slide along them at a pace that could not be achieved even by the fastest sailing shops with most favorable winds. Rheinberg had three men armed with binoculars, both at the bow as well as positioned on the port side. On the bridge, two officers carried their own binoculars and watched the waters. An expectant tension settled over the crew.

Captain Becker climbed into the bridge and joined Rheinberg. "If we have them, what do we do?"

"We threaten them. We give them a shot across the bow. If they refuse to surrender, we sink one of them. If they are compliant, we send the steam launch and board them. We form a boarding party of your best men and some of my sailors. I think for the maneuver I take my people, who have practiced boarding, and your men give covering fire."

Becker nodded. Already in the last battle drill his best shooters had been assigned good positions on the ship. Two NCOs talented with the gun had been given positions from which they could kill any enemy soldier within 100 meters. And Rheinberg had the intention to go close enough to use this advantage.

"Captain!"

Langenhagen indicated. "To port!"

Rheinberg raised his own binoculars and looked in the direction. A number of sailing ships became apparent. He handed the glass to Africanus, who had been accustomed to use it by now. He looked through and a triumphant grin appeared on his face.

"Aren't fishermen," Africanus growled. "Offshore ships, quite far away from the coast. That's how they are always escaping our triremes. It has to be them."

Rheinberg ordered a slight change of course. "Köhler! Clear for action!"

The boatswain's whistle sounded again, and the men took their battle positions with great confidence.

"I want to use a 5-inch gun. Align it and ready to fire. Wait for my command!"

"Aligning and make ready, yes."

Von Klasewitz appeared on the bridge, recognized the situation, nodded and disappeared back to control the gun crews. Rheinberg had no objection because this was the expertise of the nobleman. He knew his guns.

Renna followed the unintelligible conversation with silent attention. He noticed very well that a carefully oiled military organization was ready to follow the orders of its officers. He understood, and he didn't interfere. As Africanus asked him to port side and pointed to the mouth of the 5-inch gun, he seemed to guess what kind of power lay behind this ultimately inconspicuous device.

The *Saarbrücken* gained rapidly now that the ship had a goal. Soon the excited crew members of the pirate-ships were observed pointing toward the onrushing behemoth, obviously confused, impressed and hopefully scared. The pirates used small and sleek vessels, none longer than five or six feet, but there was a total of eighteen, and each was armed recognizably. Against this pack, a ponderous trading ship was obviously helpless, and perhaps it could also be dangerous for a single trireme.

"Navarch, it would be useful if you would ask them to surrender," Rheinberg finally said. He looked into the officer's face and was surprised by the transformation that was clearly visible. From the distant and noble navarch, the man beside him has changed into an avid sailor, impressed by the wonders of a ship that was technically far beyond everything he had known before. Renna nodded, his cheeks almost glowing with excitement and enthusiasm. Rheinberg knew that he had finally brought the man to his side, and be it because of his conviction that he must use this miracle for the good of the Empire.

Africanus handed him the megaphone, which Renna took immediately and rushed to the front deck. Rheinberg gave Becker a wink and a nod just before he followed the Roman. Africanus preferred to remain on the bridge.

Renna stood at the bow as the *Saarbrücken* slowed and slid parallel to the pirates through the water. Apparently, the pirates had not yet realized that the metal monster was after them officially and on behalf of the Roman navy. When Renna yelled his surrender request and was clearly recognizable in his armor, it finally dawned to the crooks.

Renna's call was answered with a half-hearted arrow attack. One of the missiles landed powerless on deck; the remainder hit against the ship's side or went swimming.

"I take that as a 'no'," muttered Rheinberg. "Shot across the bow!"

The well-oiled machine of the cruiser, both technology and crew, responded with disciplined precision ... Messages poured in, and then the 5-inch gun barked hoarsely. A moment later, a fountain spurted high among the leading pirate and spray flung over his railing.

"Well targeted and shot well, my commendation to the gunners!" Rheinberg said with a satisfied grin. Everyone was righteously impressed.

Renna roared again something into the megaphone. This time some yelling came back. The navarch threw up his arms in mock despair, the megaphone still in one hand, and then trudged back to the bridge. "This is silly. Fools," he cursed as he stood beside the helm.

"Can you determine which ship has the hostage?" asked Rheinberg.

"Not really. But the sailing ships have no lower deck. There is not much place to hide someone. That ship over there seems to be filled only with pirates."

"Then we have a target."

It all happened very quickly. The 5-inch turned its mouth and orders were given. Von Klasewitz himself was on deck to command the fire. Again the gun bellowed, but this time there was no fountain of water but the crashing of splintering wood, a ball of fire, screaming men thrown into water, and a very fast, very effectively sinking wreck. It was gone in an instant, without a great roar of attack, without further warning. There was nothing left where a pirate with a good twelve men on board had been – only foaming sea, a few planks of wood, and one or two desperate swimmers.

Renna stared speechless, amazed, but also fascinated by the spectacle. Now he had seen what he had been reported by Africanus and could appreciate what the cruiser was capable of. The navarch seemed to be very impressed.

Through his binoculars Rheinberg could see the terror in the faces of the pirates. He had left a lasting impression there as well. "Good, very good," he said. "Navarch, may I suggest that you renew your call one last time?"

"Sure," Renna, still shaking his head. He seemed now to truly grasp what kind of power had destroyed Africanus' trireme.

And what it meant when one opposed the *Saarbrücken.* Rheinberg hoped very much that Renna was not afraid. Caution yes – but fear was a bad counselor. He needed the man as an ally, not an enemy.

The navarch marched back to the foredeck. He picked up the megaphone, but before he could say a word, he was yelled at by one of the sailors.

"They finally surrender," Langenhagen announced excitedly.

In fact – the pirates turned in, dropped the sails. Weapons flew over the railing into the Mediterranean. These men had lost all courage, and Rheinberg could not blame them.

"Little speed," he said. "We circle the flotilla. I want us to keep an eye on each ship. Köhler!"

The NCO ran to the bridge. "Captain?"

"The steam launch. Ten-men landing company, under your command. Take Sepidus along. I want the hostage. If someone doesn't behave, you shoot without warning. No false indulgence. You understand?"

"The pinnace to water, allow ten men under arms. Take the hostage. No games."

"Wait until we are in position!"

"Waiting for message, yes."

Köhler stormed to the stern, where the men stood on the winches to allow the large pinnace to water. Rheinberg himself had previously selected the ten most experienced soldiers. When he saw the eagerness with which Sepidus now joined Köhler, a satisfied smile played around his lips. Sooner or later, when he had established a safe haven for his

Saarbrücken, he would have to take on board Romans as regular crew members.

He had no doubt that enough volunteers would be found.

It was not long before they knew on which of the hostage had been held. He was on the largest of the ships, together with the leader of the pirates, Claderius. Rheinberg gave the command to bring the pirate captain and soon deposited between the surrendered ships the pinnace bobbed toward the flagship of Claderius. The menacing 5-inch guns were sufficient to stop the crooks from any attempt to attack the pinnace as this would be associated with their immediate and complete demise. It took about 45 minutes, then Köhler was back, and he brought a maybe thirteen-year-old boy who entered the *Saarbrücken* with big eyes and was immediately led into Neumann's hospital ward. Africanus joined him. The burly, tanned giant of a man who came on board as a second didn't have to be introduced. The word "pirate captain" was figuratively written across his forehead.

Two men of the boarding company took him into their midst. His hands were already tied up on board the pinnace. The giant seemed to be scared and overwhelmed and looked up only when Renna placed himself in front of him.

"Claderius," he spoke to him triumphantly. "I've long waited for this moment. With this hostage you've gone too far."

Claderius ignored the admiral and looked at Rheinberg, who had joined them. "What is this vessel?" he exclaimed in Greek.

Rheinberg said nothing.

"It is a new ship of the Roman navy," Renna said instead. "It's the ship that brought you and your men down. You will be executed as soon as we have reached Ravenna. With any luck, we'll just sell your men into slavery."

Claderius spat on the floor. "No one executes me. You may have the upper hand now, Renna, but I have powerful friends."

Renna patted the railing with a hand. "Me too. What do you think, which are more powerful?"

Uncertainty crept into Claderius' face when Rheinberg ordered him led to the brig. Renna looked at him, suddenly very thoughtful.

"Of course he's not wrong, Trierarch," he said quietly to Rheinberg.

"Claderius has invested a lot of money in his connections to the mainland. I'll have to execute him quickly if I really want to get rid of him and his menace. But in any case, the gratitude for the liberation of the young one will be great. We should experience a lavish party in three days. You've introduced yourself well, Rheinberg!"

"Thank you, navarch. How do we want to deal with the prisoners?"

"We'll bind the ships together and tow them. Will that work?"

"We'll be slow."

"There is no more reason to hurry."

"Then I'll give the orders."

Renna was satisfied. As he walked away, Rheinberg immediately gave the necessary instructions. With luck, they would be back in Ravenna at sunset, and their return would be a triumphant one. A happy twist of fate had helped them. This mission had been easy for the men of the *Saarbrücken*, just the right action to present their skills to the test in front of an appropriate audience.

Now it was necessary to forge the iron while the fire was still hot.

16

It was a farm. It was a typical small farm, as there were hundreds of them in the area of Adrianople, and more or less they all looked the same: half-collapsed, with devastated granaries, looted store rooms, the living spaces in exactly the pitiful state the pillaging Goths had left them. It was these small farms the Roman army vainly tried to protect, and it was therefore quite close to the great ironies of history that Valens had, with his small band of scattered bodyguards, found refuge here.

He sat with trembling hands on a stool, which apparently had escaped the looters, and muttered to himself. He already sat there for a good hour, and centurion Alchimio looked at the state of his men with growing concern. Valens appeared broken, did his retreat as well as the army of the Eastern Empire, which had faced the massive attack of the Goths in the Battle of Adrianople. For hours the battle had swung from one side to the other, and the memories became blurred in Alchimio's mind. The Goths had been far more numerous than the scouts had reported. Valens' wrong decisions, especially the premature use of cavalry, waiting too impatiently under their forceful commander, who was eventually slaughtered, had contributed to this unprecedented defeat. The Roman phalanxes eventually collapsed under the onslaught of the enemies, and their arranged retreat was lost in chaos. The bodyguard and the emperor quickly had lost contact with the main army, were headless, and fled almost blindly, without paying attention to the direction. The centurion didn't know how many of those who had started fighting the battle have been left alive to leave, but it couldn't be more than a third. The East was defenseless before the Gothic hordes. With the field army in dissolution and morale broken, there was no one left outside the fortifications of cities and the border troops in their garrison forts that the Emperor could send against the barbarians.

If he would ever be able to do anything. Most recently, he was hardly capable to lead his own horse.

Pietus, as was decurion next to Alchimio, the only surviving man with command experience. He gave him a flask of water, and the centurion drunk thoughtfully. Tribune Marius Vitelius Tiberius had been slain on the run. Alchimio now carried the command of about 40 bodyguards who remained with the Emperor. A puny force. And since they didn't know exactly where they were and darkness fell quickly and everyone was aware of the fact that tens of thousands of Gothic warriors roamed about, the prospects were dim.

The meaningless murmur and the bloodshot eyes of the devastated emperor did not make things easier. Since he had lost all contact with Sebastianus – rumor had it that the general had been killed in battle – the Emperor was completely self-absorbed. This was interrupted only by an occasional mutter, and he also refused all food.

Alchimio took another sip. No need to follow the example of his master. "How are things, Pietus?"

The decurion scratched his beard. He was a veteran of 22 years' service, about to be honorably discharged. He had surely hoped to make his last years of service differently. "The property can be defended quite well. It is surrounded by a stone wall and from the roof of the main building we have a good all-round view and clear shots. I have placed guards everywhere and told the rest of the men to rest. We don't have food here, because the Goths have been here weeks ago, but there is a well, and the water is fine. If we can get through the night undisturbed, we can decide tomorrow if we continue our ride or remain – or whether the Goths make that decision for us."

Alchimio put a hand on his shoulder. "Well done. Find some rest; I'm keyed up too much to think of sleep. In addition, someone should have an eye on the Emperor."

Pietus threw a furtive, almost shy look at the crumpled figure on the stool, then made a telling gesture. "You think he's completely nuts?"

"Does it make a difference? We have sworn to defend him with our lives. And this we'll do." There was no sharpness in Alchimio's words. His sentences hadn't been more than just a normal statement of facts and the decurion nodded.

"I sleep. There in the corner, Centurion, if that is ..."

"Go on."

Pietus withdrew. Alchimio rose, took the cloak that Valens had carelessly laid aside and put it around the Emperor's shoulders. He wanted to turn away even as he heard the Emperor whispering his name.

"Sir?"

"What do you think, Centurion?"

"We are safe for the moment."

"That's not what I mean. What do you think about me?"

Alchimio hesitated imperceptibly. "You are my master, the Emperor. I have sworn to serve you and to protect you. That's all I need to know."

Valens laughed dryly. "Well done, Centurion. Very well behaved. Your Emperor and Lord has brought you destruction and death."

Alchimio decided not to comment on this. Valens also seemed to have expected no answer.

"Centurion, I was a fool. A great fool. An especially old fool, seeking to avoid any glory for his nephew and no victory for him. Ah, the great god in his wisdom thought otherwise, don't you think?"

Alchimio wasn't a Christian like Valens. Again, the centurion kept his silence.

"So I'm going to be punished, Centurion. Sorry, that you ended up with me in this. Sorry."

"There is nothing to apologize for," said Alchimio. "We will form a new army and pushback the Goths. Rome is eternal, my Emperor."

Valens made a weak gesture. "Yes, yes, Rome is eternal. The problem is that, unfortunately, I'm not. And neither are you."

For a moment, Alchimio waited if the Emperor wanted to add something, but he was lost in brooding silence. The centurion put some water, a hunk of bread and some fruit in front of his master –a meager meal, but the best he could offer.

He withdrew quietly.

The air was pleasantly cool on the roof of the farmhouse, which he had climbed by a ladder from the inside. The house was built fortified, with a kind of balustrade around the flat roof, from which one could hurl missiles at attacking enemies. This eventually happened, because there were some unused, roughly-made arrows lying around, and the balustrade itself showed signs of impacts. The Goths were remarkably unable to attack fortifications, were impatient and undisciplined in sieges, and absolutely none of them was able to design the complicated siege and attack machines available to the Roman army. The property here was simply too small, and though the lord of the courtyard also has used his servants and slaves as defenders, their resistance had obviously been useless. The building was ultimately a civilian, not a military one, and even Goths had not likely spent more than an hour or two to conquer it. And though that was already weeks ago, the trail of destruction and looting was clearly visible. The residents of this property had either been enslaved or killed, the flight hardly would have been successful. Alchimio made himself believe that a few of the brave had still managed to escape to Adrianople, to see safe shelter within the mighty walls. Even now, with the Eastern Roman field army in complete disarray, the city was safe. It had a garrison and probably more supplies than the Goths, and a wise leader like Fritigern knew that his warriors would be able to do something against mighty city walls and towers only with treason – which had succeeded one time or another – otherwise the city wouldn't be threatened for long. What remained under threat was the rural area, and the long-term food supply of the big cities. If the whole Eastern Empire consisted only of cities and the country was left to the Goths, then there was no Empire left worthy of the name. Alchimio hoped and prayed that Valens would succeed in restoring his powers. If he just could bring the Emperor to safety ...

Tomorrow morning, before sunrise, he would suggest leaving with his fairly rested and cared for horses. He knew in which direction Adrianople had to lie but didn't have any idea how many Goths they had to dodge. But he had to try it anyway.

Instinctively, he flinched when he heard a noise in the distance. At first he thought he had made a mistake, but then it became clearer and it could be by no means an illusion.

Horses. Many of them. The Roman cavalry was almost completely wiped out during the battle, so it could hardly be the miracle of a rescue. Refugees had, when very lucky, a donkey cart, but never horses, and certainly not this many.

It could only be the Goths.

Below the guards stirred, muted warning cries were heard. Curses penetrated to Alchimio's ear, when the men who had just found some sleep, rose and took up arms.

"Pietus!"

"Sir?"

"The archers on the roof. Barricade the doors."

"Yes, sir."

Alchimio climbed down the ladder and saw how Valens straightened. The Emperor's face was haggard and dejected. He was no one to give his troops inspiration and courage in this situation.

"The Goths." Just an observation, and the centurion could only nod.

"What shall I do, Centurion?"

Just don't stand around in the way, Alchimio thought to himself, but he had to be polite. "Stay in the middle of the room, sir. We will create a protective belt around you, should it be possible for the enemy to enter here."

"Maybe they want to negotiate?"

Alchmio had to admit that this was an option, although not very likely. Capturing the Emperor was an interesting prospect for the Goths, and especially when it came to negotiating the settlement area on Roman territory. On the other hand, since what happened to Valerian everyone knew what could be the fate of captured emperors, and the Persians were, in contrast to the Goths, at least somewhat civilized.

No, it wasn't an option. The Goths probably didn't know that Valens was staying here, and only expected a straggling troop of abandoned Roman soldiers.

The centurion rushed to the roof again. The sun hadn't yet entirely disappeared, and he could see the approaching fighters quite well. There were in fact enemies, and there were certainly 300, if not more. Alchimio's heart sank.

The Goths reined their horses just before the property, as if they had only now realized that it was inhabited. Without hesitation, the centurion grabbed a torch and climbed down. If there might be an opportunity for negotiations, then this would be now.

He stepped outside, unarmed and without escort, brandishing the torch above his head. With measured steps he walked across the yard, climbed the low stone wall and presented himself to the Goths. Then he left the compound, walking slowly toward the enemy. One of the horsemen rode ahead, and Alchimio could see that he was at least of low nobility. He had apparently caught the horse of a dead Roman cavalrymen; at least the bridle was of Roman making.

"Who are you and who's with you?" snapped the Goth, when he brought his horse to a halt before Alchimio.

"My name is Alchimio."

The Goth looked to the Roman breastplate.

"Centurion, yes?"

"Centurion."

"How many men do you have with you?"

"Enough."

The Goth laughed, then he shrugged and made an expansive motion to his waiting warriors.

"Enough for this?"

"We'll see. But we'd prefer not to try."

The facial expression of the Goths changed. He seemed to be interested. "No, perhaps not. You intend to make an offer, Roman?"

"What is your name?" Alchimio asked instead.

"Godegisel, son of Argaith."

The centurion had never heard the name before, but who wanted to keep track of the complicated structures of the low Gothic nobility anyway.

"Godegisel, I have the Emperor of the East here with me."

The Goth stayed calm, but the interested glint in his eyes betrayed him. "Valens himself is with you?"

"He is under my protection," Alchimio corrected him.

"Imperial bodyguard, yes?" The nobleman grimaced. To fight bodyguards, also with great superiority would inevitably cause many casualties. It seemed as if Godegisel had no great desire to test his strength and Alchimio drew new hope.

"If you grant us safe passage to Adrianople, you will not only be richly rewarded, the Emperor will consider this benevolent gesture in future negotiations with your people."

"Negotiations? I may be terribly wrong, Roman, but the way I see it, your great Emperor has just lost a battle, and we Goths flood your precious land like an unstoppable tide!"

Alchimio couldn't suffer barbarians who had discovered their lyrical vein. "You have bravely fought and won," he admitted aloud. "I'm the last person who would deny it."

"Good."

"But the cities are not taken, a large part of our army has escaped, the garrisons are filled, and Gratian, the Lord of the West, is on the way here with his troops. How long, o noble Godegisel, do you think the people of the Goths will have the power to oppose us?"

If the Gothic noble was impressed, he didn't show it. Instead, he made a derogatory gesture. "I'm not sure if I want to give your Emperor safe passage," he said thoughtfully.

"It would be to your advantage!"

"Yeah, maybe. I remember a scene when we had just reached the Danube and your Emperor promised us free settlement area. We crossed the river, with nothing in our hands than our swords, without belongings. The promised aid didn't arrive, no, and the Romans demanded of us to sell our own wives and children into slavery, and they gave us dog meat. Dog meat, centurion. Have you ever eaten dog meat? Meat, captured with great efficiency by your soldiers and supplied to us?"

"No, I haven't."

Godegisel nodded. "I thought so."

"I don't deny that major mistakes have been made," said Alchimio weakly. The centurion knew only too well how the officials at the border had squeezed out the refugees and humiliated them to the bone, rather than to faithfully execute the commands of the Emperor. Here was the root of all evil, and it didn't make things easier that the Goths had been victims twice: First they had fled from that distant enemy from the east, and then they had been cheated by the Romans.

"You know, centurion, when the Romans demanded two of my sister as a slaves, so that I would receive enough meat to feed my other siblings for another day, I slowly developed a good picture of Roman civilization."

"Not all Romans are like that."

"No, no, of course not. You're not, right?"

“I’ve never done this kind of things.”

“As an officer of the imperial bodyguard you surely never come into contact with this kind of profanity.”

“And you master the Greek language very well. I have the impression that you definitely had the benefit of education. Have you not understood since, that there are always alternatives and the chance to change direction?”

Godegisel nodded sadly. “Yes, I did, as I was full of hope, when Fritigern and Alaric put the fate of our people in your hands. So full of hope. And I didn’t like the way your people dealt with us, centurion, I really didn’t like it.”

“Give the Emperor safe passage and past injustice should be remedied,” Alchimio offered.

“My sisters were 13 and 14, centurion. How many Roman pricks were inserted in them against their will by now? A dozen? Two dozen? Hundreds?”

Alchimio didn’t know how to answer this question, so he remained silent. For a while, the two men looked at each other in silence.

Then the Goth sighed. “Oh, you know, Roman, today I’m tired of fighting. My men are also exhausted.”

“Then let’s stop the fight.”

Godegisel shook his head regretfully. Then he measured the Romans with a long view and added, “It’s not that simple, centurion, not as simple as that.”

Alchimio didn’t really see the sword that killed him. Godegisel targeted well and threw the blade from his horse in one fluid motion, like a throwing dagger. The centurion slumped, and as he fell, he saw that at the behest of the nobleman a first swarm of flaming arrows came down on the farm.

Then his gaze broke.

17

"Captain, we've got a problem."

Rheinberg looked up and into Becker's face. The fact that he saw him smiling allowed him relax immediately. Life was stressful enough. The spacious atrium of Senator Urianus provided room for around 120 guests who navarch Renna had invited to this celebration. 120 men and women who had been officially invited. After Rheinberg's good estimate as many as twice actually appeared. He had long forgotten all the names that had been presented to him, and during the last three hours he had been passed around like a piece of loot from an exotic country. Just a few faces he could remember: Symmachus, who had invited him to a four-to-one conversation later, "if the time allows," as his words had been – and then the liking of Senator Marcus Flavius, whose nephew he had saved from the pirates, and who was obviously very grateful to him. As Rheinberg had heard that the boy was the only son of the senator's brother, the gratitude of the old man seemed less silly than at the beginning.

"What's the problem, Jonas?"

"The food here is inedible. I've spoken with Volkert and Neumann, and ... ah, here he comes."

The doctor plowed his way slowly, politely, but firmly through the surging crowd of guests who ate and drank either lying or standing with plates and glasses in hand.

"Johann, what about the food?"

Neumann snorted.

"This stuff is spoiled! I have tempted the roasted pork – it is okay, but stayed definitely too long in the sun!"

Rheinberg himself had not yet found time to taste the offered food and listened to Neumann's account with raised eyebrows.

"Spoiled? Seriously? I can't imagine!"

"And this paste, which is passed with everything – unbearable. Stinks of rotten fish like the plague, comes well with the rotten meat. So this is how the Romans fed? I'm surprised that they haven't died in rows of poisoning!"

Rheinberg grimaced. "I read something about the sauce once. They called it *garum*."

"Disgusting stuff. What is it made of?"

"I don't know exactly. But fish is in there, too ... ah, Africanus!"

Rheinberg held the passing trierarch's arm. The naval officer was willing to move into their circle.

"Please tell us how this fish sauce is made which is served so lavishly with the food," Rheinberg said.

"Oh, yes – I forgot that the cooking has to be foreign to you," replied Africanus. "Well, it's quite simple: Garum consists of mackerel and anchovies together with their giblets, salt water and many spices. This is all well mixed and then placed in the sun."

"Placed in the sun?"

"In order to rot away."

"To rot?" Rheinberg asked.

"But yes. Once the sauce is rotten, it has become really thick and has deployed its full flavor. Then it can be served. I remember that my mother always quoted the great Geopon. He has written exactly how garum was supposed to be produced." Africanus set up a pose, pretending he would recite a poem. "You put salt in a vessel, add the guts of fish, and add to all sorts of small fish stuff like sardines, mullet, picarel and sea butterflies, add more salt and put the whole thing under the sun. Once it is well rotten, we pour everything through a sieve. The mass that remains in the sieve is alec; the liquid that passes through is the liquamen. Or garum."

Rheinberg, Becker and Neumann exchanged glances. "And ... and the meat, I mean, the roast ..."

"Something wrong with that?"

Neumann tried a wry smile to somewhat cover up the embarrassment of the question.

"Well, I thought, maybe it's just me, but it tasted as if the pig had also been in the sun a little bit longer than usual!"

Africanus nodded vigorously. "But yes. A good roast, just on the edge of being rotten, only just fresh and edible, but already with the aroma of decay, is a great delicacy. If you got that taste, then the cook has done his job well." The trierarch looked around and noticed the pained expression on the faces. "I suppose, that this kind of preparation doesn't meet the habits of your palate."

"You can say that," confirmed Neumann.

"Well ..." Africanus looked around. "How is the wine?"

At least here the men could say nothing but good things. They had very quickly found out that everyone was drinking wine – always. Pure water wasn't one of the usual drinks. Although the wine was usually mixed with water – to reduce the alcoholizing effect significantly – it was, even though sometimes barely tolerable and sour, without doubt the national drink. All guests had been righteously impressed, had listened expectantly to Urianus who promised in his opening talk that he would present the best wine from Greece as well as some selected Italian vineyards, and in fact, the offered product was obviously of high quality. Neumann, the only truly passionate wine drinker in the delegation of the *Saarbrücken*, seemed very satisfied.

"I wish we had something like beer," muttered Becker, who in contrast to Neumann regarded wine more as juice.

Africanus looked at him quizzically, as Becker had spoken in German.

"Cervisia," Rheinberg helped out. "My friend here prefers it to wine."

Africanus' face lit up, and then was once again full of doubt. "Beer is the drink of poor people and barbarians. But because my ancestors come from Africa, I know exactly what you like about it. And the Germans, with whom you are so obviously related, appreciate it very much. You will hardly find it on a feast of the finer circles, because it isn't a common drink here, but if you really want some, I can get it. Or let's go to a tavern, there should be no problem."

Rheinberg waved it away.

"That's a nice offer, but we don't want to act like barbarians. Becker will be able to endure it all."

The infantry officer nodded, although he didn't look very happy. Neumann, however, gathered a refill from one of the servants running around with a decanter. The medical officer had red cheeks and showed more than a little satisfaction that the circumstances might turn every one of them into wine aficionados. Rheinberg gave him a warning look.

They went back into the crowd. Rheinberg noted that few women were present. He vaguely remembered the family structure in ancient Rome and still knew that the position of the men was even more dominant than in the German Empire of his time. Probably it was owed to a certain liberality of the upper classes that maybe 15 or 20 women were invited to this festivity, many of them obviously the wives of important personalities and a few younger ones who were probably daughters of the house or prominent guests. They all kept mostly to themselves and also only spoke among themselves, not the men around them.

Nevertheless, Rheinberg found himself quickly back in the center of attention and curious glances were aimed at him, regardless of gender. He had been spending hours being passed from caller to caller, and his rather underdeveloped diplomatic skills had been subjected to a test beyond their limits. Nevertheless, he believed to have left a positive impression throughout, he behaved quietly and had been kind, had striven to respect highly placed dignitaries and dutifully laughed at the jokes he actually understood. If he had a problem, then certainly with the language, although he got used to the sound of ancient Greek and Latin more and more and much long-lost knowledge had been revived in his memory. He spoke with increasing fluency, although he could see in the faces of his listeners that he made many mistakes. But he didn't understand everything, and wherever the language was still distorted by a dialect or accent, he had to rely on the translation services of Africanus, who had accompanied him faithfully. The other Germans had similar problems, although everyone tried his best. But at the same time the Romans were willing to overlook this seemingly barbaric deficits, and the openly expressed desire by Rheinberg to hire capable teachers from Ravenna was acknowledged with pleasure. Some proposals were submitted and Rheinberg had to look at them carefully.

All in all, he felt comfortable. Many of the fears and worries he had busied himself with were gone. There were many and great challenges he was very much aware of. But the odds were now much improved.

He looked up as the young Volkert came up to him. The ensign looked a little embarrassed and perplexed. "What is it, Volkert?"

“Well ... Captain ... I don’t know whom I can ask about it.”

“What is the question?”

“I really have to pee, and I have no idea where the toilet is.”

Rheinberg grinned. “Ask one of the slaves over there. He has just showed me the way. But don’t be surprised ...”

The ensign’s eyes followed the outstretched finger of the captain, and he nodded eagerly as he turned away gratefully. Rheinberg looked at the young man. He would soon discover that defecation and socializing in Rome were not opposites.

18

The way to the toilet wasn't far, and although Volkert had understood only half of the directions given to him, he could ultimately identify the locality because he wasn't the only one walking there.

When he entered the room, three surprises waited for him. Firstly, in Roman villas there was apparently no privacy on the toilet: In a square room with marble benches a total of probably twenty holes were visible, and above them were already sitting a dozen guests. They talked animatedly. Two men in a ripe old age were bent over a document paper and appeared to discuss a business transaction of some kind. Secondly, Volkert realized that there was no separation between the sexes, at least not here. Directly in front of him were two massive matrons who groaned heavily on the toilet holes and with a strained expression in their faces, fully occupied with their excretions. Volkert decided not to get irritated, and anyway, there was no alternative, as he was already quite desperate.

The third surprise he found when he looked into the toilet before sitting. He saw a steady stream of water splashing within. Permanent water rinse. Damn, he had to revise many a prejudice about the ancient folks and their devices. The Romans had water rinse. Just as there had been warm running water in the hall before the bathroom. This was necessary because there was no toilet paper – one obviously used the left hand to clean and then washed it thoroughly afterwards. Volkert braced himself. This was a part of the Roman hygiene habits with which he would have problems. Luckily he was here only to conduct a small business, so that this problem wasn't so immediate. Yet.

He pulled down his pants. The matrons decided not to look at him, remained very focused and turned inward. A lot of effort there. He sat down. The marble bench was warm, and the smoothly polished stone dispensed a comfortable feeling. As a rich senator, by Volkert's assessment, you could make a very comfortable and pleasant life in later antiquity. Would he ever come to such wealth, he would've liked to make some changes in his villa. A loo only for himself would be included, among other things.

Volkert relaxed. Just as it began to splash, he saw the door open and someone entered.

Every relaxation disappeared from him as he looked up.

In came ...

No.

In floated a young woman, certainly not even eighteen. She wore a tunic that covered her whole body, however, as it was well tied to her slender waist, her full breasts clearly loomed below the fine fabric. Her heart-shaped face was dominated by two large, dark eyes. Under a small nose, gently curved and delicate lips parted in a smile.

A wonderful smile. Volkert couldn't even look elsewhere. He forgot a little why he was here, where he actually was, and could do nothing more than to look at this face. His heart pounded. That wasn't good. That wasn't good at all. What happened had never happened to him before.

Completely against his will, his eyes wandered from the young woman's face, as she pulled up her tunic casually, and revealed two slender, light brown legs with perfect calves, which were adorned with fine jewelry.

God, he wanted to look away, yes! Really! But it just wasn't possible!

She turned around and sat next Volkert. As she slid back and forth to be able to sit pleasantly, the soft warmth of her hips touched his for a moment. A powerful surge seemed to blow through the young man, and now he felt exactly the opposite of relaxation.

Volkert decided not to stand up until further notice.

He stared with emphasis on the floor decorated with mosaics, in order to pretend that he wasn't completely baffled by her presence.

"I'm Julia, daughter of Michellus!" a soft voice said beside him. She spoke to him directly. No doubt about it. And no one seemed to mind that.

"I ..." stammered the young man, searching for the right words, more difficult because he had to track down the Latin vocabulary.

"You are one of the strangers."

Volkert understood Latin better than he spoke it. And he spoke Greek better than Latin. So he tried it.

"I'm Thomas Volkert, from the *Saravica*."

"Glad to meet you, Thomas," Julia replied in Greek and smiling. Volkert was lost, yes, literally drowning in that smile. "A boring party," she said and scratched her chin with a totally un-ladylike attitude. "I hate it when my father drags me to these things."

"Yes," Volkert brought forth barely, trying not to look too stupid. He found the festivity rather interesting and instructive, but who was he to contradict a goddess?

"Are you finished, Thomas of the *Saravica*?"

"Finished?"

Julia grinned and nudged him. Then she pointed to the toilet bowl, on which he sat. Volkert looked down at himself and everything he saw were his cheesy white, hairy legs under the shirred tunic. Why did he have to meet this woman in this deplorable state? And she actually expected him to just get up now? He probably wouldn't be able to, because his butt was currently locked down in quite narrow opening due to an uncontrollable bodily reaction between his legs.

Julia, daughter of Michellus, didn't seem to share those concerns. She got up with ease, allowed Volkert – intentionally? unintentionally? – another look at her thighs, which not insignificantly increased his mobility problem, and dropped the tunic.

"I know a nice place," she said softly. Her voice was murmuring and virtually undiscernible in the surrounding noise. "I'll wait for you outside the portico. There's an ancient statue of Jupiter with a small fountain."

Volkert knew the place she mentioned and managed to offer an affirmative gesture. Julia gave him again that magical smile, turned and disappeared lightly into the hallway.

It took ten minutes for Volkert to dare rise.

He washed his hands thoroughly in order to regain control over his excitement and realized that a fine film of sweat stood on his forehead. For a moment, he wondered if he should inform Rheinberg of his date, but he suspected that he was busy with something more important.

And somehow, in this moment there was nothing more important in Thomas Volkert's mind than Julia, daughter of Michellus.

He didn't even think about the fact that this condition may have very little to do with any "mind" at all ...

19

As a servant begged him into the study of Urianus, Rheinberg knew that he had to take the next step to increase his chances of being accepted in this time. He was already a little tired, but the stamina of the Roman upper class at such festivals seemed to be endless. Half-hearted, he regretted having to miss the current show presenting some dancers and jugglers, who accompanied by flute music had begun to entertain the guests. But now there were more important things to do.

Though spacious, the office he entered was spartan. It was dominated by a giant marble table, which was crowded with parchments. No one even took one look at the documents, as an unwritten law was applied, a kind of code of honor.

Near the table close to a fireplace, four chairs were set up. It was getting dark and a little bit chilly, and a slave had kindled a fire. On a side table were several carafes of wine and a tray of cups. A second table was cluttered with all sorts of sweets. Rheinberg saw mountains of candied fruits, for which Urianus apparently had a special passion, because they had been omnipresent on the buffet – and tasted, as he could confirm, quite excellent.

Three men were waiting for him. One he knew: it was Navarch Renna, a cup in his hand, which he raised in greeting. To the second Rheinberg was briefly introduced – Symmachus, Roman senator, and a well-known figure in history. He was especially famous through the centuries because of his comprehensive collection of letters, above all the correspondence with which the pagan senator had tried to convince both Gratian as well as his successor Theodosius to show tolerance in relationship to the ancient cults. The biggest opponent of Symmachus had not been the emperor, but the bishop of Milan, Ambrosius, who had been canonized by the church afterwards. In this time, however, he was anything but a saint, but a shrewd church leader and fanatical catholic, for whom the unity of the Church and the dominance of what would later be the Papal hierarchy was more important than anything. St. Ambrosius would later be honored for something that was, in Rheinberg's conviction, a number of deadly shocks that had weakened the already quite sick Western Roman Empire. As such, it was ironic that probably Symmachus would most likely be his ally in the endeavor to secure Western Rome and the empire as a workbench to maintain the *Saarbrücken.*

A Christian civil war had to be avoided as well as the numerous tax privileges that Theodosius had given to the clergy. Rome needed the money. And Rome needed inner peace.

Rheinberg had desperate plans for both issues, and there was no alternative for him. The alternative of the history he knew ended about 100 years from here in the complete collapse of Western Rome.

The third man, prone to obesity and in expensive clothes, he didn't know. He had been introduced to him, but the names and faces were too quickly rushed past him that he could remember all of them.

"Rheinberg, good that you found some time," Renna greeted him. "Symmachus here you've already welcomed. I'm not sure if you have been presented to senator Michellus."

"I remember," Rheinberg lied and bowed slightly.

"There's a reason why I have consulted these two gentlemen," Renna said now and meant for everyone to sit down. "Symmachus and Michellus both represent the same fraction in the Senate, but at the same time they also differ with respect to one important issue: Symmachus is a friend of traditional Roman religion, Michellus is Christian."

"Catholic," added the man and smiled. "And all of this is a lousy political move of the estimated navarch. I'm shocked."

To give his horror emphasis, Michellus scooped a handful of candied fruit in his mouth and chewed it with a crashing sound.

"Of course, the esteemed senator is correct," said Renna. "This conversation has a political note, because the emergence of the *Saravica* under your command has a political dimension. We have won some respite by the fortunate incident with the pirates, but already now exorcists and fanatics gain ground all too quickly. In fact, you have proven your usefulness as well as your potential threat."

"Thank you."

"But that leaves many questions unanswered," Symmachus said. He touched neither wine nor sweets. "Where do you come from, and what miracle has brought you here?"

Rheinberg nodded. It was clear that he had to tell the truth, if he wanted to achieve anything. "The first question I can answer easily, Senator. The second ... the second is a mystery to me."

With a gesture, Symmachus told him to continue.

Rheinberg was looking for words. "I come from the area you call Germania. The port of origin of my ship is where the Frisians are hailing from."

"Frisians have built this ship?" Michellus doubtfully said after chewing again.

"No. The fact that the said land is the home of my ship is only half the truth. The other part of the truth is that I come from the year 1914, about 1500 years in the future." His words were important now. Before anyone tried to interrupt him, he continued quickly. "I'm not a demon, not a devil worshiper, and I conjure no magic. The *Saravica* is technology, craftsmanship, built and developed by well-trained ... guilds. But from the future. Just as Rome is superior to the barbarians, my country in my time is superior to Rome – maybe not in civilization and art, but certainly in the progress of science."

The senators looked at Rheinberg in silence. Michellus interrupted his chewing for a moment.

"How did this happen?" Symmachus said finally.

Rheinberg told him the whole story. He reported on the impending war between his empire and other powers and of his mission to distant provinces – all concepts that the Romans could understand very well. He reported on the strange phenomena that they had met on the trip and about what had happened since then. He left nothing out.

After he finished his description, again silence returned. Rheinberg throat was dry, he used the time to take a sip of watered wine.

"If that's true – and I cannot otherwise explain a ship like yours – then you know the future." The simple observation of Michellus showed that behind his jovial and quite naïve demeanor he hid brains and had listened well.

"Well ... one might assume so," replied Rheinberg. "The fact is that my past might already have been changed by my presence – it is your and now also my future. In my time, the appearance of my ship at Ravenna 1500 years ago isn't known. However, I believe that I know a few things to come ... and it could be beneficial."

"Does the empire still exist in your time?" Symmachus wanted to know.

"No. The western Empire will dissolve in about 100 years and in the year 476 the last Emperor will be a man named Romulus Augustulus."

Shocked silence was the response.

"You say ... Rome will perish," Renna said in a husky voice.

"The East is more fortunate," continued Rheinberg in a low voice. "The East of the Empire will even experience a revival, with successful military expansion and ascension to great power. It is later called the Byzantine Empire. The capital will be Constantinople, renamed Byzantium, and it will vanish with the conquest of the city in 1453."

"1453?"

The tone of Michellus had contained something like relief.

"Yes," confirmed Rheinberg. He waited for the inevitable question.

"Why had Western Rome to fall?" asked Renna.

"There are many reasons. A key reason is what you are currently witnessing. The attack by the Goths in the East."

"The Goths destroy Western Rome? But Valens fights against them! He will be victorious for sure!" Michellus claimed.

"The Goths are not the problem. It is the whole process ..." Rheinberg searched for the right words. "We call it ... the great migration, the *Völkerwanderung.* It is caused by a people who you already know as Huns. They push all the others in the East from their ancestral territories, and so a constant pressure on the Roman frontiers is building up. That would perhaps be endurable if the empire would still be strong and prosperous as under Traianus, but ..." Rheinberg broke off when he saw the knowing smile on the features of Symmachus. "Anyway," he took up the thread again, "this is Western Rome's undoing. Valens is about to die. That is, he is already dead, and his army has been defeated at Adrianople."

Again, silence filled the room.

“The Goths overran the East?” Renna said. “But I thought you had said ...”

“Theodosius the Great will prevent the worst.”

Symmachus frowned. “Theodosius? The general’s son?”

“That’s the one.”

“The Emperor of the East?”

“He’ll become emperor of the entire empire after Gratian’s untimely death.”

Now the horror was almost tangible.

“Gratian ...” stuttered Renna, who was now clearly struggling for composure.

“Gratian dies in a few years, after the appointment of Theodosius as emperor of the East, killed by traitors who intend to make one provincial general the new emperor.”

“Ah,” Michellus sighed. “Will this curse never end? Gratian had just restored the tortured relationship between throne and the Senate and settled the strife his father had started – and now this.”

Rheinberg didn’t comment. He sat back and let his words sink in. He would add nothing to his credibility by divulging more details at this time – especially not when he had the firm intention to prevent many of these developments.

It was Renna, who broke the silence.

“If all this is true and if the events have already been changed by your appearance, as you guessed – then does it mean that the downfall of the West is not inevitable, just as the death of Gratian isn’t?”

“I assume so.”

“We should approach the Emperor with your knowledge in order to encourage him to take certain actions that may change the course of history so that things would go in a ... satisfactory direction.”

“Sounds smart.”

“That’s not so easy,” said Michellus, who had obviously calmed enough so that he was again able to honor the sweets with some of his attention. “If it is true that Valens is dead, then Gratian must now organize the war in the East.”

“He can only do that by naming a new emperor in the East. He will feel overwhelmed to govern the whole empire,” Symmachus opined.

"This is consistent with what I know," confirmed Rheinberg. "But here's the point: That must be prevented. I have come to the conclusion that Emperor Gratian must remain Emperor of the entire Empire, and much longer than a few months."

"Explain!" demanded Renna. "I know the young Theodosius. If he is at least a bit like his father, he is likely to be passable emperor."

Rheinberg collected his thoughts before he continued. He knew that he would have only one chance to find the allies he needed so badly.

"Theodosius is in fact not without talent," he finally admitted. "As far as I recall the history, he will be quite successful in rebuilding the armed forces of the East. He will make a treaty with the Goths and add them as foederatii to the Empire, which establishes a precedent – the Goths will be allowed to keep their own government and are no longer subjects but allies of Rome. This is bearable. Theodosius will also ultimately defeat the usurper who kills Gratian – of whom we'll have to take care in any case! – and ultimately preserves the unity of the empire as a whole, being the last emperor of all of it."

"That sounds pretty good," said Renna.

"Theodosius is called 'the Great' in our time. And that has nothing to do with his undoubtedly impressive diplomatic and military successes, but the fact that he is going to adopt extremely rigid religious laws that not only prohibit the pagan cults and expose their followers to persecution, but also put pressure on Christians deviating from the Catholic mainstream, especially on the Arians. He will extend the privileges of the Church, foremost the tax exemption and exemption of priests from all military or civilian duties. Theodosius will lay the foundation for an ongoing internal instability of the empire as well as the final financial collapse of the West. Sure, he will restore the unity of the Church, at least for a certain time."

Rheinberg had no intention to report the Romans about Martin Luther yet – or the fact that he himself was a Protestant and as such would certainly incur the wrath of any true Trinitarian of this time.

"Theodosius is certainly no fool, although he has been known for his sudden outbursts of anger. But Gratian, at least this is what I know, was quite willing to exercise a greater tolerance toward other religions and factions within Christianity – at least currently. Bishop Ambrosius will soon take him completely under his wings. But even then, Gratian was always more cautious in church affairs than Theodosius. I don't really care why, but is has always been quite obvious to me that Constantine's idea to promote the introduction of Christianity as the state religion in order to foster unity has proven to be a fallacy. We cannot and we do not want to undo anything – but the costly and time-consuming persecution, disturbing the life of the people and working of the state, must end. There are bigger problems, and those can only be confronted by a united and focused Empire."

Rheinberg paused, his mouth dry again. The speech was longer than he had planned. Many ideas he had developed for the first time as he spoke. Everything seemed a bit half-baked and ill-conceived, but many of the considerations that he had made when he had been thinking about the fall of Rome already in school had come back to light.

It didn't seem to be complete bullshit. That good Symmachus sympathized with Rheinberg's words wasn't surprising. The senator looked pleased.

All eyes turned to the chewing Michellus. Rheinberg long suspected that his behavior was a mask to hide his thoughts and reflections. The senator could be a shrewd politician, if he wanted. And now he did.

"Well," the chubby Roman finally muttered as he had swallowed the last bite, "what you claim here isn't totally absurd, Rheinberg. Not that I've been doing a lot of thinking about such issues – certainly not as much as my friend Symmachus here, who surely considered all this also from a slightly different point of view. Still, your words sound convincing. But whatever we're saying here, we have to win the Emperor's ear first, and currently he has a problem."

"He has two problems, at least," added Rheinberg. "Are you familiar with the name of Magnus Maximus?"

"Sure," said Renna, "the military prefect of Britain, an able general. Are you ... he is the one who will grab the purple and fight against Gratian?"

"Even worse, he will not only trigger a civil war that kills Gratian, he will not be outdone in religious fanaticism by the Emperor Theodosius until his defeat, if only to gain its recognition. No matter what they say about Theodosius, he has never recognized Maximus and always demonstrated a certain formal loyalty to the house of Valentinian, probably mainly because he had received his crown from the hands of Gratian and has cooperated well with him. It is Maximus who ultimately failed. But this was a civil war, which has weakened the empire more than the attack of the Goths, which has now led to the death of Valens."

"We still don't know if you are correct," Michellus said. Rheinberg bowed his head. There was nothing to add to that.

"Anyway," Renna now took up the thread. "Gratian will be only be convinced if Rheinberg achieves something like what he has done for us with his victory over Claderius. He will simply have to provide another proof of his usefulness."

"That is correct," agreed the captain. He knew what was coming. Becker would be thrilled.

"You have a big ship, but that will not help in the fight against the Goths."

"It will. It can move troops quickly."

"Too few troops."

"Not legionaries. My soldiers. If Gratian agrees, I'll bring them to the East in a few days, to wherever it should be necessary. Or I let them march together with Roman troops across the country, if it is conducive to our mutual trust. Someone can reorganize the rest of the Eastern Roman army against the Goths, while Gratian pushes forward slowly from the west. Or ..."

"Or?"

"Or we solve the problem without the army of the West."

Renna looked critically at Rheinberg.

"How many men and weapons do you command?"

"The number isn't important," Rheinberg replied. "The weapons' quality is."

"And they are superior to anything we know," Renna confirmed. "I'm considering just what these weapons can do against a formation of Goths. The result would be devastating."

"The Goths will learn and adapt – but the first battle will come as a complete surprise and is therefore decisive," added Rheinberg. He didn't go into detail what Becker's company could accomplish with the four MG 08, firing into a horde of storming barbarians from a safe position. It would be a massacre, and one that would never be forgotten by the surviving attackers. Of course, an army of 20,000 warriors against maybe 200 German soldiers would result in a corresponding determination to defeat the soldiers, although massive losses among the attackers would be the price to pay. But it should never come so far. The morale of the attacker, shot to pieces by a seemingly invisible meat grinder, would collapse very quickly – and then it was time for diplomacy.

It just had to all fit together at the right time at the right place. To achieve this, he needed the help of the Romans, and he also had to be there in order to transform the spirit of the victory into influence and support at court. Rheinberg noted with dismay that his idea required a parallel tactic at two very distant places, a plan that was rarely successful.

"Communication," he murmured absently. "I need the ability to communicate."

"You say?"

"Nothing, just a thought."

Rheinberg looked around.

"That was all a bit much, I fear. We should think about all this and meet again, maybe tomorrow. But time is short. Once the message of Valens' demise has arrived, Gratian will start looking for a successor. If we want to persuade him to proclaim himself as overall ruler of the empire at least for now, we must act quickly and decisively."

"That is true; however, I really have to make my mind up in peace," Michellus replied and looked into the fire.

"There is much to consider," Rheinberg said. "Gratian will first appoint Theodosius as general, but already by January of next year he will be raised to the status of Augustus. I have no problem with General Theodosius, if it really has to be, but once he wears the purple, it gets difficult."

Symmachus nodded to Michellus. "My friend here is right, we need to think. These are important decisions that you cannot make on a balmy summer evening. We meet again tomorrow ... On your ship, if I may suggest."

"You're welcome."

"Then we can discuss, if ..."

The door flew open. Visible was a stout, tall and in all very impressive-looking older woman. She pushed a servant aside, who wanted to fend them, and that with playful ease. In her face everyone could see that she was angry.

Senator Michellus wasn't too amused. "Lucia, my dear," he greeted the matron weakly as she rushed into the room and gave both Symmachus as well as Renna a welcoming nod, ignored Rheinberg and placed herself terrifyingly in front of Michellus, which slumped visibly on his stool.

"Michellus!"

"My little dove, I'm busy ..."

Rheinberg recognized Lucia now. Maybe she was someone who had to be included in important decisions. Her voice was of cutting energy, and her tone reminded him of Köhler when he shooed recruits around.

"Michellus! Julia is gone!"

The senator winced, his eyes widened and he seemed now fulfilled with righteous anger. "What?"

"Disappeared! That happens once you allow her out of sight! I told you: We leave her at home! But no, you have to be so endeared by her! And now look what you've done!"

Michellus became even smaller. Very small. He threw begging glances to the other men. Renna looked into the fire. Rheinberg looked at the lady Lucia.

Symmachus lifted the wine decanter. "I'll pour you one, my friend!"

20

"It's beautiful here."

"This is wrong."

"What?"

"You used the wrong form. You said: You are beautiful here."

Thomas Volkert felt his cheeks grow hot, and it wasn't because of the wine. He was grateful that the darkness had arrived and here, on a wooded hill on the outskirts of Ravenna, nothing but the twinkling stars lit up the scene.

"Well, I'm still learning."

"How to make women compliments?"

"How to pronounce Greek without making bad mistakes."

Julia's small hand patted Thomas' shoulder, causing the burning in his face to increase. He tried to distract himself by looking downhill at the city, which had some street lighting, even though it consisted mostly of the torches and lamps in front of the public buildings and taverns. From here one could see the villa of Urianus quite well, because it was right on the edge of town, and the ongoing reception was brightly illuminated by all kinds of lamps.

"Good idea to leave," Volkert said. "It was very stressful. One of the guests even asked me if our ship could not escort his grain cargo from Africa. He would pay us well for it."

"Well, you all will need to do something to earn your living."

"I think my captain has something else in mind but boring escort from Africa."

Julia said nothing, and so they both just sat there and looked at the panorama of the city at night.

When Volkert had met the senator's daughter at the party he had immediately been struck by the impression that she radiated a degree of self-confidence that was almost an insult to many of the other guests. In fact, even in the higher society of his own time, this not too decorous behavior of a "schoolgirl" would have been extremely unbecoming. Especially the older men – and of which there had been too many in the villa – had sent her quite disapproving looks. Julia had finally met with Volkert at the statue of Jupiter, where he had waited shyly as agreed and since then she hadn't questioned him about the *Saarbrücken*, politics and the strange weapons, but only about himself. Quite a surprise.

A welcome change, and not only because of her toga, which, while covering the whole body, was for some reason not at all that demure so that he could at least imagine that Julia possessed stimuli that exceeded her obvious self-confidence. Exceeded them significantly.

When Julia had finally proposed to leave the festivities and to disappear with a few supplies from the buffet to the nearby hill, he agreed immediately. Whether due to a mistake or because it did simply not come to his mind, the captain certainly hadn't forbidden anyone to leave the house. The senator's daughter had unerringly selected food from the buffet that best corresponded to the palate of the German, which in turn spoke of her observational skills, for this particular problem he hadn't discussed with her.

"How are the women in your time?" asked Julia and shoved a piece of bread into her mouth. Volkert cleared his throat, wondering how he could answer the question.

"It's not very different," he said lamely. "But it depends on where you live. If you're invited to a noble family, the women are usually just as ... cautious as here. And also in my time, the man is without a doubt the master of the house." He frowned. "But lately there's been some change, because more and more women demand rights ... I think there are even some in the parliament."

"Parliament?"

"Ah ... something like the Senate. But all members are elected by the people. They decide mainly about the money that the state may spend."

Julia processed this information. "Sort of like in ancient Athens?"

Volkert was thankful at that moment that he had enjoyed a reasonably good education and was able to remember a lot of it. "Well, not quite like that, but something like it. I believe in ancient Athens women had nothing to say."

"They don't speak in the Senate as well. I think my mother talks about some issues with my father, and sometimes his opinion expressed in the Senate is what she has ... advised. But that is probably not comparable."

"In my time, there are many who do this ... the women who demand more rights ... many men find this strange and inappropriate."

Julia looked at him from the side, a pensive expression on her face. "And you? Do you consider that as inappropriate as well?"

Thomas Volkert controlled himself. It was bad enough that he had apparently traveled with his ship 1500 years into the past, now he also had to take on a most winsome young lady who seemed to be the Roman equivalent of Clara Zetkin. Or close to it.

On the other hand, he knew that he had to be very careful how he answered that question. No, he had an issue with these new, self-confident women, as many of them also were inclined toward socialism. He preferred the good old tradition that the man in the family was the boss, and of what he had noticed of the familiar conditions in the Roman Empire, he liked quite much.

However, Julia he liked even more.

Very much more.

Perhaps too much.

He cleared his throat. "Well, I'd say that times change and we learn from history that nothing remains as it once has been."

This cumbersome and ultimately evasive answer seemed to satisfy Julia, or she had simply decided, for the sake of her own peace of mind, not to press the issue. "What will you do now?" was the next question.

"I ... I will perform my duty."

"And what else? Even in your time, your life must have consisted of but more than duty."

Volkert impulsively wanted to answer, as this assumption wasn't quite true. He remembered suddenly that there was no longer an emperor who had to give an officer the permission to marry. How would this problem probably be solved now?

And why the hell came this to his mind?

"I will certainly not lead a relaxed life of a senator's daughter," he replied.

Julia snorted. "A relaxed life, indeed. With parents who want to permanently marry me to a snob who wants to have a well-behaved, obedient girl and as many male offspring as possible. If I'm unlucky, I wouldn't see my toes for years after marriage."

"Your mother didn't seem to be so terribly obedient," Volkert said.

"But she is terribly conservative. In these things she is in full agreement with my father. I had the opportunity to get rid of spouses so far only because my father likes me."

Volkert didn't comment. Based on her descriptions he guessed that the idolatrous father loved his daughter and despite all her lamentations wouldn't be able to refuse her anything.

Well, perhaps within certain limits. And possibly Julia began increasingly to test these limits.

"Something is going on there," muttered Volkert and leaned forward. Torches were moving through the night and all around Urianus' villa.

"They're looking for us," Julia stated calmly. "Of course I shouldn't have left."

"What?"

"No, it was not only improper but also dangerous. A senator's daughter is a beautiful booty."

"What?"

"My mother will be furious."

Thomas Volkert was dumbfounded – speechless at Julia's callousness and his own carelessness. If their trip caused so much commotion, and it came out that he was part of this conspiracy, it would fall back to Rheinberg. To the *Saarbrücken.* To the unstable, provisional agreement that protected the ship in this city.

Volkert looked at Julia from the side. She seemed completely unaffected by the commotion. A spoiled brat who got everything she wanted and didn't care for others, Volkert suddenly thought. He stood. "We have to go back before they mobilize the whole city!"

Julia stretched. Volkert tried not to stare at her breasts. Beautiful, perfectly shaped breasts, big like ripe fruit, such as ...

He shook his head. This led to nothing.

Julia slipped her hand into his and pulled him back to the villa.

Ensign Thomas Volkert stumbled behind her. He refrained from any comment and only thought about what he would be able to present for his defense. As they neared the villa and some of the searching servants and slaves saw them from afar and shouted the news to the property, he still didn't have any idea.

When he, in tow of a young woman, stepped with a red face into the illuminated area of the villa, he knew that he had just lost a war before he was ever able to compete in the first battle.

And although he walked under the disapproving gaze of the guests, he felt at the same time the feeling of strange satisfaction and ... happiness.

He saw Captain Rheinberg built up before him, scowling and angry.

And Volkert was happy. *Damn*, he thought.

This could not end well.

21

"There can be no doubt?"

"As far as we can determine our information to be reliable, yes. Your uncle is lost on the battlefield. Last time we saw him, he had been on a the wild ride with part of his bodyguard, but the chaos was big."

"What about Richomer?"

"My Lord, he survived the battle, and with him half of our advance guard. He has been lucky. Serious mistakes were made, o Lord. The cavalry was sacrificed without any sense. A slaughter without equal, and so pointless."

The Tribune lowered his head as if he'd suddenly realize that he had criticized the orders of his superiors, even those of the emperor of Eastern Rome. Gratian sighed.

"Speak openly, Tribune. Tell me everything."

The man looked up again. His face was covered with dust, his clothes looked torn and he was tired. He had to ride all night to convey the news to the Emperor. Gratian looked around, saw some servants who stood waiting and waved them. "A chair for the Tribune. Wine, meat and bread. Help him to take off his armor."

"Lord."

"Sit down, Tribune. Once you're done with everything, you shall rest. And do not hold anything back."

The man allowed a servant to remove his breastplate, and sat meekly when another one pushed a stool toward him. On a small table a servant placed food and a carafe of wine. Gratian sighed. With forced marches he had pushed his troops eastward, and yet they were only as far as Sirmium, where the tribune had reached them. They had just crossed the Danube and had been ready to advance further in the direction of Adrianople, when the little troop of lone riders had emerged under the command of this exhausted officer, and he had carried the seal of

Richomer, the commander of the cavalry division, which Gratian's own legions had sent ahead to get in contact with Valens.

Too late now as it turned out. And the consequences were not foreseeable. Emperor Gratian looked at the Tribune and felt in his limbs the same fatigue that he saw in the officer's eyes. He wouldn't follow the advice of his men and remain in Sirmium, where he had a palace and all the amenities, because he preferred to remain in the camp. Sirmium was the city in which he was born, and he had good memories of it. He didn't want to pollute them with concerns of the present.

"Eat and drink," he asked the officer. "Valens won't be brought back to life if we hurry you. Eat and drink!"

The tribune bowed and let it not be said again. He dug his teeth deeply into the cold meat, took great sips from his cup, and got himself a refill. Gratian had meanwhile turned away in order not to unnecessarily force his lingering presence on the man and joined Malobaudes, who stared on the great map of the Empire, which was clamped on the tent's wall.

"Valens is a fool," growled the Frankish king and general.

"Valens is dead."

"That happens to fools a lot," replied Malobaudes. He could afford this disrespect because Gratian had to agree with him.

"Why didn't he wait for us? Together we would have beaten the Goths," the Emperor said.

"He wanted the victory."

Gratian spat. "Valens isn't like my father."

"Your father always listened to his advisers, and then he made his own decisions."

"Valens decided as well."

"Your father was a wise man, a good general, loved by his troops. Valens was a fool."

"You said that already," Gratian replied mockingly and put a hand on his shoulder. "The consequences are what make me worry. I'm now the Emperor of the East and the West. The army of the East has disassembled. My troops are the only ones that are currently organized and powerful, but I tarry to lead them immediately into the battle against the Goths."

"And you rightly hesitate, my Emperor. The Goths are many. The Eastern Roman troops were the best of the Empire, let's not dispute that. We need time to gather the units of the East again, dig for new recruits and then go to the field together."

"I cannot take care of everything myself. It's not that the West is suddenly an island of peace and security."

Malobaudes nodded. "We need a new emperor in the east."

"First of all, we need a new general in the east."

Both were silent, staring at the map, lost in strategic and political considerations. As the smacking had stopped in the background, both men turned as if on command.

"Tribune, how are you?"

"My Emperor, I thank you. Your mercy is great."

Gratian smiled. "My uncle had sent many good soldiers to their doom. I have to maintain all that remained to me."

"Once again my thanks, sir."

"Then my reports. Who is in command in the East?"

The tribune, who now seemed much more relaxed than before supper, walked armed with a cup of wine to the map. "Richomer belongs to those who have taken command of the remaining troops, sir. The highest surviving leader is Flavius Victor, but he is seriously injured. Sebastianus has remained on the battlefield. In Constantinople the consistory rules, until further notice, under the chairmanship of the Minister of Finance and Praetorian Prefect."

"Modestus – not a fool but little military experience," Malobaudes commented. "He lacks the knowledge to make the right decisions at this point of time."

"Where do the remaining troops gather?" asked Gratian.

"Nowhere, at least not when I was sent by Richomer to you. It is a shambles. The Goths are out of control. They plunder the villages and avoid the cities. Fritigern has completely lost control of some of his men after defeating us. They are intoxicated by their victory."

Gratian had expected little else. Fritigern was a Gothic king, and as much as it was the case with the Alemans, a man with fluctuating, vaguely defined authority. The victory had contributed to his prestige and of course if he would call for another battle, he most likely would able to unite the various tribes under his banner again, no doubt about it. But in the meantime, sub-chiefs and nobles would see what could be gained for them from this victory, and this probably even with the discreet acceptance of Fritigern. Gratian thought it even possible that Valens' death had been occurred without knowledge of the Gothic king, and without his command. It wasn't the time to connect the leader of the Goths with all the misdeeds. Revenge was a feeling that you could indulge in very easily, but it didn't make political sense, not as a rule.

"What will the Goths do next?"

The tribune looked perplexed. "Lord, no one knows. The situation is out of control. When we ..."

He paused, and something like guilt crept into his face.

"We have treated the Goths certainly wrong."

"Can we negotiate with Fritigern?" asked Malobaudes.

"Lord, I don't know. Fritigern always made quite a reasonable impression to us ... until we had gone too far. If you make the right offer, he might be willing to negotiate."

"Doesn't mean that all of his subordinates are of the same opinion and will join a deal," Malobaudes said.

"That wouldn't be a problem," said Gratian now thoughtfully. "Fritigern has prestige. Many of the Goths would follow him. Even if it would be only two-thirds, that would be sufficient. With the rest we can deal militarily. Imponderable is what the smaller groups of Alans and Huns will do, as they fought with Fritigern. Can he control them? I don't know."

Malobaudes nodded. This variant of the good old Roman strategy "divide and rule" had worked well several times. Gratian had internalized the lessons of Ausonius well. With this approach, they would actually be able to succeed.

"Tribune, you rest now. Tomorrow we will hold a council of war and talk more and I want to you to join us."

"I'm at your service, my Emperor."

"Retire now, if you please."

There was no need for any further invitation. Constantly bowing, the exhausted officer left the tent.

Gratian looked after him.

"We need a new emperor in the east," he affirmed. "I cannot do this alone."

"Nothing to hurry about, sir," suggested the General. "Let us all have some rest now. There is no use to make these decisions too quickly and being tired."

"You're right. Tomorrow morning. We cancel the march eastwards until further notice. It makes no sense to move into the unknown and endanger our forces unnecessarily."

So everything was said and the tent emptied. Gratian stopped in front of the map of the Empire, and wondered for a moment how it felt to be sole emperor of the entire Roman Empire. Then he thought back to how his famous predecessors Traian or Diocletian or his father Valentinian felt once, crushed by the power of memory, thinking of the deeds of their forefathers. Even the Empire under Diocletian had been different than the one he now ruled. His reforms had helped to continue its existence, but more and more the spirit of his policy was undermined and Gratian knew with every day less what he could do about it. If the constant threat on the frontiers wouldn't persist, perhaps he could finally stabilize the peace and the structure of the empire from within. But his energy was depleted by riding from one battlefield to the next.

He remembered a saying that was awarded to Marcus Aurelius, the philosopher emperor: "Often the one who does nothing, does wrong. Who doesn't fight injustice, if he can, commands it." This statement haunted him since the time when Ausonius had read the works of the old emperor to him. If he did wrong by omission, then hesitation was another step into the abyss. But when he made the wrong decision in haste, then the disaster could be much greater. Gratian had respected his step-uncle Valens because he was named co-emperor by his father and he earned respect as the older one. Yet he had never doubted that Valens' procrastination and his dependence on the advice of his court – well-meaning officials as well as charlatans – would cause his downfall. That it had been hasty speed and lack of self-control which caused his defeat sounded like the kind of irony of life, for which Marcus Aurelius had always been very understanding.

"It would be silly to fret over the world," Gratian murmured dreamily. "She does not care."

Another insight of the old emperor.

"Elevius?"

As if by magic, the old manservant appeared out of nowhere.

"You called, sir."

"I will go to bed early."

"You have need of rest."

"I need to think about many issues indeed. Prepare my bed and ..."

Gratian hesitated.

"... and fetch my edition of Marcus Aurelius' *Meditations*. I feel the need to learn from the wisdom of my forefathers."

Elevius bowed.

22

Thomas Volkert was pale. Deathly pale, as some would say. It wasn't enough that Captain Rheinberg had summoned him to express his anger about the behavior of the young ensign. No, he'd have to do this before the assembled officers. His speech was quite short. He used words like "irresponsible" and "reckless," and those had been the most polite terms. He had made it clear what he thought of Volkert's stupidity, and he had announced full arrest for him on the ship and three weeks of double-shifts. After the ensign had been allowed to sit with a red face, the discussion was immediately drawn to other issues, of which Volkert had been quite grateful. But the stealthy, partly joyous looks of his comrades hurt. It took him several minutes to be aware that the biggest pain was triggered by the fact that he had no chance to reunite with Julia in the foreseeable future.

It was a kind of pain such as he had never known before, very deep and upsetting, combined with a longing whose strength was also new for him. The feeling contributed to his confusion as well as to his sorrow.

Thomas Volkert felt quite miserable and listened with limited attention to the discussion of the "War Council," as Rheinberg called the inner circle of officers.

The real topic of this meeting had not been Volkert's misstep, but a first report of the chief engineer.

"Captain, firstly I have a list of all crew members who enjoyed some kind of technical training."

Dahms handed Rheinberg a sheet of paper, which he accepted with a nod.

"Give us a summary," Rheinberg asked him.

"In addition to three marine engineers, we have a carpenter on board. A trained carpenter who never actually passed his master-exam, but apparently quite competent. We have seven men with good training: Two turners, a blacksmith, a carpenter, a baker, a cook and a butcher. Another fifteen claim that they had some learning and practice, but never passed the journeyman's examination, and from four I know that probably this is true, including a blacksmith apprentice, who works pretty well with me. We have seven men on board who have worked in mining, each with more than two years work experience. They have learned all sorts of clever things that we can use. I have in my department three good machinists and two coal-workers who both have been steelworkers, one with a decent education, but without any examination. All our men have sniffed into one or the other craft. We even have two charcoal makers on the ship, who could prove to be very helpful to us."

"In fact," confirmed Rheinberg. "What do we lack most?"

Dahms looked as though he wouldn't know where to start.

"Captain, we need just three things: We need something for firing, so that the machines run. We need lubricant. And we need spare parts. The first problem can be solved: the *Saarbrücken* can also burn wood if needed. The efficiency is ghastly and we need tons, but it is not impossible. Moreover, we can easily produce charcoal by ourselves, which increases the efficiency again – and even better with appropriate assistance from the officials here in Ravenna. We know that there are exposed coal reserves in the Empire, which are even used sparingly, not on a large scale. With the support of the Emperor, we could get access and be able to cover this our greatest need in the long term."

"That sounds pretty good," commented Rheinberg.

"This was the easiest problem. I have no idea what to do about the lubricants. Our machines operate with superheated steam, so we cannot use natural fats and oils. We would ideally need refined mineral oils to keep the machines running. But I'm still looking for substitutes."

Dahms stopped. Rheinberg wasn't inclined to comment further.

"Well ... So, to find oil itself should be possible. As I have heard there is something like open oil sources, if I'm not mistaken. Again, once the Emperor helps us to gain access to crude oil, the problem is solved. Second one is: We lack the chemical industry to even begin to make somewhat like usable mineral oils. Therefore, I still have no solution."

"What about naphtha?" asked Joergensen, the second officer. He wasn't known for his exceptional knowledge of history, so he drew surprised looks. The young lieutenant turned a bit red, but when he saw Rheinberg's nod, he continued.

"Naphtha was used in ancient times for something similar to a flame-thrower."

"So?" asked Dahms.

"If I remember correctly, it was nothing more than mineral oil made from rape."

Dahms' face showed understanding.

"I would like to suggest that when it is heated to over 100 degrees, you can drive out the water, and if you then add vegetable ash, so that the sulfur is bound as sulfide ..."

Rheinberg frowned. "You are a chemist, Joergensen?"

"No, Captain. But I admit to had certain pleasure in experiments with fire as a student, which meant that my friend Karl and I have made some inquiries ... We wanted to, if I remember correctly, recreate a flamethrower of the Greeks. We were 14. Maybe a bit precocious."

The second officer looked convincingly embarrassed, but did notice with relief that everyone present grinned broadly.

"Then you have chosen the right profession," said Dahms. "And your idea has merit. I'll sit and discuss this with the artificer of our infantrymen. I have a feeling that he could contribute to the discussion. I have it written down in any case and we will as soon as possible begin with our experiments. Ultimately, I fear, there will remain no choice but to try to convert the boilers from steam to saturated steam. Thus, the *Saarbrücken* will be slower, but the heat is much lower and we can therefore also work with poorer oils. That will mean a lot of effort, but it is possible."

"I don't expect miracles, Dahms," affirmed Rheinberg and nodded gratefully to Joergensen. "How long will our supplies last?"

"With great caution and lower load on the machines – about a year. Probably less."

"The third problem."

"Yes, exactly. Steel production is a difficult field. We have a good workshop and well-trained crewmen, and we can provide some of the necessary replacement parts and produce molds. The problem is that we unfortunately don't have a furnace on board. We can replace a few things through cast iron, but when it comes to the really reliable parts, only steel will help us. We don't need tons, but we need to have something like a steel production get going if we want to keep the cruiser running. Again, in about a year things get critical if we don't have serious damage because of strain even before."

"Steel. There is no furnace in the Roman Empire, which can generate the necessary temperature. Iron ore is not a problem, even the other commodities should be accessible," Rheinberg said with a thoughtful tone. "But we have to heat up to about 1600 degrees, and that is only possible ..."

"... if we build a puddling furnace," Dahms completed the sentence. "We need many workers, plenty of space and a certain infrastructure. The underlying principle is not that complex and I think we have the necessary knowledge on board. We won't resurrect the Ruhr region, we need a single puddling furnace, which covers our own needs. Here, too, Captain, we need a safe harbor. You must arrange things with the Emperor."

"I'm working on it. Fine, these have been the three urgent problems. Now a few more: weapons and ammunition."

Dahms put his forehead in sorrowful wrinkles.

"We can't produce the ammunition for our guns. Also the guns themselves, any replacement, will be impossible. If we have steel – maybe I can work something out. Ultimately, however, all will be irreparable and we can't fix everything endlessly. Therefore, I have a very different proposal."

"We listen."

Dahms took a deep breath.

"What I say now, ultimately, covers the basics, Captain. Also for the *Saarbrücken.* Even if everything goes perfectly, I don't think that we can keep our ship functional for more than three or four years. Until then, we need an alternative. And that can only be in it if we make cuts."

"What kind of compromise?" Becker wanted to know now.

"We have to make a technological step back, which is for the Romans still a giant leap forward. We need to see what can be produced with local resources, if we provide the necessary knowledge. There are materials available: Bronze is not a problem. We can build anything from bronze, even steam engines. Let us build steam engines and develop new ships – timber ships. Let us instead of guns and assault rifles think about what we can build with local resources realistically and in good quantities – black powder we can produce quickly. We have bronze. We probably have a bunch of perfectly capable blacksmiths."

"Muskets," muttered Becker. Dahms nodded brightly. Becker, however, didn't seem to share this enthusiasm throughout.

"We can provide the whole damned legions with muskets," the chief engineer said eagerly. "We can build cast-iron cannons and manufacture corresponding balls with propellant charges of black powder. We can begin professional mining – with a bronze steam engine we can drive a generator and produce light, heat, or make ice. We can build pumps and drive tunnels into the mountains. So much is possible. We don't even have to start building cannons; let's begin with steam catapults."

Rheinberg looked pensively at the table. "The Western Empire was finally doomed when Genseric conquered Africa's breadbasket with his Vandals. A fleet of ocean-going steamships with catapults and musketeers could prevent this without us having to show up with the *Saarbrücken* everywhere. Against other enemies the profit is less: The Huns under Attila will not be impressed by a few musketeer-legions, so we have to think of something else."

Becker nodded. "Muskets are inaccurate and don't fire far. The idea doesn't make me happy."

Rheinberg looked up and directly into Dahms' excited face.

"This is still awesome. We have to succeed. We'll find alternatives. A step back for us, but a great leap forward for Rome. Let them all come, the Huns and the rest of them. They will have no chance against the *new* Rome."

Dahms nodded. "But to do all that we need more than just a base, Captain. We need the full support of the Emperor. We need many workers. We need time. We need to stomp a whole industry out of the ground. I ... I can't foresee everything. And we need a dry dock."

"A dry dock?"

"We need to have a place where we can put the *Saarbrücken* for an overhaul. The water in the Mediterranean is very aggressive, the rust will quickly turn worse. Fortunately, we got the hull overhauled before our departure from Wilhelmshaven and we have a lot of special paint on board, so it will last a while. But once it is finished ... the old lady will slowly but surely rot away. I don't even know what we can use as a substitute to prevent that. I fear that no matter what we do, eventually the rust will break our neck, simple as that."

Dahms threw up his arms in mock despair.

"One after the other," calmed Rheinberg the visions the engineer had apparently been infected with. "First we need to come to good terms with Gratian. Renna wants to send a delegation to Sirmium, where the Emperor resides with his troops. We have to send a strong fighting troop there, and very quickly. And then we have to convince the Emperor that he allows us to solve the problem with the Goths for him. And once we accomplished that, we will be able to make further plans."

"Where is this Sirmium? I've never heard of it," Becker asked.

Rheinberg rose. In a closet at the head end of the room lay curled up all kinds of maps, and once the captain found a specific one, he immediately rolled it out on the table. All bent over and followed Rheinberg's forefinger on the map.

"Sirmium was an important garrison town in the east of the Mediterranean," said the captain. "She was even at a time imperial residence. Today ..." He paused. "In our time there are only a few ruins. It was about here ... west of Belgrade, near the Danube."

"We go over the Adriatic sea and land at ... Spalato?"

Neumann's idea was quickly accepted as a good proposal.

"As far as I know, there is a considerable port in Spalato at this time," confirmed Rheinberg. "I can give my maps to Africanus. There is a village called Salona. Emperor Diocletian built a palace there in which he intended to retire. At least, that was his original idea, but it didn't quite work that way. In any case, an important building. It should now no longer serve the old purpose, but there is definitely a port. And there is a road to Sirmium, where we are likely to do well."

"We could use the truck," suggested Becker.

"For the material, yes. The men have to march."

"How many soldiers do we take?"

"The whole company," Rheinberg replied immediately. "We have to deliver a very impressive show. We get an official pass and two of Renna's tribunes as a companions, they know the area well. In addition, Africanus will continue to serve as a liaison officer."

"That one will leave the *Saarbrücken* only if forced," Dahms said grinning. They all nodded. Africanus was without doubt the Romans with the slightest fear of the technical marvel presented by the cruiser. He tried to understand everything he was shown and sucked up explanations like a sponge. He was obviously fascinated with the ship's possibilities.

"When do we leave?" Neumann finally asked.

"And who?" added Becker.

That was the most important question indeed. Rheinberg's hesitation didn't go unnoticed. Everyone knew what the problem was – or at least who. Only von Klasewitz himself seemed unaware of the hidden looks that everyone gave him. He had behaved remarkably calm throughout the meeting.

"I ... we'll worry about that later," Rheinberg evaded the answer. In fact, there were several options that he had already discussed with Neumann. "We mustn't forget one thing: Although Renna seems to trust us, there are plenty of others who will establish a cooperation with us. I think that this also can mean the imposition of hostages."

The word seemed to awake von Klasewitz from his rest. He opened his eyes and said, "Outrageous!"

"No, not really," replied Rheinberg quietly. "During these times that's a totally normal political action. Many hostages have lived for years at the court of Rome, were trained there, lived in quite luxurious circumstances, and made great careers after their return. And it went both ways. I'm thinking about a very famous man who has been Roman hostage at the court of the Huns for many years, only to beat them afterwards during the battle of the Catalaunian fields: Flavius Aetius, the last great general of the West."

Apparently, few had heard of this particular man, because many eyes were directed full of curiosity at Rheinberg. He decided not to reveal the little historical detail that Aetius, after decades of de facto sovereignty over Western Rome, was betrayed and killed by the hand of his own emperor, Valentinian III. The men would lose some of their illusions soon enough.

"So, I assume that we need to give hostages, and senior ones, too. Let us, therefore, talk some other time about staff issues. Once we get the green light from Renna and the Senators – and I think we will find out within 24 hours – I want the *Saarbrücken* ready to move so we can get started. So full readiness. All right then?"

The captain looked around. Many of these men had left behind families, beloved women, and children. All had experienced dark hours full of self-doubt, since they came here, and many more were to come as it sunk in that in all probability there would be no way back. But now he saw in the eyes of many feelings like hope and confidence, saw them making plans and developing a vision.

He ended the meeting and allowed all of them to think about the issues discussed.

As he stood alone in the mess, his eyes fell on the map. "Sremska Mitrovica." He read the name of the local Serb community, which was in his time located where currently Sirmium was to be found. He put his index finger there. Regardless of how to finally answer the questions about any staff distribution, one answer was already very clear to him.

He would travel to the court of the Emperor.

He would stand before the face of Flavius Gratian and try to persuade him to start a revolution.

He was definitely mad.

23

"What exactly is going on in Ravenna?"

Secundus looked up from his scroll. The secretary had been so engrossed in his text that he needed a moment to notice that the question had been addressed to him. The slim man with his thinning hair wreath leaned back and looked longingly at the wine decanter. But it was highly improper to overdo it with the wine. Ambrosius had patience, much more than the secretary, 20 years his senior, would ever be able to apply in his life.

The Bishop of Milan was 38 years old; he was a man who had already reached the zenith of his life. The narrow face was decorated with a well-kept, thin beard and dominated by a large, downward nose. But most obvious was the fact that his right eye was slightly lower than the left, which the Bishop didn't stop from throwing a questioning look at his secretary.

"Your Eminence, I only report what has been told to me. A strange ship of unknown type has appeared out of nowhere, destroyed an imperial trireme and yet has been hospitably received by the Navarch in Ravenna. Well, at least they didn't immediately attack it."

"Nothing is known about the origin?" asked Ambrosius to be sure, as he stroked his beard. He certainly was convinced by the decorative elegance of his face.

"The rumor says that they came from Germania."

"Germania? That seems absurd. A ship that destroyed a Roman war galley and then enters the port of Ravenna? Guarded by the legionaries of the city garrison?"

"A ship made entirely of metal, and with demonic magic bullets," Secundus confirmed eagerly.

"Demonic wonder weapons, yes." Ambrosius looked thoughtfully out of the high windows of his study. The warm summer wind carried the chants from the nearby church into its walls. "Demons are always quite handy if you don't understand something, my friend."

"I don't know more than you, Your Eminence."

"I'm much more interested in what to think of the rumors that Renna has invited Symmachus to Ravenna. Symmachus hates the city, and he has held no public office for years. Why does he endure this? What's behind it?"

Secundus knew that these questions were rhetorical. As much as Ambrosius was as Bishop of Milan famous and recognized for his firm beliefs and vast knowledge, everyone also knew that he had been a politician before his election to this high church office and had taken a civil service career. For some years, he had even been prefect of Liguria and Aemiliaand helped to govern the Empire. The bishop had, despite his move to the church, never forgotten where he came from and that the church carried political significance in the Roman Empire, and so his questions for his longtime secretary were anything but unusual.

"Should we investigate further, Your Eminence?" asked Secundus.

The bishop hesitated with an answer. His hands lay flat on a paper on which he had been working since the early morning hours. Today, he had at last roused to start with a script that once and for all should explain the dominance of the doctrine of the Trinity over the Arian heresy, yet now such issues disturbed his progress. Ambrosius secretly wished to be able to spend more leisure for the really important things, but politics caught up with him again.

"This is not what Constantine planned," he growled and began to roll up the papers.

"What do you mean?"

"Well, when he promoted Christianity, he had hoped that it would strengthen the empire as a unifying bond and secure its position forever."

"Oh yes," said Secundus, who got up and helped his master in the proper storage of their morning's work. He knew what was coming, it was the litany of the bishop, since he had taken office, and it was getting worse every year. Once he was elected bishop, he was expected to show considerable religious neutrality in the dispute between the Arians and Trinitarians. Few had expected that Ambrosius would become one of the strongest and most convincing fighters against the Arians. Many already regretted their choice.

However, before Ambrosius could elaborate his musings about the strange occurrences in Ravenna with a monologue about the worthlessness of his opponents, a priest stormed unannounced into the study. The bishop stopped in his intended censure immediately, because the man seemed completely out of breath and in a great hurry. Something important was happening.

"Your Eminence, I just overheard a very important message in the palace of the prefect!"

"Speak!"

"Emperor Valens has fallen against the Goths before Adrianople! The armed forces of the East are in disarray."

Secundus and Ambrosius exchanged glances.

"Is it the truth?" asked the bishop.

The priest was breathing heavily. "I got it directly from the Secretary of the Prefect. The message has just arrived. Gratian is in Sirmium. The Court seems to be in great excitement."

"Yes – thank you, you can go."

The monk turned and hurried out. Ambrosius went to the window and looked outside.

"Valens was a heathen. God has punished him."

Secundus said nothing.

"At the same time he punished the entire East for its Arian heresy and delivered it into the hands of the Goths."

Secundus grunted something.

"A just punishment, I'd say."

Ambrosius turned. Secundus was still silent.

"You say nothing at all."

"Your Eminence, it may be as you say ..."

"But?"

"But it seems once again that we have a more political and less of a spiritual problem here."

The bishop smiled gently. "Of course that's true – and it will turn out to be a real opportunity for us. Gratian, an emperor with deep faith and the right attitude, now reigns in Rome. And whether he continues to govern alone, or a man of his mind will be appointed, I see that we have a very good chance to win some battles for us."

"The fight against the Gothic hordes?"

Ambrosius waved. "With those we will deal in time. I'm talking about two different fronts: the Arians and of the remaining old cults. Have I not just talked about the fact that Emperor Constantine had made a mistake long ago?"

"Yes, Your Eminence."

"He made a mistake in many ways. His biggest mistake was to pass here, in this city, a decree that obliges the state to tolerance toward other religions. Jews, pagans, heretics all are still under the protection of the edict."

Secundus saw that Ambrosius unconsciously clenched his hands into fists.

"The edict has to go," exclaimed the bishop. "And now we have a good chance to get this done." He seemed to think for a moment, the smile on his face grew wider. "And the fact that my special friend Symmachus has hastened to Ravenna because of our mysterious visitors might even prove to be beneficial."

Ambrosius straightened himself. One could see that he had made a decision.

"Secundus, we must act. First, send a courier to Liberius, Archbishop of Ravenna. I want to know every detail about the foreign visitors, and I don't mean hearsay, but the facts. He should send one of his best confidants to the strangers, and he should question them. I want a full report as accurate as possible."

"I'll arrange it at once."

"But this is not enough. I have to do something myself and seize the opportunity. Let's immediately make all necessary travel arrangements. I want to leave as soon as possible. At this hour the Emperor has the spiritual need of the counsel of the church, and I feel that God has chosen me to fill that role."

He looked into the still somewhat uncomprehending face of his secretary.

"We travel to Sirmium, and the fastest way. We are visiting the court. We shouldn't waste time."

24

"I'm Fulvius."

The Roman was in his late forties and a mountain of a man. Sure, there were also one or two pounds of excess fat on his massive body, but Dahms was not fooled. Fulvius was with about six feet height someone he didn't want to struggle with. Dahms wasn't a weak man. But the Roman was as wide as tall, with broad shoulders and apparently aware of his power, visible in the way he moved. His hands were like shovels, torn and scarred by hard work, and his legs sticking out under the loose tunic looked like tree trunks. Dahms took a while to get used to the fact that pants were not popular, although not unknown, and certainly not in the warm late summer of 378.

Dahms gave Fulvius his hand, and he grabbed it without hesitation. The grip was firm and strong.

"Navarch Renna said that I should sit down with you. I'm a messenger of the city guilds. I represent the artisans. I myself have been a blacksmith for over 25 years. I own the largest forge in the city, I have 22 men working for me, and I own two factories outside the city walls, which I run for the Empire."

Dahms now knew enough about the organization of the Empire to guess that Fulvius was actually the owner of the forge, but the factories were used for weapons production, established by order of the emperor. In any case, he was the right man, if he had some knowledge of the other crafts as well. The artisans of Rome were organized into guilds and were subject to increasingly restrictive legislation that allowed sons no choice but to take up their father's profession in order to prevent bottlenecks due to too many individual preferences for specific trades. Rheinberg had told him that this had been part of the legislative reforms introduced in order to ensure in particular the supply of the army. No one had to explain to Dahms that this benefit was ultimately bought with large losses in productivity. It was another thing they had to change when the Empire should be preserved in the long term.

Later.

"I'm glad to meet you," the naval engineer returned the greeting. The intense lessons with Volkert and Neumann had at least significantly improved his knowledge of Greek, and Fulvius seemed to be just as familiar with this language like with Latin. "Please, follow me!"

Dahms led the man down the hatchways into the belly of the *Saarbrücken*. The almost reverent silence of the craftsman said it all. As they entered the engine room and stood in front of one of the impressive steam boilers, Fulvius' mouth stood open. Dahms sat and gave the man some time to absorb all the impressions. To give explanations now would be wasted effort. It was a plus that the expansion engines were running idly at low pressure to be ready to leave the port if needed. By this he could offer Fulvius the full spectacle.

He looked into his face after the Roman sat down heavily beside Dahms.

"No magic, my friend," said the engineer. "I'm the same like you, a kind of blacksmith. A better blacksmith only in the sense that my teachers have had more to teach than yours, but I stood at the bench, and I swung the hammer like you. No magic."

Fulvius wiped the sweat from his brow.

"This is depressing and overwhelming," he finally blurted out, and could not keep his eyes shut. They seemed intended to absorb every technical detail. "But it's a machine. No doubt about it. A machine." He now looked Dahms directly. "You built it?"

"No," laughed the engineer. "I couldn't do this alone. I have neither designed nor built it. I just make sure it works, and therefore I have to understand how it functions."

Fulvius nodded sympathetically. "But you could build one given that you would have the necessary men?"

"Yes, I could. And that's one of the reasons why my trierarch has asked the navarch to establish contact with you."

The eager glint of barely restrained enthusiasm in Fulvius' eyes spoke volumes. Just as Aurelius Africanus couldn't be removed from the bridge of the *Saarbrücken*, the blacksmith's interest burned intensely, almost in every meaning of the word. Over 1500 years separated them, but Dahms immediately felt a deep kinship between himself and this man, acting as they were both cut from the same wood.

No, Dahms involuntarily corrected himself. Hammered out of the same metal would be more adequate to say.

"Say, Dahms. Ask me what you wanna know!"

The men smiled at each other, each false formality was gone. The smell of sweat, oil and steam impregnated the air. A member of the coaling-crew came in, the face smeared, the upper body completely naked and sweaty, the wild chest hair sealed with grease on his skin. Johann Meyer was more than just a man shoveling coal; he had been a journeyman to become a blacksmith in civilian life. Dahms waved him to join.

"Fulvius, this is Johann, a blacksmith like you."

Unfortunately, Latin lessons so far yielded little success with Johann, who was otherwise a quite gifted young man. He raised a hand in a somewhat helpless greeting. When Fulvius seized his hand and the two men silently began to measure their strength, a wide grin flashed across their faces.

"We'll get along," said the Roman, when Johann got up and went to work. "No magic, Dahms. This man looks like me, when I have been a young apprentice of my father's. Mages look different."

"Even though I sometimes wished I could conjure a little magic when all the problems occur at once."

"Yes, I know. So, again: What do you need?"

Dahms took a deep breath. "I cannot list everything and much of it you might not understand without lengthy explanation."

Fulvius accepted this without being offended. The panorama in the engine room had convinced him that he had a lot to learn.

"It'd be nice if you could show me what you can, then I can tell you what I need," Dahms said.

Fulvius grinned. "As if that would make things easier. I've heard rumors that your ship will leave soon. Otherwise I would suggest that you join me with some of your men, and I'll give you a tour of Ravenna – with visits to all the guilds, the great workshops and such. There you could see all sorts of work pieces and ask questions. We would certainly make progress."

"Yes, that's true. Unfortunately, I cannot do such a thing currently, because I have to keep myself ready for departure. But the *Saravica* won't be gone for long."

The plan was that the ship, after it had delivered the infantry company and Rheinberg to Spalato, should return to Ravenna. In particular the idea of letting the cruiser touring around in the Mediterranean without any supervision didn't sound too attractive to the Roman authorities. Rheinberg and Dahms both knew well that they were all still moving on very thin ice. It would only become thicker and therefore more resilient when the emperor was on their side.

"Once the *Saravica* is back, we'll get back in touch, and we'll do it the way you suggested," Dahms said. "And now I give you, if you do not mind, a tour of my empire ... and you can look at some of my problems."

Fulvius got up and made an engulfing motion with his arms.

"This, Dahms, is the greatest piece of work I've ever seen in my life. And I tell you, I want to build something like this one day!"

Dahms stood beside him.

"That's what I want, too, Fulvius. And I promise you, we will succeed."

25

"So this is supposed to be wine. I call it piss."

The fact that Sergeant Behrens could utter these words clearly and without caution had primarily to do with the fact that no one understood him. He sat with Köhler in a tavern, which was frequented by dock workers, sailors, fishermen, craftsmen, and legionaries, a beautiful hodgepodge that not only led to vociferous disputes, but also to occasional brawls. The latter lead to the permanent appearance of two strong slaves who had apparently been acquired only for the purpose of being visible, to act as a deterrent. They were huge guys who looked fatter than muscular, but both were almost two meters tall and in Köhler's perception nearly as wide. Apparently, they were preceded by a reputation, because as soon as they took on one of the revelers with a watchful eye, who was too loud or whose cries sounded too aggressively, the observed were quickly subdued. That the looks alone were enough, spoke for itself, otherwise the two just sat at a small table in the middle of the taproom and ate. Of all the slaves in Ravenna, these two certainly enjoyed the best of all possible fates, and the fact that some of the dispensing maiden changed clearly ambiguous glances with the guards, also pointed out that it was not the food alone they cherished.

Köhler and Behrens did get these looks too, and it was the boatswain who remembered the teachings of Rheinberg that in pubs like this the border between female prostitutes and waitresses was indiscernible. Until further notice, the two men, however, did not feel the need, remembering the vivid descriptions of Neumann about rampant STDs. Another time perhaps. If they both were desperate enough.

Until then they desperately drank the wine, and as Behrens pointed out so correctly, the drink tasted like rotted grapes, and that it contained alcohol was probably the only reason why it still was popular among revelers.

"What is missing here is beer."

"It exists; cervisia it's called," Köhler taught his comrade. "I would advise against it. Limp and barely digestible. In contrast, a good glass of wine is easily available."

"It would be more drinkable if accompanied by a shot," muttered Behrens. He stared at the pot in front of him, who had been served recently, and poked morosely with the wooden spoon in it. The soup was doubtlessly hot, but that decreased Behrens' distrust little.

"Yes, I find it odd that they offer nothing stronger here," said Köhler and waved the wooden cup back and forth sulkily. "Actually, to turn the wine into brandy shouldn't be that difficult."

"I know enough companies who operate their own distilleries, mainly in the colonies. It's not that much of a challenge," muttered Behrens. He pushed the bowl with the stew careful away, as he would fear that the brew would rise from its container and attack him.

"Since you say that," Köhler muttered suddenly with a very thoughtful expression on his face. "We would need a few metal pipes and a few other materials, but some of the men of Dahms' department might give us as a hand ..."

"What are you thinking?" Köhler had the full attention of the infantryman.

"Well, I guess if you offer the audience here an alternative to this swill, they will not say no. Some of the guys here look as if they are willing to drink plenty, and they all seem to have money for that."

"I see. Half the people here are professional drunkards. And they have a lot of silver to invest in wine in order to achieve a decent level of bliss."

"Yes?" Köhler grinned. "One can achieve this faster and cheaper – and with more flavor. Perhaps, then, even the beer might suddenly taste well."

"Not to talk about medical appliance," Behrens emphasized with exaggerated seriousness. "Disinfection is sorely needed here. A few shots might work wonders."

"Nothing is closer to the truth," confirmed Köhler. He looked pensively at the innkeeper, a broadly built man who stood behind a roughhewn bar and observing the clientele all at the same time with his piggy eyes. Köhler's attention wandered from the man to the half-open door, behind which he suspected the kitchen. He saw a woman who carried food back and forward again and placed it on the bar where the waiters picked it up. She was about the age of the innkeeper and didn't give the impression of an employee, especially when she insulted one of the waiters loudly. Kohler suspected that she was the wife of the host. Every now and then young ones could be seen peering curiously into the tap room, before they were chased back by their father. After ten minutes, Köhler had identified five different faces.

"This innkeeper here has a full house and a big family," he said, and bowed his head toward the counter. "The prices are moderate and I don't think that the customers always pay. The man can write, you see? He keeps a tab."

Behrens nodded. The landlord clearly maintained a list at the back of the counter where the names of regulars were written on a blackboard. Although he didn't know exactly what the cryptic abbreviations behind the names meant, one could surmise that the accumulated debts were not negligible. The fact that the innkeeper sometimes directed very clear words to one or the other of the regulars and consequently smaller amounts reluctantly changed hands, confirmed this. Afterwards, the man changed the entries behind that name, but didn't wipe them away, which indicated that only a portion of the debt had been settled – just enough to move the innkeeper to honor a new order.

"The pub needs better customers, and more of it. An extension of the range of products could help," Behrens said, observing the surroundings with open eyes. "There is no back room. This is bad, because where do you meet undisturbed to gamble for the high stakes?"

Köhler nodded.

"How good is your Latin?" he finally asked.

"Crappy."

"Then we'll get us a translator. Someone from the crew. And we return before the *Saarbrücken* will leave. We should have a serious conversation with the innkeeper."

"What do you suggest?"

Köhler grinned. "A partnership that could prove to be extremely lucrative for everyone involved. Are you in?"

“Definitely. Don’t you think we will encourage evil by this?”

Köhler made an innocent face. “Evil?”

He lifted the emptied wine jug and waved it.

“This is not a prerequisite of evil; we expand the technological base of the Roman Empire for the sake of our mission and for the benefit of all Roman citizens. We do civilization building!”

A barmaid came over to their table and smiled shyly. From Köhler’s assessment, she was barely 15 years old.

The filled pitcher stood before them, and they poured on.

“Then for the sake of civilization!” said Becker, raising his cup.

“You got it,” Köhler said, smiling.

They toasted.

26

Decisions flowed like water down the Tiber. When the *Saarbrücken* finally left, the military authorities, as far as they could have been contacted, entrusted Navarch Renna with the management of the new challenges – not least because he had promised to put all of his decisions in front of the Emperor for scrutiny as soon as possible. The personnel on board of the *Saarbrücken* had increased again: Both Senator Symmachus and Michellus had decided to make the trip to Sirmium, Africanus and two officers of the staff had also embarked. To find accommodations for extra guests was remarkably simple: As expected, one of the central demands of the Romans was that the *Saarbrücken* had to give hostages. Rheinberg had taken the opportunity to get rid of Klasewitz elegantly, while also giving the impression of doing him a favor. Von Klasewitz, reassured of his importance as a highly prominent hostage, stalked the ship like a general after his triumph. He was accompanied by some men, who Rheinberg couldn't really do without, but he had to put together a suitable group at least for appearances. Volkert was among them, though he had provided impeccable service since his reprimand, two non-commissioned officers, including Sergeant Behrens, one of Becker's most experienced men, who'd provide with one of his corporals something like an unofficial bodyguard, and finally Köhler. All hostages were allowed to remain armed, which was a leap of faith on the part of the Romans, and Rheinberg had impressed with all of them, especially von Klasewitz, that he expected proper behavior. The first officer, apparently delighted with the prospect of further public receptions and festivities, had solemnly promised to do the *Saarbrücken* honor. Symmachus and Michellus were quartered in the cabins of Rheinberg and von Klasewitz, while Rheinberg would now bunk with Becker in another cabin. The crossing to Spalato would take a day to complete, so the possible inconvenience was limited.

It was this early August morning, when the *Saarbrücken* finally got ready to sail when Rheinberg was approached by someone he had almost forgotten.

"Trierarch!"

Rheinberg stood at the rail, watching the bustle on the quay when he heard the voice. He turned around and saw the fisherman, Marcus Necius, and his son Marcellus, both in fresh tunics. They had actually left the *Saarbrücken* when the cruiser entered the harbor for the first time, and Rheinberg had almost forgotten the two Romans, but the fact that the guards had let them come on board, reminded him that he still owed both of them.

Rheinberg greeted them warmly. "I am delighted that you visited me. Unfortunately, we'll leave soon and I don't have much time."

Marcus waved. "I don't want to take your time, trierarch. I've heard that you have done a great deed by defeating a notorious pirate."

"We tried to be of service," replied Rheinberg.

"Well done," said Marcus and Rheinberg immediately felt that negotiations had begun. He suppressed a smile.

"What can I do for you, Marcus?" he asked right away. "Since our first encounter there hasn't been much time to talk to each other."

"There is in fact something that I want to ask of you," continued the fisherman. Since his hands, which he had placed on the shoulders of his son, pressed Marcellus' bones while saying that, Rheinberg already knew that Marcus had no wish for himself.

"Speak!"

"I have seen many wondrous things on your ship, trierarch. Very wondrous things I don't understand and I won't understand in my life. I have the feeling that a new era has dawned."

"I'm not sure yet. Much will depend on what we'll achieve in the near future." Rheinberg remained vague. That they left to meet the Emperor hadn't been a secret in the strict sense of the word, but at the same time also not a piece of public information.

"However, I feel that way," insisted Marcus. "I would therefore ask you to take my son Marcellus as a cabin boy on your ship. He is hardworking and intelligent. He can work and needs little sleep. A corner and a blanket will suffice as a place to rest. He doesn't eat much.

Please, I want him to learn from you, and from your men. These ... machines, these tools, all this is more than we Romans ever knew. I want Marcellus to learn all of it."

Rheinberg nodded slowly. "You understand, Marcus, that this is a warship in the first place and all the crew are soldiers?"

"Yes, Trierarch. I understand that well."

"And we are, at least until now, neither Roman citizens nor official members in the armed forces of the Empire."

Marcus smiled gently. "My feeling is that this will change soon."

"The opposite also can occur."

"The benefits outweigh the risks."

Rheinberg then looked at the boy, who had followed the conversation with a straight face. "What do you think, son?"

"I'll do what my father says."

"That wasn't my question."

Marcellus looked questioningly at his father, who apparently didn't mind that his son spoke openly and honestly.

"I'm afraid, Trierarch," Marcellus said finally. "But I want to be more than a fisherman."

The way how the pride in Marcus' eyes sparkled revealed that his ambition was quite the same like his father's.

"And I don't want to be a soldier either," he added firmly. Marcus' eyes asked for an apology. But Rheinberg liked the boy. He looked forward to an uncertain fate on a strange ship with even stranger men, and yet he had enough courage to express his will.

"You're anyway too young to be a soldier," said Rheinberg. Before the disappointment in Marcus' face was too strong, he raised a hand. "But you're not too young to go with us and be properly trained. You are ready to work and sweat?"

A rhetorical question. Marcellus had during his stay at the *Saarbrücken* visited the engine room in every free minute and admired the great machines. Dahms had even accepted him like a kind of mascot. And Marcus had quickly made friends with the other ship's boys, who worked mostly in the engine room and ensured the continuous lubrication of the big machine. They were about his age.

Rheinberg would fulfill his desire because of his own considerations.

Marcellus was a chance and he wanted to spare him just to work as a helping hand. Recently, he had already told Dahms that the ship's boys had to undergo a stronger learning regimen, as they now had to consider each crew member as a precious and irreplaceable resource. Unlike the Romans, the boys knew the cruiser already. One could train them well, but they had to be released from their duties more than before.

And that had to apply to the young fisherman's son right away.

"You will be hired as a ship's boy," Rheinberg said. "You shall serve at Dahms' department; he and his men will teach you about machines. You start at the beginning. You have to learn mathematics and geometry. That's pretty exhausting."

Rheinberg immediately realized that he had underestimated Marcellus. His father waved his hand. "Sir, I have sent my son to the best teachers I've been able to afford. He couldn't go to school too long because of the money, but he has learned a lot of mathematics. He can count up to 10,000, and he can read and write. He knows a lot, he just needs some encouragement to learn now and then."

"Not here, Father. Here I'll learn voluntarily," the boy said eagerly.

"I hope so," growled Marcus.

"He will be well," Rheinberg reassured him. "He has to learn, but he won't become a soldier. He will be a machinist. The first Roman machinist. I offer him a three-year term on the *Saarbrücken.* Then he can disembark with all that he has learned. I pay in food, clothing and lodging, and once we should get any money he will receive some payment. Also, I promise to do everything I can to ensure his safety. That's all I can offer you ... Marcus ... Marcellus."

It was clearly evident that he met both the expectations of the father as the son more than enough. Rheinberg waved Köhler, who immediately joined them.

"Mr. Köhler, this boy here is added to the crew."

The older man nodded and smiled calmly at Marcellus. The boy looked up at the massive bulk of the NCO and returned the smile rather timid.

"You'll see if we can tailor an outfit for him and find a hammock. He will be registered as a cabin boy and civilian apprentice, not a soldier. Dahms has to find someone who takes care of him and set up a training plan, Neumann has to give him a safety briefing. Bring him to Neumann and tell him my regards, he should examine the boy properly and create a record."

Köhler tapped his index finger against his forehead and rested a broad hand heavily on Marcellus' shoulder.

"Marcus, of course your son will be allowed to go ashore, when we are back in Ravenna. Do not worry!"

"I don't," replied the fisherman, though his eyes didn't hold quite the same determination like his voice.

"Köhler, go ahead!"

Marcellus left without resistance. Rheinberg pointed to the quay.

"I'm sorry, Marcus, but we'll actually leave soon."

The fisherman swallowed hard. "Thanks," he finally said quietly. "Thank you."

"He'll make you proud. He's a good boy."

Marcus nodded and turned away. Rheinberg watched him and wondered how quickly the news of Marcellus' hiring would make the rounds in the city. He smiled. At least for the more adventurous, the curious, those who were willing to try anything and to do something new and different, this news would hit like a bomb.

Rheinberg looked at the bridge and waved. Only Köhler had to leave the ship, then they were ready to go.

Commands echoed across the deck, as the lines were prepared to be cast off.

They embarked toward Spalato.

To the Emperor.

27

Petronius Ascellus had everything he could wish for. Three things filled his life with joy and great satisfaction: The knowledge that he had found the true faith, certain that this knowledge would prevail over all other opinions on that matter and the fact that he had the ear of the Archbishop, something which was of no insignificant importance. These three things filled him especially with satisfaction because they enabled him to achieve his three main goals in life: to clean his soul from impurity so that he could face final judgment with joy and anticipation, to clean the lives of others so that they could also be saved, and to ensure that his pure life would be most comfortable until judgment would be spoken.

To be the closest confidant of Liberius of Ravenna helped in all this. When the messenger from Milan had retired and the old archbishop humbly contemplated the message of Ambrosius with obvious confusion, Petronius just waited to be asked for advice.

Liberius was old, in fact not far away from his very final days. He was without doubt a pious man of high standing and with a firm faith, even if he, as his adviser silently thought, confronted the heresy of the Arians with too much indulgence and a mild manner, a behavior Petronius explained with the advanced age of the Archbishop. In addition, Liberius was in worldly things ... the word that Petronius preferred not to use was "helpless." Liberius loved the early hours of prayer he celebrated despite his age, embraced profound worship and he knew the scriptures like no other. He was well educated, spoke and read Hebrew beside Greek and knew many of the scriptures in the original text. Ambrosius, himself a highly educated man, had a long and fruitful relationship with Liberius and learned from his knowledge, and so a very good connection had been established between the men quite early. Petronius respected the high education of his master, but he knew that the message from the Bishop of Milan would lead to puzzlement within the old man.

So the inevitable happened.

"Petronius, my friend," groaned Liberius, waving the parchment in the air. "What am I supposed to think? The city senate has assured me that the aliens are neither risk nor threat, and that they have freed the area from the scourge of bloodthirsty pirates. I heard the senate considered all this and left dealing with them to Navarch Renna, and they intend to ask for the Emperor's word on the matter, which seems like a wise counsel. Now why this sudden interest of my brother Ambrosius?"

Petronius put quite a bit of acting talent in a facial expression of deep contemplation before answering. "Your Eminence, I don't presume to be able to follow the thoughts and reflections of our brother in every case. Between him and me are worlds, and as much as I take after him, so far I'm still beneath him. Still, if I may say this: Ambrosius has always been able to focus special attention to a problem that has later proven to be worrisome, and he acted accordingly."

"Hmm, probably true, probably true," murmured Liberius. "But my brother has never lost his secret passion for politics, and it seems to me that he has once again succumbed to temptation."

Petronius had to control himself in order to act righteously surprised by this sudden brainstorm of his bishop. He reminded himself not to underestimate the old man too much. Complacency, he told himself, should be on the list of deadly sins, and would make number eight easily.

"Quite right," he said submissively and inclined his head. "I think there has to be someone in the church who at least sometimes pays attention to these horrible but necessary worldly affairs. As long as the Empire and the church are divided between those of the true faith and the heretics of Arianism, no man of god can disconnect himself from secular considerations completely."

"Yeah, well, maybe," muttered Liberius. He hated to talk about this topic. He was very convinced of the Trinitarian doctrine, but at the same time reluctant to oppose the heresy with all the necessary power, which sometimes also required sacrifices. He probably assumed that the

Arians would eventually die out by themselves, a view that couldn't be further from the truth as strong Arian bishops dominated the east of the Empire. Petronius was convinced that a good dose of fire and iron should be used against all the enemies of the Church – Arians included – but was careful not to say this too loudly. The ear of Liberius was a valuable asset, it was important not to unnecessarily put this at risk.

The old bishop sighed. "Petronius, you go and take care of this. I charge you with this task. You'll report to Ambrosius; you will know what is important and what is not. For me this is all too much, and you have my trust. Go, take this burden from me."

Petronius hid a smile of triumph behind a deep bow, as he left the audience room of his bishop, the letter of Ambrosius held tightly to his body.

He wasn't going to miss this wonderful chance of making himself known. Liberius was old, and would retire or die. The flock of Ravenna would have to choose a successor in a few years. The word of the bishop of Milan, should he make a recommendation, had great weight in Ravenna.

Petronius smiled as he hastily left the seat of his Lord and approached the harbor.

Bishop Petronius.

Yes, that was something.

28

The crossing was uneventful. The sea was calm, the *Saarbrücken* progressed without problems. Rheinberg stood on the bridge when the landline of Spalato, or Salano, as it was called during the Roman era, emerged on the horizon. Diocletian, the great reforming Emperor, who had made the last comprehensive albeit flawed effort to reorganize the Empire in order to secure its boundaries, had built a palace here. In his own time in the future, as Rheinberg recalled, this palace had transformed itself into the entire old town. Diocletian had intended to build this gigantic building as a place of retirement. In the assumption that the Empire was put in order by his efforts, he left it divided into equal parts for his sons. Immediately after the resignation of their father from his office, they had nothing better to do than to fight each other. Diocletion remained to be the only Roman emperor who ever had abdicated voluntarily. But he was forced to intervene as an arbitrator for several times. The system created by him eventually fell apart and it was Constantine, called the Great, who ultimately reintroduced complete autocracy. Diocletian also failed in his determined and brutal persecution of Christians and couldn't stop the rise of the new religion, so that ultimately his successor Galerius proclaimed the famous edict by which the existence of Christianity was in fact recognized and which often was wrongly attributed to Galerius' co-emperor Constantine.

The edict was still in force, and if Rheinberg couldn't change history, Gratian would lift it in a few years – although to very specific ends: As a prelude to the pursuit of heretical Christian movements and the complete suppression of all other religions which would lead to civil strife, a struggle that would weaken Rome massively, and this at a time where the Empire couldn't afford this kind of infighting and the associated loss of substantial resources.

The list of challenges seemed to grow longer and longer each time

Rheinberg thought about it. He'd have to try to handle one problem after another. And at first he had to prove his usefulness for the emperor.

When the *Saarbrücken* sailed into the harbor of Salano, curiosity was high. The residents of the city gathered at the harbor wall and stared in amazement, but not without fear, at the mighty ship, which came in very slowly. The first thing after the cruiser was moored was for Africanus and the two tribunes to disembark. The fact that Roman officers left the ship seemed to soothe the anxieties of at least the port authorities, and as senators and their servants went ashore, armed with letters of recommendation and orders, the fearful amazement turned more into something like a carnival atmosphere.

For the crew of the cruiser, there was no time to lose. Even before the falling dusk, Becker ordered his people to heave chassis and body of the truck to the pier where mechanics immediately began to assemble. Port guards and infantrymen Becker secured a wide circle around the landing site, but generally behaved passively. If the port guards were nervous about the presence of the strange, foreign soldiers, they couldn't show it. The collaboration seemed to function fairly well.

When it got dark, the truck was assembled and ready to go. Rheinberg ordered to keep him guarded until the next morning and to retain the valuable cargo on board. In addition to the equipment of the infantry a box of 10,000 Goldmark would accompany them. Gold was in short supply in the Empire, no matter in what form it was coined. Rome was chronically broke, especially the West, and it didn't hurt to take some change along, as Neumann had sarcastically remarked.

Rheinberg and Becker shared their cabin alternately so that everyone theoretically got five hours of sleep. Practically, both lay awake most of the time. Too many things had to be considered in order to prepare for too many contingencies. Ultimately, both realized independently that it made no sense to consider all possible developments in advance. It was simply not possible to mentally prepare for everything – or even to imagine what could happen.

It was no wonder that all were awake early. At 6 o'clock in the morning, the infantry was ready to leave. Sergeants barked commands, and the proper formation for a long march was taken. The port guards as well as any early observer of the ceremony were neither impressed nor surprised: if one army in this world could march in formation, it was the Roman one. Rheinberg had to admit that the field-gray infantrymen behaved not half as impressive with their backpacks and rifles slung compared to a similar Roman formation.

The truck was loaded quickly. In addition to the gold and three MG 08 in the load, one machine gun was set ready to fire on the roof of the truck. All sorts of other stuff as well as ammunition completed the equipment. Becker, who had slept the second half of the night, joined Rheinberg yawning. The captain of the *Saarbrücken* would provide the naval contingent together with Neumann and Köhler. The cruiser remained under the command of second Officer Joergensen and would return to Ravenna after two days – another condition laid down by Renna. A sailing-ship of the Roman fleet would arrive in Salano soon and break the news of their eventual return to Ravenna, once they arrived back in Diocletian's cozy place of retirement

If they returned here. If all went well – and it was strange to speak of it as something good – the Emperor would send his new ally into battle against the Goths. Rheinberg was quite confident that they would eventually come back to the *Saarbrücken*. But he wasn't sure how many would return.

"You sit with the driver, Jan," Becker mumbled as he watched his officers and NCOs counting the infantrymen before the march began. "You can doze off a little. I will march with my men the first few hours, which is good for morale. Also, I have a feeling that the time on your luxury cruise ship has made me a little rusty."

"Thank you," sighed Rheinberg, stifling a yawn. "I won't turn down the offer. Also, I certainly don't tell you anything new when I say that marching isn't part of everyday life within the navy."

Becker smiled. "Yes, it's good for once that real soldiers call the shots."

Rheinberg sat next to the driver, a very young corporal, and shook his head. The young man nodded hesitantly.

"Corporal?"

"Maszcak, Captain."

"Good. Just ignore me."

The young soldier looked at him as if he couldn't imagine exactly how he could accomplish this, but nodded again and started the engine. The truck awoke to life with a roar. Soldiers of the port watch as well as spectators jumped aside with startled faces as a gray-blue plume hovered over the pier.

Rheinberg heard Becker's order to march. The captain had made it clear that he would obey Rheinberg's commands in all matters of fundamental importance, like political issues and overall strategy, but had asked not to be questioned in regard to everything that had to do with military matters on the ground. Rheinberg had agreed without hesitation. His infantry training had been a while. This was Becker's profession.

The truck jerked loose when Maszcak released the clutch. The shouting was great once the vehicle began to follow the two tribunes and Aurelius, who rode on horses ahead. The animals reacted visibly nervous in the presence of the unknown and frightening vehicle, but the riders had them reasonably under control.

Behind them, someone broke into a marching song. Rheinberg wanted to close his eyes, but he was curious about the Palace of Diocletian, the city Salano and everything else that was there to see. He had to learn to get used to this time and even thought to change to one of the spare horses during the journey. After all, he had learned to ride quite early, as it was expected of a cavalry officer's son.

His gaze fell through the windshield of the car, wobbling after the horse before him. He looked at the tribune sitting on the animal and riding it slowly and frowned, pulled out a notebook in which he had grown accustomed to note sudden ideas. He set the pencil down and wrote only one word: *Stirrup.*

"Captain?"

Rheinberg hadn't noticed that he had voiced the word aloud. He put the notebook away and smiled at the corporal.

"Look yourself, Maszcak. No stirrups."

The driver frowned.

"You can't ride?" asked Rheinberg.

"No, I'm sorry."

"It is essential. You'll have to learn it."

Rheinberg listened to the chatter of the truck's engine. "To refine gasoline will present us with considerable problems."

From the corner of his eye he saw how the corporal shifted restlessly back and forth in his seat as if he wanted to say something but wouldn't dare. Rheinberg frowned. He knew the common soldier had been trained to have one hell of respect for officers, but too much respect didn't help him here in the Roman Empire. He was dependent on the knowledge of everyone. And everyone had to be aware of it.

"You know, Corporal, what happens when we all keep our mouth shut with our proposals and ideas?" he asked abruptly.

"Um ... I ..."

"If no one dares to address one of the officers about something he has learned or just came to his mind, to simply express an idea or make a suggestion – no matter whether it actually makes sense at the moment or not?"

"Well, I don't know ..."

"Exactly. That's the problem. I don't and no one else does. And then we may have a problem and a solution, but both don't know each other, because the one who could make the connection doesn't feel like talking. This affects us all. I need each and every idea. And what we can't do now, maybe later we can."

Rheinberg showed Maszczak his notebook.

"This is my memory, Corporal. I have just written down that the Roman cavalry knows no stirrups. Stirrups secure the rider in the saddle. He can more easily swing his sword, he can push a lance and hurl it free, he can control his horse better. He could fire a rifle or a musket and throw grenades. Without stirrups this would be difficult. So what do we need to improve the Roman cavalry?"

"Stirrups."

"Exactly. And when do we need them?"

Masczak shrugged.

"Exactly. I don't know either. But I wrote it down. And as soon as the opportunity arises, I'll conjure the idea up from my notebook. And now it's your turn!"

The corporal was pale and focused on the road. But there wasn't much that called for his attention: The road was free, legionaries guarded the track, and the speed of the truck was barely faster than the brisk marching Becker had ordered. Enough opportunity to think about other things.

"Well ... Captain, what you did you say about gasoline, well, that isn't true."

"Explain!"

"My father works at Opel in the machine design-shop. He once told me that the first engines were run with salad oil. I mean ... our truck swallows diesel, but I guess ..."

Rheinberg squinted. "Who among the crew can know more about this? We don't have a fucking chemist among us. And our library also won't give up too much."

The corporal shrugged. "I can't say, Captain. I just had an idea. Probably not much help."

But Rheinberg had already opened his notebook and scribbled something into it eagerly. When he had closed it again, he nodded to the driver.

"It'll not help us now maybe, that's true. But it may in the future. And if you or one of your comrades have a good idea – you tell me or Captain Becker. We have an open ear. We listen to everything and there are no stupid ideas – only those that we can't use now. Tell that to every comrade, everyone who seems to have something of an idea just on the edge of his mind and maybe doesn't dare to express it."

The corporal nodded hesitantly.

"You promised me, Maszczak."

The driver cleared his throat.

"Yes, Captain."

Then he stared back on the road, as if at any moment the Roman pavement might explode in their way.

Rheinberg smiled and leaned back.

They made slow but steady progress. While the morning sun climbed up the sky, more onlookers accompanied the marching column. Rheinberg saw faces in which curiosity struggled with fear. He looked at stony expressions and at parents who ushered their kids off the street, priests in long robes, who kept clutching their cross. He saw young men who got bright eyes at the sight of the truck, and artisans, squinting their eyes at the slowly turning wheels with their tires, like they'd be able with no more than mere inspection to improve their own designs. It was all remarkably quiet, and whether it was the fact that many were intimidated by the noise of the diesel engine, or just didn't know if they should applaud or express their fear, couldn't be seen from the cab of the truck. But the range of emotions and reactions observed by Rheinberg gave him cause for optimism as well as fear. He noticed, beyond the protective hull of the *Saarbrücken*, just how much he needed the help of the local authorities, and how little their superior technology meant out here.

After two hours, they had left the town and followed a good road toward Sirmium. Traffic on the road was slight – a few horsemen, a few carts, a few pedestrians – and they all respectfully gave way as the column approached. After three-and-a-half hours of moderate march, Becker ordered a break. The men sat on the grass by the roadside. The captain had deliberately chosen an area where only a lonely farm was discernible from far. Thus, the safety of soldiers was easier to ensure.

Rheinberg left the cab groaning. When he joined Becker and Africanus, who were talking quietly, the infantry captain handed him a metal cup of coffee.

"Enjoy it, Captain," he said half-jokingly. "I have tried to ask our friend here about the coffee bean, and he didn't know what I was talking about."

"Ah ... yes, it will probably remain so for a while, if we do nothing about it," Rheinberg said, smiling. He pointed to the coffee pot hanging over a hastily kindled fire. "We are lucky to have a good load of coffee with us, but even the best stock is going to run out. Africanus, will you try it?"

The trierarch looked suspiciously at the black liquid in the cup. "I'm not sure."

"It's inspiring. With something sweet, maybe?"

Becker scooped some sugar into the cup. Africanus, under the encouraging gaze of the two men, finally took it hesitantly then brought it gently to his mouth.

The two Germans looked curiously at the Roman officer. Africanus sipped. He rolled the liquid in his mouth back and forth. He swallowed.

Then he grimaced. "That's disgusting," he said. "This is something you like to drink?"

"Ah, and what about this fish sauce ..."

"Garum."

"Yes. Now that's disgusting!" affirmed Becker.

"A delight!" contradicted Africanus, took another deep sip of coffee and closed his eyes. Then he finished the cup, handed it to Becker and looked at him triumphantly.

"What?" the captain asked.

"I drank it all."

"Yes."

"You have left the garum untouched. I have seen how you dropped your bowl full of good meat, probably in the hope that nobody would have noticed."

Becker looked a little embarrassed. "Hadn't thought that someone was watching me."

Africanus showed a broad grin. "I had a good view on your sins."

"I promise I'll try it again ... in Sirmium."

"If the Emperor invites you to dinner, then be well advised not to criticize the cooking too much," Africanus added. "That would be ... undiplomatic."

Rheinberg received a descriptive view from the trierarch. The German apparently had little pleasure to look more closely at this aspect of their mission.

"I'll cross that bridge when I reach it," Becker said finally.

Africanus seemed to understand the idiom, as he returned the grin and pointed to the saddlebag of his horse. "Not that I can't help you with this, my friend. If you lust for it immediately, I'd be happy ..."

"No, no!" Becker raised his hands defensively. "This really isn't necessary ... but thanks for the kind offer."

Africanus' grin indicated that this offer was supposed to be anything but friendly.

Less than half an hour passed before Becker ordered the men to commence the march once again. This time Rheinberg decided not retreat lazily into the cab of the truck, but instead to keep marching at least for a while.

About an hour later, he found himself on the back of the one of the spare horses. His feet were sore, and his boots suddenly appeared to be too tight nearly everywhere. He was definitely out of practice and had become increasingly been the subject of joyful glances by his comrades from the infantry. Finally, he had accepted Africanus' offer to ride with him, although he had a big problem to cope with the horse without stirrups. On his personal priority list, this technical innovation slipped a great step upwards.

As night fell, they had made a good first day, but Sirmium was still at least two more days away.

29

The men had possibly imagined something else connected to the term "hostage." Ultimately, they were very happy not to be accommodated in a dark dungeon, but in the guest wing of a very distinguished town house. Their host wasn't in the city, the house belonged to a Roman senator, who currently held an official position in Gaul. But his family had made the property available, and so the guests were billeted there. Volkert and von Klasewitz each received a very spacious suite, Köhler and Sergeant Behrens shared another nice room, and the two infantry corporals could make themselves comfortable in a third room – and comfortable they were, because all rooms were nicely decorated with fresh fruit on the tables, soft beds and furnishings. Von Klasewitz warned them to deal carefully with the furniture, and it was one of the first of his commands about which Volkert had nothing to complain about.

The ensign's mind was elsewhere anyhow.

The men in the villa were guarded only subtly. The doorway, the only passage through the wall enclosing the property, was one of the few places where soldiers were recognizable. They were also searched only fleetingly. At their service were a number of deliberately silent slaves, and one of these, an older, bareheaded man, had slipped Volker in an unguarded moment a piece of paper with a message.

Volkert didn't unfold the papyrus immediately as he instantly knew from whom it came.

Julia!

His heart pounded as he excused himself for a moment and finally disappeared in an unused room, carefully paying attention to the fact that no one was watching.

He unfolded the paper with trembling fingers, only to immediately determine with great disappointment that the doodle was not for him to decipher. He quickly found that between the normally written Latin and careful inscriptions on walls and columns, a large difference was visible and this caused him great trouble in reading. Unfortunately, Julia had not thought of that fact.

Volkert felt a bit desperate, sat heavily on a stool and rested his head in one hand, while with the other he ...

The back!

Volkert looked up. Julia had indeed not acted without thought! On the back she had apparently repeated the same text in Greek! Volkert was getting along with that language so much better, and with newly awakened ambition he started to decipher the Latin text as well. He had the feeling that he would quite appreciate this ability in the future. He read the Greek text several times, and a hot joy rose to his head. After some time, he had also deciphered the Latin part, investing some diligent effort.

"Scribenti mii dictat Amor mostratque Cupido: A peream, sine te si dea esse velim!"

"Amor dictated what I should write and Cupid led my hand: Ah, I would rather die than to be even a God without you!"

Volkert smiled. Then a date and time: The third hour of the evening. The date of tomorrow.

And the sentence: *"Virum vendere nolo meom ..."*

Volkert mused. This sentence was not in the Greek version. He found the translation after some thought and muttered the phrase silently. "I will not sell my husband ..."

What was the purpose of this? Thoughts whirled through his head. Why should she ... and why did she call him ...? He didn't understand. He hoped she would tell him, because date and time left no doubt Julia was still in Ravenna, although he had last heard that her father had banished her to a country house. And she wanted to meet him.

He would wait for her.

His heart beat. He remembered Rheinberg's warnings, his status as a hostage, the conduct expected of him. But what should he do? Ignore Julia's message? A secretive conversation couldn't hurt! He felt that his confidence in the senator's daughter was larger than the binding force of his orders or the memory of the reprimand he'd collected.

And he had to know the meaning of this last sentence. Everything in him yearned for an answer. He couldn't let it rest. He would meet Julia. And then they would see, yes, then they would see ...

Volkert was lost in thought, and in his dreams he felt Julia's lips gently on his skin. He kept the dream tight for a while, like almost every night before he went to bed, since that fateful evening.

"My lord!"

The ensign was startled, automatically pocketed the note. A slave stood in the doorway.

"Sir, the other gentlemen are looking for you. Guests have arrived."

Volkert rose. "Visitors?"

"Someone from church. An envoy of the Archbishop!"

It was less the fact itself that elicited the Ensign's suspicion – it was more this mixture of respect and fear vibrating in the slave's voice. Volkert followed the man through the corridors of the sprawling villa until they arrived in a tastefully decorated room in which the homeowner apparently used to receive guests. Von Klasewitz was there, as Köhler and Sergeant Behrens.

"We have been waiting for you." von Klasewitz greeted the Ensign with a critical undertone. "We have a guest."

The attention of the ensign was aimed at the man in robes, standing beside von Klasewitz and bowing. The courtesy didn't hide the impression the visitor made on Volkert: The pointed nose, close-set eyes, his face haggard-looking, none of it elicited great sympathy.

"Father Petronius is the authorized representative of the Archbishop of Ravenna," drawled von Klasewitz. "He has come to meet us."

"To get to know us?" asked Volkert. "What a great honor."

"In fact," said Petronius. He had a penetrating voice. The priest was certainly a great preacher or a gifted demagogue. Volkert wasn't sure whether there was always a very big difference between the two.

"What can we offer you, Father?" von Klasewitz said with oil in his voice. Volkert had to concede that the officer's language skills improved steadily since their arrival. To find recognition among the rich and powerful of Rome had spurred the first officer's interest.

"Water, thank you," Petronius emphasized his modesty, which corresponded to his appearance. "My master, the Archbishop, has heard many wondrous tales about you. He is eager to find out to what extent they are true."

"What kind of stories?" Volkert asked, ignoring the punitive look of von Klasewitz.

"Stories of fire and thunder, of a steel ship without a sail and oars, from the ease with which the alien visitors have crept into the hearts of those who rule in this city – and beyond!"

"Anything else?"

"My master heard that Roman senators are accompanying your captain to present himself to the Emperor and to find favor in his eyes."

"Whether they will find favor we'll know only for certain once the emperor has made his decision," said Volkert. He got a bad feeling about this man, and it was only reinforced by the false smile on his lips.

"I assure you," interrupted von Klasewitz and pushed himself between the priest and the ensign, "that we have only good intentions. In fact, we have proved this, as we have eliminated the threat posed by a notorious pirate."

Petronius took a cup of water from a slave. "Yes, I've heard. Either a noble act that deserves the applause of my church or a clever trick to gain confidence and to take advantage of it later."

"Exploit – for what?" asked Volkert. The ease with which Petronius formulated his allegations in this room disturbed him and he wondered why von Klasewitz didn't respond accordingly – until he admitted to himself that this was exactly the conversational style of the first officer. The nobleman didn't even seem to be bothered.

Petronius looked searchingly at Volkert, before he answered. "What, indeed ... what?" the priest repeated pondering. "A very good question. Can you give me an answer?"

"We don't really beg the question," replied Volkert. "We entertain no dark intentions, if you're accusing us of any."

Petronius held up his hands. "Nobody wants to accuse anyone. Absolutely not! I only collect information for the Archbishop, nothing more. I make no judgments, which alone is the task of my Lord."

Volkert didn't believe him. Petronius appeared here not just as a mere agent of his master, such as a lower henchman who listens and faithfully reports. The man before him was more than a simple priest, and the way he asked his questions led to the conclusion that he had a very accurate opinion of what he intended to report to the Archbishop.

And that meant he had a plan, a purpose, had planned more with this meeting in his desire to learn to know the Germans.

"Maybe we should have a conversation with the Archbishop," Volkert suggested.

Von Klasewitz nodded enthusiastically, although the ensign suspected that he did so for very different reasons than Volkert would have liked. "An excellent idea, ensign! An audience with the Archbishop! With pleasure I would also visit a church!"

Petronius nodded measured. "Yeah, sure, such an audience can be arranged in due time. And I'm delighted that you want to celebrate mass with us. There should be an opportunity as soon as possible. What kind of service is it you prefer?"

Von Klasewitz looked a little confused. "Well, one celebrated by the Archbishop himself would be preferable."

Volkert sighed silently. Von Klasewitz dodged, without knowing it, a skillfully laid trap. He himself hadn't noticed much of the church dispute that threatened to split the empire at this time, but he knew that Rheinberg had ordered extreme caution when discussing religious issues. On this topic one very quickly walked on brittle ice.

Petronius seemed to accept von Klasewitz's answer for now.

"I'm pleased. I'll send you a messenger with an invitation when the time comes. I hear you're hostages – you may not be allowed to walk around freely in the city."

"We are hostages, but they treat us like guests," said von Klasewitz. "To attend a church service should be no problem."

"Good, good. But if you are hostages, against which danger is it the authorities want to be guarded by inviting you as ... guests?"

"It's a precaution, I would say," replied von Klasewitz not without cunning. "We'll have to, I admit, show our good will. To give hostages, without complaint, is a proof of such, wouldn't you agree?"

Petronius smiled sourly. One could see that he would like this part of the discussion to be steered in a different direction. But he couldn't do more than to agree with the first officer's assessment.

The conversation continued for a half an hour. Volkert was hardly forced to intervene again, because von Klasewitz kept the good priest occupied. Rather than be interviewed by him, he asked his own questions, especially with regard to the impending schism in the church between the Arians and the Trinitarians. Volkert listened attentively, because he himself had not yet grasped too much of it, although it was a very important discussion in this time. Petronius himself was a convinced Trinitarian, and everyone in this century seemed to be entirely convinced of something. That he presented the Arian view slightly less euphoric, and found all sorts of derogatory words for their position wasn't surprising. It was a bit strange for Volkert to find out that the dispute ultimately rested only on one specific question: What was Jesus – God Himself as the Son of God, and therefore divine, or a person subordinate to God? Arius, one of the church elders, took the latter view, so his followers were called Arians, while the other party, which insisted on the divine trinity, was designated as Trinitarians. Volkert saw that this dispute had a long history and knew the Trinitarians would achieve victory – sometimes by quite violent means. Here, however, in the year 378, the outcome was still uncertain. Currently, the Trinitarian doctrine even seemed to be in a defensive position, because while in the west Trinitarian and Arian bishops were spread throughout the Empire, eastern Rome was dominated by the Arians. Volkert remembered from school how this dispute ended in the complete defeat of the Arians. As with the entire Church policy, this discussion had a lot to do with power and political intrigue. The successor of the current emperor, Theodosius, in cooperation with the bishop of Milan, seemed to have been instrumental in the defeat of the Arian "heresy." Rheinberg had indicated his intention to prevent the appointment of Theodosius by Gratian, and for Volkert it has been clear that the captain saw this type of restrictive religious policy as a serious problem. Volkert wouldn't interfere, especially since he himself was a Protestant: to explain the reformation to a bishop of this time, would likely cause him to be accused of heresy. Volkert therefore abstained from any commentary, but had the feeling that Petronius had a very vital interest to know the position of the Germans in this matter.

Von Klasewitz was a Catholic, as Volkert knew, and when he finally confessed his sympathy to the Trinitarian cause, Petronius' eyes lit up. Volkert suppressed any reaction. The remaining ten minutes of their meeting consisted of a presentation of religious beliefs by the priest, to which the first officer reacted fully supportive. Volkert couldn't interfere, because that would have made things worse, but the behavior of the nobleman would, he was sure, have very unpleasant consequences. Von Klasewitz didn't seem to recognize the sensitivity of this issue and made flippant remarks, which would cause repercussions for him – and thus Rheinberg. Petronius eventually left with a happy grin on his face.

And Volkert saw dark clouds rising on the horizon.

30

The weather had changed somewhat. The once radiant sky became misty and clouds built up. The few farmers on the way of the marching column stared in amazement not only at the strange travelers but threw appreciative glances at the sky, because the ground was dry.

It was a little cooler, which made marching pleasant, and the column was progressing well. They had been on the road for quite a while now and Rheinberg could only be grateful for the good street-network, which at this time still characterized the Roman Empire. He knew that the preservation of this network had more and more diminished, because the cities and towns were bled more every year with high taxes, and the gold ended up either in the pockets of corrupt officials or in the financially insatiable machinery of the armed forces who sought to protect the boundaries. Another problem on Rheinberg's to-do-list, and one of the largest, because it was connected to numerous other difficult issues.

It was already evening and the light was diminishing faster than usual due to the low hanging clouds; and the silhouette of Sirmium loomed in the distance. Sirmium, in his own time no more than ruins, belonged to the illustrious line of imperial capitals and stood in line with Trier, Milan, Ravenna and Constantinople. Unlike its sister cities this hadn't brought her a lasting future. Rheinberg had been looking for information in his small library before his departure and learned that city remained of certain importance until the 12th Century as part of the Byzantine Empire, but disappeared after the conquest of the Turks from the history books. This fate was now, in the late summer of 378, still a few hundred years in the future, and currently the town, in which once also Marcus Aurelius had taken residence, presented itself as an extensive and quite sizable urban settlement and a witness of the remaining strength of the Roman Empire.

"We can make it before nightfall," said Africanus, who rode at the head of the column next to Rheinberg. "Our arrival has been announced and won't come as a surprise."

"Will we meet the Emperor in the evening?"

"No. The Emperor isn't in the city. He has already crossed the Danube and established a field camp. We will stay in the garrison and approach the camp tomorrow morning. They are expecting us."

"What reactions has this caused?"

"Well, at least we are allowed to present ourselves. Gratian and his war cabinet still debate whom to entrust with the fight against the Goths."

"They will choose Theodosius," Rheinberg reiterated his prediction.

"That's not a bad choice," Africanus pointed out. "He is an experienced military leader and ... well, there is such a thing as poetic justice, by the way, if we recall how they treated his father."

"Don't get me wrong, Aurelian," Rheinberg said soothingly. "What happened to his father was certainly wrong, and yes, Theodosius isn't an idiot."

The elder Theodosius, father of the candidate under discussion, had been a highly successful and loyal general under Valentinian, Gratian's father. Immediately after the death of his master he had been dismissed from his battle against a rebellious prefect in Africa, charged on flimsy pretexts and executed. Power plays at court and settling old scores – the real reason was not important. His son recognized the signs of the times and retired to his country estate in Spain to pursue a silent and private life.

"He's a reasonably able diplomat," Rheinberg continued, "and he showed the right judgment on important problems during his reign. He resolved the problem with the Goths as well as was possible. I'm not saying that his choice is totally wrong. Gratian has taken a decision, and his choice could have been for a worse candidate."

"But?"

"But he's too easily influenced by the whispers of Ambrosius, and this will result in rigid, oppressive religious policies and thus weaken the inner strength of the empire. He paid dearly for the unity of the Church, for which he has been given the title 'the Great' later – especially by trinitarian historians. And he has pursued at least one completely unnecessary civil war. It certainly could have been worse – but also much better."

"Gratian listens to Ambrosius as well."

Rheinberg nodded thoughtfully. "Yes, and we will have to do something about that. In a few years he will remove the Victoria altar from the Senate and denounce Galerius' Edict of toleration. He will give great privileges to the churches which will exacerbate the financial crisis of the empire. Theodosius will continue this policy. Ultimately the issue is about the money that is available to the state."

"You are against the unity of the Church?" Africanus wanted to know.

"Not at all. I'm absolutely of Constantine's opinion that the Empire needs a unifying bond. He has seen great potential in the church, but he also has miscalculated and had afterwards even intervened often in the disputes of a disunited Church now freed from all constraints. This has cost him a lot of time and effort. But it's not the Church that can act as the unifying bond Constantine envisioned – it is far from that. And violence cannot force it. This works only if the State who tries to enforce it is strong and can focus on these matters, without any external threat. That's really not the case currently. No, the church can try to achieve unity as it wants, but not by decree."

"And what can unify the empire against foreign enemies alternatively?"

Rheinberg pointed to the city faintly visible in the evening haze before him. "That's it, my friend. The idea of the empire. The power of civilization as a counterpoint to barbarism. A civilization that connects all and everyone, whether Trinitarians, Arians or followers of other religions. An idea that leads all kinds of Christians to the battlefield along with followers of Mithras or Jupiter, united to defend the Empire and the idea behind its creation."

Rheinberg turned to Africanus, who listened thoughtfully.

"You are the best example for my argument, my friend."

"Me?"

"Yes. In my time, our Empire has conquered and enslaved your people. In my time, your people have no chance to obtain citizenship, even if many serve in our army. Your dark skin is seen by many as evidence of inferiority. And I see you here as a trierarch, an Imperial officer with full civil rights, riding next to me to see your emperor. Explain that to a chief of the Hottentots."

"The what?"

Rheinberg waved. "Never mind. What I'm saying is this: the fact that everyone strives to live in security and prosperity, has a lot to do with the idea of Empire, and this, properly applied, should be the unifying bond that holds everything together. Religion should not be as important as the common welfare. This should also be understood by a well-educated and intelligent man like Gratian."

Africanus smiled. "I remember something my grandfather once told me. His father had been a simple peasant, and joining the fleet had been his greatest dream. He was the second son of his father, and would not inherit the land where he was born. So he moved to Alexandria and went to the recruiters. They wouldn't take him because he was limping. He finally settled down in town and worked in the harbor, but this desire to be something more than a farmer without rights he has transferred to his son, my grandfather. And that one was accepted by the recruiters. He began as a simple sailor, rowed for ten years, and at the end of his 25-year period of service, he retired proudly as proreta."

Rheinberg was by now familiar enough with the Roman naval ranks to know that this is was an important position on a war galley, and it was only acquired through formal qualification and exemplary service.

"He retired and settled near Ravenna. He had already started a family, and enjoyed the Roman citizenship because of his service. He then married a girl from Gallia, my grandmother. And the moment he joined the fleet, he looked for a Roman name, and discarded his old one."

Rheinberg looked at Africanus. "What was his name before he joined the fleet?"

"He was Benipe, son of Nakhti. His name means 'iron,' and there could be no name more appropriate, because he has made it through his determination."

Rheinberg smiled. "Let me guess – he rocked you on his knees as a little boy and he hasn't called you Aurelianus, right?"

For a moment it seemed as if Africanus was embarrassed. The memory of his grandfather, whom he had apparently adored, touched a sentimental chord in him.

"Well," he replied, clearing his throat. "He called me Wakhashem."

"And that means?"

Africanus' embarrassment was now obvious. "Little fool."

Rheinberg laughed and slapped his friend on the shoulder. "Then let us see that we can reach Sirmium today, little fool."

Africanus grimaced.

"Jan, you've never had a sword between the ribs, right?"

"By God, no!"

The trierarch smiled wryly. "Then you better think about how to address me ..."

31

"I'm pleased that we have the opportunity to speak privately."

Von Klasewitz smiled at the priest and looked around. After the service the hostages had been allowed to attend, the envoy of the bishop had come up to him with an invitation to a little conversation. The service itself had been similar in many ways to those which von Klasewitz knew in his time. There had been a reading and a sermon, but no prayer of intercession. Although there had been a few songs, they had nothing to do with the church music he remembered, and the songs weren't sung by everyone. The service lasted almost two hours and had been quite tiring. Nevertheless, the nobleman has had the feeling to have been very close to the roots of what he experienced as modern Catholicism in his time. Petronius, who had accompanied the group to church, was never tired of warning the hostages not to attend a mass of the Arians. Although the worship was almost identical, he explained sourly, the basic beliefs on which it was based were consistently of a heretical nature.

"Let's sit down!"

The small chapel in which they had retreated was deserted. The thick walls and the massive wooden door Petronius had closed firmly behind him guaranteed that their conversation would remain undisturbed. Klasewitz was curious what the episcopal envoy had to discuss with him.

Petronius opened the conversation. "The service seems to have impressed you."

"It reminded me in many respects to those in my time," admitted von Klasewitz. "These are actually the roots of the church that I know well."

"More than a thousand years in the future, if I have understood correctly? I'm reassured to hear that. It shows that our struggle for the true faith and the eternal church will not be in vain, and everything that applies today is of truly epochal character."

Von Klasewitz couldn't disagree.

"But this is also a good start with respect to what I wanted to share with you."

"It's surely about our ship and our intentions," surmised von Klasewitz.

Petronius shook his head. "Yes and no, yes and no. First of all, I care for you."

"For me?"

"Sure. I have the impression that this very strange journey through time your men and yourself have experienced is difficult to understand and accept. And I'm not just talking about us Romans. I refer to your men – and leaders, officers like you."

"It's confusing and perhaps sometimes even frightening," the first officer replied.

"Isn't it? The more it should be our job as your host to give comfort and encouragement. No matter how much time may separate us, we have something that connects us – you only just mentioned it yourself. It is faith. The true faith. The legitimate faith. The only faith."

"That is true," von Klasewitz said. "There is something familiar in this strange environment. I felt reminded of it several times today. That's quite reassuring for me."

"And for me," replied Petronius with a pleased smile. "For me, it shows in fact that you are not at all wild demons, but Christians, though ..."

"Though?" von Klasewitz repeated.

"... though not all of you seem to be of equal commitment and purity of beliefs, if I may say so."

"I can hardly disagree. I assure you though that this is not true for all, so yes, it applies only to a minority of our people."

Petronius nodded eagerly. "I would like to believe you. But I have the impression that this minority is very influential on board your ship. And prominently represented in the person of your trierarch, who probably already sees himself as a future emperor."

"I don't always agree with him, that's for sure," admitted von Klasewitz. “He makes his own decisions and follows my advice less than I would want him to.”

Petronius made a sad face. “This is regrettable, but already I begin to imagine how much wisdom escapes him thereby. And is the true leader not characterized by his request for the opinions of his charges and carefully weighing all options?”

Von Klasewitz snorted. “Rheinberg thinks he knows better and is inaccessible to any argument,” he blurted. He felt understood by the priest and didn’t want to cloud his true opinion behind polite words. The friendly face of Petronius and his pleasant way of listening to von Klasewitz made him relax. There was no one stopping the nobleman, and he gave his frustration free rein, speaking with loud words, gesticulating. Example after example of his humiliations by the hands of Rheinberg he described, ranging from ridicule to incomprehension.

“And all for you, a man of nobility,” was one of the typical objections of the priest, with whom he sprinkled salt into the wounds. Von Klasewitz’s outrage was understood, yes, the priest participated in the German’s rightful anger, and it was as if Petronius really felt the pain caused by the lack of respect the first officer suffered. For the nobleman this was a liberating moment, as he could speak unimpeded about his feelings. He didn’t notice the passage of time, so much had his rage captured him and so willingly and patiently Petronius listened to his words, even as he began to repeat himself increasingly toward the end.

It was getting dark. As Petronius lead him back to the house, accompanied by some torchbearers, von Klasewitz felt exhausted. Finally, the priest began to speak, slowly and calmly, then faster and more intensely. He had taken up much of what the nobleman had said, but put it in a different light. Von Klasewitz’s head quite buzzed. The feeling of being understood, however, remained strong in him. The priest had begun to give a new perspective to his life. The fact that he couldn’t return to his time moved into the background. New challenges and recognition and social advancement, all this seemed to be not such a bad idea. Petronius had presented him a bouquet of flowers from which he could choose the most beautiful ones, and some were more sweet-scented than others. Some had thorns, but wasn’t he a soldier and of nobility, man enough to take risks and survive adversity?

When they reached the villa, Klasewitz took Petronius' forearm.

"We need to continue this conversation! Tomorrow," he said urgently. The priest nodded, made no effort to free himself from the grip.

"We will speak, my friend," he said, and it sounded like a lot more than just a promise. Von Klasewitz had a headache. He needed to think. He had to weigh the options.

He had to decide.

32

It was already dark and Thomas Volkert had remembered much too late that Julia's message didn't contain an important information: namely, where they should meet. Still, he felt a strange confidence in the abilities of the exceptional senator's daughter and was sitting on the hour alone in his room, ready for ... for whatever.

He was quite happy to have had a reason to excuse himself. The men hadn't talked a lot after the departure of Petronius, but on the next day the visit had been an important talking point. Von Klasewitz gave the other soldiers only a very brief version of this first discussion, he seemed to take the view that not everyone was supposed to be bothered with details. To say this in the face of such an old, experienced NCO like Köhler, who enjoyed the confidence of the captain, bordered on an insult. But Köhler knew von Klasewitz and how to take it. Volkert had led him and Behrens aside and gave them an extended version, spiced with appropriate commentary. Behrens who had barely managed elementary school and regarded himself heartily unaffected by education, had just shrugged his shoulders and made it clear that Volkert should tell him in time when and whom to shoot, and that he would rather take commands from Volkert than from "this silly twerp" von Klasewitz. Köhler, who had traveled around a lot and got educated by life, regarded the matter clearly as not to be taken lightly. His bad opinion about the first officer had been reinforced, if this had ever been possible.

The day had been otherwise boring, especially since the men were under house arrest. They lacked nothing other than distraction. The subservient slaves followed every command without hesitation – especially von Klasewitz seemed increasingly to be fond of the idea of slavery, which was not surprising, as he treated his subordinates mostly the same way. But that was already all they could do. In conversations, the servants did not engage, and although they feigned lack of understanding, Volkert suspected that they had been instructed in this regard.

The Romans were not fools, even if the ensign had the impression that von Klasewitz still regarded them as somewhat primitive. Von Klasewitz could not keep technology and common intelligence apart. A people who had managed to build a gigantic empire over a period of hundreds of years one should not underestimate.

He had eaten an early dinner – slowly, he'd almost gotten used to garum – and then excused himself, pretending he wasn't feeling well. Since both von Klasewitz as well as at least one of the corporals behaved still basically hostile toward the Roman cuisine, the excuse was acknowledged with understanding nods.

And here he sat. He held Julia's note like a jewel in his hands. The mixture of excitement and fear, and ... longing that filled him made him nervous. Whatever the senator's daughter had done with him, it worked like a charm, who had taken possession of him entirely. There was no doubt that he was terribly in love and this feeling clouded his senses.

The enjoyment he found in it was greater than any fear or the voice of reason.

The door opened, and Volkert winced. A slave came in; he looked around, then waved. He was followed by a hooded figure, covered with a wide cloak. A slender hand appeared under the cloak, some coins changed possession, and the slave disappeared with an expressionless face.

Volkert didn't have to wait until the cover was removed. He knew so well that it could only be Julia. He got up, ran to her, and she hugged him back with equal fervor and power. Their lips met in a long, intense kiss that seemed to last forever. As they parted, panting and smiling at each other, Volkert recognized the traces of tears in her red-rimmed eyes. He pushed her to half arm's length, looked into her face more closely and now saw signs of exhaustion.

"Julia," he mumbled awkwardly. "What happened?"

As if the question would have brought a dam to collapse, tears flew from the young woman's eyes, but she fought them bravely. She pressed her lips together and wiped her hand across her cheeks, leaving a wet trail. Then she sighed loudly and took several deep breaths.

"Let us sit down," she whispered finally to Volkert and he led her to the sofa, which dominated a large part of the room. Julia came plainly to the point. "My mother has made wild threats," she said with a bitter undertone. "She explained that the parents alone would decide which men I will meet from now, and that she is tired of my behavior. Father would support her viewpoint in everything. I opposed her however, and there have been ... unpleasant scenes."

Volkert knew what that meant. Especially in a Roman familia, in which at least theoretically the father had the final decision in everything. Julia seemed to cherish these ancient traditions rather little and had possibly gone too far this time, even in the eyes of her doting father.

"What happened?"

"My mother said that any visit to the strange visitors is not permissible, even if the Emperor would accept your presence favorably. For me and in any case only a man of Roman nobility should be good enough, a senator's son. She was also willing to consider a high-ranking officer or someone from the Imperial court or maybe a rich businessman. She said that my decision for you would be immediately interpreted as *infamia*."

"As what?"

"Ah, yes, you might not know. The law of *infamia* explains the circumstances under which someone can lose his civil rights. For example, if a senator would marry the daughter of an innkeeper, that would be a reason to deprive him of civil rights. Or if a widow remarries, without waiting the one-year period of mourning to pass. There are many cases and marriage with someone of lower social status who pursues a profession which is regarded as particularly dirty and repulsive, is one of them."

"Innkeepers?"

Julia threw a meaningful glance. "You'll know what I mean. In any case, I replied that surely this didn't relate to you, but she said you didn't even had the right of citizenship, and therefore they couldn't allow it in any case that someone like me ..."

"... should marry you," Volkert completed the sentence.

"Yes. That might change one day. But by now you're simply ..."

"... quite strange."

"Very strange."

Volkert pressed his lips on each other. The feeling of despair and anger clamped his throat. He took Julia's arm and pulled her toward him. For a moment she just held on tight and they gave each other comfort. "What have you told your mother then?" the young man eventually wanted to know.

"I have made it clear that I'm not interested in any of her marriage-proposals and that I had made a decision."

Now it was the mixture of sudden joy and warmth that made Volkert's words stick in his mouth. He locked Julia's mouth with a long kiss. The happiness seemed almost overwhelming. But then reality crept back into his mind and he pulled away from her.

"My mother was angry," Julia went on. "But my parents have finally realized that they cannot do anything against my expressed will even with their own stubbornness."

Volkert hid a smile. The word "stubbornness" in Julia's mouth, and then meant negative, was quite a bit ironic.

"She has made me an offer," she said.

Volkert frowned in confusion. "An offer? What kind of offer?"

"She told me I could take every free decision that I wanted, including the choice of my husband. And she told me she would never again complain about anything, if I would simply forget the guy from the future."

Volkert's eyes were round. "That's what she said?"

Now the last sentence in Julia's message suddenly made sense.

"Thomas, I suspect that behind all this is more than my parents are willing to tell me. After the conversation with your trierarch, Symmachus and others have been in many consultations. My father may not be an avid politician, but he is not without influence, and he operates within certain constraints. Something is brewing, and I rather think that's why he especially doesn't want us to be together ... in order to protect me."

"Protect? Against what?"

"I don't know."

Volkert looked pensively into nothingness for a moment. He remembered the visit of Petronius. The uneasy feeling that he felt ever since intensified. Julia's interpretation couldn't be dismissed out of hand. "What remains for us to do?" he finally said quietly.

Julia seemed to have been waiting for this question. The vehemence with which she pressed her full breasts against his chest was surely equally passionate as calculated, but the ensign couldn't care less. They kissed again, long and hungry.

When they separated from each other, Julia said it. "We must run away. Otherwise we have no chance to remain to be together, Thomas."

"Running away?" Volkert asked half incredulously. This seemed to him too much like one of the bad romance novels which he had read as a young man. "Where to?"

"Someplace where no one knows us."

Julia seemed to notice the hesitation in the young man. She looked deep into his eyes. "Thomas, I love you!"

Volkert's heart leapt again. He blinked as tears wanted to shoot even in his eyes. "Julia ... Julia ..." he whispered, burying his face in her hair. "I love you, too!"

"Then we should not be separated from each other," she whispered back. "We really shouldn't."

"No, that's true."

"My father will not allow our relationship, and your trierarch will certainly have his objections."

Volkert thought back to the sharp rebuke that the captain had administered and could not help but once again accept Julia's insight and intelligence. "And that's true as well," he had to confirm.

"So what do we do?"

Volkert was thinking, but he couldn't deny the logic of the woman. And that he should be separated from her, perhaps forever, became a more and more unbearable thought with every second the young man spent in the presence of the beloved. Melodrama or not, he came to the conclusion that this was now a different time and a different place. No more formal permission to marry by the Emperor needed and really no Empire to defend for him. It pained him for a moment, having to behave disloyal, but ultimately he felt that the priorities began to move in his life.

He felt the beautiful woman's warm and soft body in his arms and realized that he had already made his decision.

"Very well then," he heard himself mutter. "This is probably really the only way. But where are we going? Of what should we live?"

Julia smiled at Volkert, obviously more than happy. "I have saved and hidden, and I can do work a bit. Embroidering, sewing, mending clothes, I can even cook."

"Did you have to learn all this?"

Julia turned up her nose. "I wasn't allowed to learn anything except languages and philosophy. But I was hanging around with the slaves and some taught me. My mother was horrified when I patched my first tunic myself. She feels that it is beneath the dignity of a senator's daughter to have to do this kind of work."

"But I ... I have no skills that can help us," Volkert admitted sadly.

"You're healthy and strong. That's enough. We have to travel quite a distance anyway, because my father's arm reaches far. If we want to escape from him, we should go to the East. I know my father's possessions almost better than himself, he has long since lost any overview and leaves everything to his administrators."

She reached into a bundle, which she carried along, and took out papers.

"Here: My family controls manufactories and estates throughout the East, although significantly less than in the West. I cannot remember that my father has ever visited them, he may actually not, except that he went to the east of the Empire to buy some special wine in Greece. It was easy for me to use my father's seal and to write some letters of recommendation. Here ... you are now Lucius, from Gaul, and my name is Paulina. I'm a seamstress, and you a worker. With the letter of recommendation we will get a job anywhere in the eastern farms and estates of my father, without him ever knowing. He churns out such recommendations regularly – for freed slaves, clients of his friends and so on. There is absolutely nothing that calls out any attention."

Volkert noted with a mixture of admiration and suspicion that Julia had not only prepared everything well, but apparently hadn't even for a second doubted his own decision in the matter. He wondered for a moment if he hadn't just replaced one captain with another, although after giving her brown eyes a closer look it became obvious that the authority of his new superior had a slightly different basis than Rheinberg's.

"And how do we travel?"

"Trading caravans constantly travel to the East. One buys a place in a cart. Or we go by sea, directly to Constantinople. In the capital of the East, we have the greatest opportunities to immerse ourselves and build a new life. The only problem is that the sea journey is arduous and my father has many good links to the owners of merchant ships – the chance that someone recognizes me isn't low. The land route takes longer, but is also safer."

Volkert nodded. If they were unlucky, their escape would already falter in the harbor. He had little desire to take that risk. "Over land then," he confirmed. "When do we start?"

Julia Volkert pressed the bundle in his hand. "Here, put this on. I have another one hidden outside the city, with money and food."

Volkert unfolded the bundle and looked at clean, although a little worn-out clothes that would make him a Roman. Even his size was well measured. No, Julia had indeed not doubted for a second how he would decide. "So that means ..."

Julia shut his mouth with another kiss before she said, "That's right, Thomas. We leave immediately!"

33

"It's a miracle that you survived, my friend!"

Richomer crouched beside the divan on which Flavius Victor rested and was careful not to beat the Master Equitum on the shoulder. The man was pale, with sunken cheeks, but he managed to give a weak smile to the officer from the West. He was the only surviving commander of the East, and has been close to death.

"No gangrene," he uttered quietly. "The physician is a butcher, but he knows his business. Has learned in the Gallic schools, he said. Seems to have helped him. I'm not the only one he saved."

Richomer nodded and looked at Victor's injury. The left arm had been severed from the middle of the upper arm, a quick, well-aimed blow by an enemy, who wielded a well sharpened sword. The breastplate of the equestrian commander had finally stopped the blow, and a soldier from Victor's guard had stretched the Goth down, but for the arm, it had been too late in any case. They had tied the stump and fled like everyone else.

"When will you be fit for duty?" asked Richomer.

"I need another week of care, says the Medicus. I've lost a lot of blood. Currently, he fills me with all sorts of potions and lets me eat overcooked meat. But it doesn't seem to be completely ineffective; I feel a little stronger every day, and the frequent attacks of weakness are becoming less. A week seems to be realistic. And you yourself?"

The German made a derogatory gesture. "Nothing serious, just a few scratches."

"And even though you have really tried to get hurt. You fought like a madman."

"My time has not yet come."

Victor smiled a little wider, and it seemed as if some color returned to his cheeks.

"Valens has burned the cavalry, Victor," muttered Richomer. "He ordered us to run into a drawn knife."

"He and Sebastianus," Victor agreed. "But ultimately it was the rashness of incompetent officers who didn't held back. Sebastianus has whipped up the confidence so much ... and everyone was thirsty."

Richomer nodded. The army had gone without food and water in position and the wait certainly dragged on the nerves of all. The thirst had made them very impatient.

"They both have not recognized the importance of the cavalry. And they were too confident. Fritigern may well be a barbarian, but he's not an idiot. Until recently I have been talking about this to the Emperor. And then the barbarian lancers ... they have made mincemeat out of the ground troops. We will have to rethink."

Richomer put a placating hand on his friend's chest. He waved a worried-looking servant away. Victor had been lucky that he had his own villa in Adrianople, and the house had been immediately opened for all the injured who had reached the safety of the city walls. Only this single suite allowed a little privacy, otherwise the whole place had turned into a military hospital.

An attempt by the Goths to take the city had failed because of two factors: Their inability to besiege a well-fortified city and effectively attack the walls; and the combat readiness of the Roman citizen militia, which offered the Goths defiant resistance. Ultimately, the attackers had to withdraw.

"Don't get excited. Valens is dead. Sebastianus is dead. We have not heard from them since the battle, their bodies were never found, but would Valens be alive somewhere, even as a hostage to the Goths, we would've known by now. He is dead, and Gratian is our emperor."

Victor nodded. "A wiser emperor, I hope."

"He is young but not a fool either. And he won't forget the East. He is at Sirmium and holds a council of war. I'm supposed to ride there and meet him. You should join us once you master a horse again."

"What are his plans?"

"If I could read the thoughts of the Emperor, I would be a rich and powerful man, Victor. I guess that he will appoint a new general for the East, who, if he proves himself, will have a good chance to be promoted to Augustus. I don't think the young Gratian has a strong interest to carry the whole empire in its entirety on his shoulders for too long. The West is difficult enough."

"Very true."

"We will have to inform him properly. First we need to know how many soldiers have survived."

"How many have reported back?"

Richomer pulled out a paper. "I don't have exact figures. Luckily, most of them had the good idea to retreat into the safety of the city. I guess that the one or the other might still be sitting in one of the villages."

"Or have deserted," Victor added with some bitterness in his voice.

"Or that, yes, unfortunately. Our estimates suggest that one third of the army survived. We currently expect 22,000 dead."

Victor looked even paler now. Valens had led around 30,000 men to the field.

"This is the biggest loss since ... since Cannae?" he asked.

"Since Varus battled against the Germans."

"This is more than 350 years ago! And he lost only 20,000! What a great honor for us! The second largest massacre in Roman history, and we have been witnesses!"

Richomer didn't respond to the bitterness in Victor's words. He could understand that feeling very well.

"The problem is the structure of the survivors."

"Tell me about it!"

Richomer summarized it in one sentence. "Most of the survivors are officers and NCOs."

"Ah, damn it," Victor muttered. "We have an army of heads but without a body."

"That's it."

Victor closed his eyes and thought for a moment. "We urged the Emperor to recruit more for years," he muttered darkly. "Long gone are the days when a young man has found his way into the armed forces in order to gain citizenship or to obtain a piece of land or to achieve fame and glory. We force the sons of soldiers to take the same job, even if they don't want to. We press men into the service, and the only reason for them to oblige is us threatening reprisals. We plunder the farms of their labor-force and even senators and former officers have started to protect deserters in order to have at least someone who can work on the land. Slaves gain their freedom by betraying deserters to the authorities. The system, my friend, is sick and only works with brute force. What will happen now? We will scour the East for new recruits. We will take every criminal with a promise of pardon and free slaves to enslave them again. Maybe we'll even get another army assembled. Maybe we can hold back the Goths until this army is more or less ready for use. And then what?"

He sighed.

"Then comes the next enemy. Have you heard the stories that the Goths told us? That giant hordes of Huns have driven them from their lands? That even more will come and then eventually these barbarians will also arrive at our borders? How we will oppose them? How much gold will we throw out to bribe barbarians, so they stay away from our borders? How often can they blackmail us, because we are weak?"

Richomer smiled and shook his head rather sadly. "You are a philosopher, my friend. That must be because of the injury."

"Every soldier with some brains in his head is a philosopher when he noticed for long enough how the empire slowly but surely goes down the drain."

Victor ran his hand across his forehead.

"I'll try to make you a more complete list and bring it to Sirmium – as soon as I'm able to travel. Then we can present accurate numbers to the Emperor."

"Very good. Let us solve one problem after the other: first we take care of the Goths, then the salvation of the empire against all future threats."

"I would like to see the empire to develop into a state in which everyone wants to live and where we wouldn't need to force anyone with the threat of death to join the legions. I'm tired of leading men into death who have no interest in fighting. I would really like to command a voluntary and motivated troop."

"Our cavalry was quite motivated."

"Their bodies are lying around the city."

Richomer patted the general's shoulder and forced a smile. "You can really cheer one up, Viktor."

"You cheer me up by telling me in a week that Gratian has found a way to save all our asses."

Richomer rose. "I'll try. Make me happy by actually showing up in a week and have some color in your face."

"I promise."

"Then I'll do what I can."

The glance Victor sent after Richomer didn't speak of much confidence.

34

"A beautiful villa."

Godegisel carelessly threw the chicken bones on the floor and wiped the grease from his chin. Fritigern gave him a disapproving look and gestured expansively. "Enjoy it as long as you can. We can't reside here forever."

The young Teuringian nobleman nodded. Fritigern was the judge and general, erroneously dubbed as *King* by the Romans, and they had followed him to the territory of the Eastern Roman Empire, battered by the onslaught of the Huns – notwithstanding the fact that a great splinter-group of those fearsome warriors has allied with the Goths and fought alongside them in the last battle. He had learned to trust his judgment, and in this case the reasons were clear: the Gothic troops – even after the battle with Valens numbering a good 20,000 warriors – and all civilians associated with them were running out of food again. As long as their status was not secured, it wouldn't do good to start a place of settlement; also it was necessary to use the military advantage quickly. One had to march further in order to plunder and especially to try to finally conquer one of these damn well-fortified Roman cities. At the battle of Adrianople, they had been bloodied, despite their decisive victory. They had to learn a lot, and on top of Godegisel's list was the need to build siege equipment and use it properly.

Fritigern and his close followers currently housed in a deserted country mansion formerly belonging to some rich Roman snob but abandoned by the administrator and his people once the Goths had approached. There had been food, even wine, so here the Gothic leader had opened a temporary headquarters while his lieutenants tried to keep the Gothic convoy together, preventing that too many started to explore individually. Those would constitute an all-too-easy prey for the Roman forces, whatever was still left of them.

“The Huns create problems for us, judge,” said Godegisel now. “I have talked with their leader yesterday. Today I hear that he was found dead in his tent, and a new one is now in charge. I don’t know if we can maintain an alliance.”

“How should I know? The only thing that connects us with the Huns is that they have equally escaped the attack of their main host after some ... disagreements. They are rebels, we are victims. They feel superior to us. It wouldn’t surprise me if someday they return back to their leaders, especially if those continue to be as successful as they are now. I wouldn’t rely on them as allies even if they’d stop to exchange their chiefs so fast.”

Godegisel had, as so often, little to oppose Fritigern’s argument. “So I shouldn’t try?”

“Yes, yes. Talk with each new leader who comes out of their tents. Flatter them and understand their concerns. I don’t want them to turn too early against us. The Huns are fierce warriors and no fools. They will realize that they have no future within the borders of the empire without the protection of all three peoples who are united in our alliance. We need each other. If they ride off to plunder, they will eventually encounter an opponent who will crush them, especially if the Romans will get their act together.”

“Well, I’ll continue to talk with them. When do you think a new Roman emperor will emerge?”

Fritigern looked warningly at his young friend.

“You tend to underestimate Rome, my friend. You think they are without leadership? The Emperor of the West is now Emperor of all. He commands a fully intact army, which, if I have heard correctly, recently successfully defeated a full-blown invasion across the Rhine. Gratian has capable generals and seems – unlike his uncle – to be open-minded toward good advice. We have defeated one half of the moveable army, that is true. We have not taken a city, we prefer to plunder the country. While the officers of the East can rebuild a new army, Gratian can lead his troops against us, and we have ... nothing. Our people are euphoric – too euphoric. As if the victory now decided everything for us. I’ll tell you what we have achieved at maximum: a good negotiating position.”

"You want to negotiate, judge?" Disbelief sounded from Godegisel's voice.

"But yes. The Romans will send their envoys and suggest an amicable solution, once we have driven them to despair sufficiently. We will continue to plunder through their land. The rural population is terrified and will flock to the cities. Famine will break out. Their cities are safe from us, but within their walls terrible things will happen. And we need a second great military victory. One more, Godegisel, so we put the dagger to Rome's chest and can negotiate peace terms in our favor. The threat of the Huns, which has driven us here, is also real for them."

Fritigern leaned forward. "We need Rome, Godegisel, because we need the protection of its strong walls. And Rome needs us, because they need the strong arm of our warriors. It will just take a while for the Romans to really understand, and until then we have to prove our strength."

The young nobleman nodded thoughtfully. "I can see much wisdom in your words, Judge. And our hostage will certainly be of great help to us also."

Fritigern smiled. "That is probably true. How fares our guest? Let's hope that he will soon be in a condition to represent Rome in a slightly more honorable manner."

"Look for yourself," replied Godegisel, pointing to the other side of the courtyard.

In the shadow of a wall was a strange construction, guarded by three soldiers sitting listlessly on the ground and engrossed in a game of dice. They were hardly to blame, because what they had to guard didn't look too threatening at the moment.

In a solid cage made of wood struts lied a body. It was the body of a man, clothed with a thin tunic. His chest rose and fell regularly. The face was very peaceful and relaxed in sleep. His head rested on a pillow, his body was covered by a thin blanket.

Flavius Valens was asleep.

– To be continued –

Printed in Great Britain
by Amazon